My Road Is The High Road

Gene Suttle

ALSO BY GENE SUTTLE

My Way is the High Way
My Life is the High Life

This book is a work of fiction. Names, places, characters, events, and incidents are the product of the author's imagination or are used fictitiously. Any resemblance to actual persons, living or dead, or events is entirely coincidental.

Copyright January 2018 Gene Suttle

All rights reserved.

My Road is the High Road is the third book in the My/High Trilogy. *My Way is the High Way* and *My Life is the High Life* were previously self-published and can be found at Amazon.com

My Road is a prequel, an attempt to take you back to the beginning where the story began. Thus it is the beginning and the end of this trilogy.

If you have not read the other books and wish to read in chronological order, start with **My Road**, then **My Way**, followed by **My Life**. Each book stands alone, however, and can be read in any order at any time.

For your enjoyment and entertainment.

Dedicated to the men and women
that have chosen the life of an educator.
Blessed are those that toil
tirelessly for the student's sake.

In the beginning...

1

"...was the Word, and the Word was with God! Amen? In the beginning, all things were made by Him! Amen? John 1 tells us that the light shineth in the darkness and the darkness cannot over come it! Amen? Praise God! The darkness can NOT overcome it. Hallelujah!" The radio evangelist's voice rang out through the speakers raising the level of participation through his listeners to a fever pitch. Billy was listening, not feverishly, but because in Waymor, in the desert, there were three stations on a Sunday morning and since this particular evangelist was syndicated throughout the southwest, he was coming to Billy on two of the three. The other station was a Spanish program that Billy felt quite certain was a similar message aimed at the Spanish speakers in West Texas and northern Mexico. The right reverend intended to touch unsaved souls wherever they may be since radio waves had no boundaries and the message of salvation was meant for all.

Billy turned onto the packed caliche pad and parked the company pickup near the pump jack. He switched the engine off right in the middle of another amen and praise God. As he sat listening to the silence, interrupted only by the occasional insect and wind gust that kicked up dust, he folded his hands together across the top of the steering wheel to form a pillow for his chin. Billy looked across the vast expanse of nothingness stretching as far west as the Rockies and south into Mexico and wondered when God was going to come back and finish up this part of the world.

From where he was sitting the vast emptiness couldn't be the finished product. It looked like a blank canvas in every possible way. God obviously had been more focused on the mountains, hills, and daffodils, because all Billy saw was sand, yucca, and scrub. As he continued to stare randomly through the windshield, he saw the outline of Waymor shimmering in the rising heat off to his right.

Waymor, Texas. Located strategically in the middle of nowhere and a long way down the road that goes on forever.

People outside of Waymor referred to it as Weighmore, or Fat City for short; poking fun at the fact most of Waymor's citizens were large, bordering on obese. The fine citizens of Waymor did love their chicken fried steak, fried chicken, donuts, gravy, and fried potatoes. Beer was the main drink of choice at any time of day served in cans, bottles, mugs, cold, or not. To be fair the water from the tap had an oily sheen to it and tasted like 30W motor oil. Bottled water was for sissies. If you're paying to drink, drink beer. Catsup was their favorite vegetable.

The grease and alcohol was comfort food since a person could look outside their windows and actually see the horizon, the curve of the earth, in every direction with few other signs of life. Tumbleweeds rolled past matching the speed and direction of the prevailing winds. Chasing tumbleweeds was the favorite activity of school-aged kids, being blindsided by one during a sandstorm was not as much fun. The joke about watching your dog run off for days was written about Waymor. People had been known to see winter coming in August.

Billy arrived in Waymor almost five years ago with all his worldly possessions packed in his car. He had been hired to coach at Waymor High, home of the fighting Sand Crabs. Billy was excited to join a staff made up of a few of his buddies that he met in college. They had set out to work their way up the coaching ladder right into the NFL or at least to a major college program. It was only a matter of time they felt until their coaching talent became evident to the whole world and offers would be pouring in. They had made a pact that they would all make it together, but . . . you had to have chickens to have a chicken ranch and as large as the Waymor kids were, they were slow as Christmas. After three straight 1-9 seasons and riding a few thousand miles in a school bus across the desert to play teams that actually had talent, the grind had taken its toll and killed their dream. All his buddies, his coaching friends, left town. They all went back to civilization, except Billy. He took a job as a pumper in the oilfield.

Those events and circumstances found him sitting beside a pump jack on a Sunday morning listening to a televangelist exhort and inspire. The pump jack had broken a rod and was redlining its motor as it bobbed up and down without the weight of thousands of pounds of sucker rod to provide resistance. Billy carefully hit the kill switch before the crazy thing launched itself out into the desert. His job was to check it out, call in a crew to fix it, and make sure it was brought back on line. Unless the horse was rocking up and down, pumping oil, no one was making money.

Billy had a recurring thought each time he saw a pump jack. He was reminded of the ending to the **Last Picture Show** and wondered whether it would be fun to ride the iron horse or was that how stupid people died. He radioed in to the dispatcher to schedule a pulling unit for the repair. His work done Billy, cranked up the Beatles' **Why Don't We Do it in the Road** on his tape player, threw off his hard hat, and did the chicken dance right there on the hard packed white rocks startling the gophers and the lone coyote that had been trotting by.

Finding himself considerably out of shape, due to his own affection for chicken fried steaks, French fries, and Lone Star beer; Billy only lasted through the first verse before collapsing in the dirt gasping for air. He rolled over on his back and stared at the endless blue sky and wondered how the train wreck happened in his life. What had caused the derailment?

Billy had married Crystal, his high school sweetheart, in a storybook wedding following a storybook romance. As it turned out the storybook was **Grimm's Fairy Tales**. In a matter of months, Crystal was long gone. Billy knew that many things led to the end of their short-lived marital bliss. Not being fully open about his career path had certainly played a large part in their disagreement. She was expecting lawyer, he was thinking football coach. She left and went east, Billy went west to the desert, wide-open spaces, coyotes, full moons, cactus, beauty and an honest paycheck. What little he and Crystal had collected in their brief time together left in the U-Haul attached to his former father-in-law's Ford pickup. He was okay with that. He liked traveling light and living simple.

Five years later, divorced, and lying in the dirt in the most desolate part of Texas, Billy was 27, in a dead end job that would be phased out and taken over by computers within a year. Billy stared at the wisp of clouds that did nothing to soften the glaring rays of the desert sun. He looked left and saw the heat waves rising out of the sand and realized there was only one thing left to do. He dusted himself off, walked to the back of his truck, grabbed the cooler of Lone Stars, slid his pistol from under the front seat, and walked up the sand dune in the distance to its highest point. Cracking open his first beer of the day at his usual 9 A.M. beer break, he took aim at the nearest gopher and pulled the trigger.

2

William Robert Masters had graduated at the top of his high school class. He was smart enough to be on stage, but not smart enough to give one of the speeches reserved for the Valedictorian and Salutatorian. He was a varsity athlete, named Most Likely to Succeed, and had dated everyone on the cheerleading squad except the two dudes. Life was grand; the future was boundless. His folks thought banker or lawyer when he was born and had anointed him appropriately for the highest level of society. In their minds, he would be addressed by all three names out of respect for his position in business and in life. A solid name indeed.

His stately moniker lasted until Little League. His coach, a mechanic that loved baseball and kids, changed it to Billy on the first day of practice. Looking back, it probably had more to do with efficiency and a little to do with making everyone friends and equals.

By high school his friends had managed to keep him humble by calling him Billy Bob, which stuck with folks in Texas a lot easier than William Robert.

Things continued well during his first year of college as he went off to Texas Tech and declared his major as pre-law. Crystal, the cheerleader he had chosen after sampling the bunch, his high school sweetheart since junior year, immediately began planning their wedding. Billy was a traditionalist and would have preferred to propose first, but that evidently was just a forgone conclusion to her as well as their friends and neighbors back home. They were the perfect couple. Like a fairy tale.

The day he graduated he sat well back from the summa cum laude graduates. He wasn't even close to the magna cum laude. In fact there was no praise whatsoever to his rank or grade point. If it had been given an award it would have been for scraping by. He wasn't even able to see the stage from his seat without the video board behind the dignitaries. His diploma, however, was the same size. Good enough.

The very next day he walked down the aisle before 300 of his bride's closest friends and his family. The whirlwind of celebration should have been exciting, but he felt nothing but dread and disillusionment. For the last four years he felt pressured to march to the rhythm laid down by others and live a life they had designed. None of that appealed to him; yet, here he was getting married and expected to go off to law school.

What no one knew was he had blown his LSATs and he wasn't going to any law school anytime soon unless he registered online for a distance learning degree. He actually could buy a law degree for just under $500 if he had been interested, but he was not. He knew after the honeymoon he had to have a serious talk with his new bride who was already planning their home and social calendar once he was hired by the most prestigious law firm in Dallas. The sun, sand, fruity drinks and romance under the stars were great. Just like a fairy tale. They flew home and that was when the wheels fell off. He made the mistake of starting the conversation on the plane. He immediately saw his mistake. He had nowhere to run, and she had no door to slam. They were asked twice by the stewardess to lower their voices and on the third time threatened with arrest upon landing. Only the thought of mug shots and publicity calmed Crystal enough to salvage the rest of the flight.

He never did understand why wanting to coach football should have been that much different than being a lawyer, but it seemed to make a difference to her. He tried to explain the money would be less, but he would be doing something honorable and helping kids. Something that made him happy. She made it clear that he could take honor and kids and shove it where there was no sunshine. She had no intention of sitting in bleachers on Friday night waving pompoms while she froze her ass off instead of attending some society ball.

There were lots of tears, a few things were broken, an attempt at making up, and pleading, but eventually she realized she bet on a losing pony and the only smart decision was to cut her losses and start over. Annulment was considered since the union was dissolved shortly after it had been joined together, but they had both been of sound mind, sober, and agreeable at the time. Divorce was the only option. Crystal considered it a blemish on her stellar reputation, but she managed to play the victim well and her family and friends rallied around to console her.

Billy should have felt worse. He didn't. He felt unburdened and free for the first time in years. He liked Crystal and hoped she would find the happiness she was looking for. He hoped he would as well.

3

When Billy woke up, beer cans littered the sand dune; many were riddled with bullet holes. Sand was stuck to the side of his face, as drool cut a river through it much like the Nile through Egypt. A scorpion was crawling up his arm. Alcohol numbed his reflexes enough so he didn't overreact and get stung. He watched the creature meander about before taking a hike across his sleeve, down a beer can and back out into the desert.

The next thought that managed to claw its way past the hangover was, "Is that a snake in my pants leg?" His breathing became very shallow as the different electrical impulses in his brain tried to formulate the correct answer and response. At one point he dozed back off only to wake with a start remembering what he was supposed to be deciding. Finally, he reached down and grabbed at the legs of jeans and choked the life out of the yucca stalk that had lodged itself there during one of his impromptu leaps during the air guitar concert he remembered performing sometime during the afternoon. That was the last memory that came to mind.

Fueled by adrenaline and sufficiently awake, Billy managed to stand and survey the damage. Twenty Lone Star cans lay .

crumpled where they fell. Some were wounded during target practice; many simply lay empty and crushed. 9 mm casings that had been ejected in every direction reflected the sun that was sliding towards the west. Billy remembered he had turned on the cans in frustration after the groundhogs chose to move . . . quicker than he did.

Billy did notice the windshield of his truck was still intact after the two errant bullets had passed through both front and back panes of glass. He actually was kind of proud of those two shots since he had managed to take out a grasshopper in the process. The panes held up, but cracks were starting to form. An explanation would be needed before getting back to the office. He still had time, but decided to start back to the office before somebody started worrying about the truck. His welfare was immaterial. The truck was important. God forbid anyone cared about his well being. When the night watch came on, all that was necessary was that a truck was in each assigned slot and all was well with the world.

Billy gathered his cooler with the four remaining beers and his pistol that gaped open from its last valiant effort only to be clogged with sand as it fell from his comatose hands at the conclusion of the last encore of **Stairway to Heaven**. It would need to be thoroughly cleaned. His pistol was cleaned more often than his apartment and more important to Billy.

By the time Billy pulled into the company yard and parked his truck in the appropriate slot, he had made his decision. He took the keys into the dispatcher and on his time sheet wrote the words by Johnny Paycheck that he had been listening to on the tape player driving in, "Take this job and shove it! I ain't working here no more" and headed back out into the darkening night. He figured the money he was owed would be enough to replace the windshields. He was willing to call it even if they were. He wasn't waiting to find out.

As Billy drove home through the streets of Waymor, he knew he could continue to spiral into the abyss or choose to claw himself back out of it. His beer and heat induced epiphany was that he loved football, and win or lose . . . he wanted to be on the sideline. The last he heard, they were still looking for coaches at

13

Waymor High. Under the hot shower in his apartment with dirt and grime swirling down the drain, Billy felt excited about the possibility of coaching again. Hope and excitement were feelings he hadn't felt in a long time.

Billy woke early the next morning to the sound of his heart beating loudly in his head. The throbbing was like Morse code reminding him that stupid had a price, and it was usually expensive. He slowly dragged himself out of bed and into the shower once again with the cold water pelting his brain this time. When his head was numbed by the cold, he toweled off and sorted through his clothes to find a decent shirt and pair of slacks. He assumed he was unemployed and remedying that needed to start first thing. His daylong binge and impulsive resignation from his oil field job the previous day didn't sound like the best idea in the glare of the July sun blasting down through his apartment window. What was done was done. Billy now had a chance to reconnect with the school and be coaching again in the fall.

Dressed in a polo shirt and slacks he had found in the back of his closet, Billy loaded his golf clubs in the trunk of his car. With it being the middle of July, he knew the superintendent would be running his business from his golf cart out at the country club. Cracker Jack Daniels was a legend in Waymor, which is why he had stayed around. In the oilfield he would have been just another tool pushing, rig chasing, middleman, but in Waymor schools, Cracker Jack was king. He had gone to school at Waymor High, been hired as head coach before he finished college and won district three times. If you didn't know this about him he had the banners hanging everywhere to remind folks of this unmatched achicvement. From there it was a matter of rightful ascension to the Superintendent's office when the Honorable Shorty Black passed away twenty years ago after having served Waymor faithfully as Superintendent/high school principal for 40 years. So either Shorty or Cracker Jack had been running Waymor ISD for almost its entire existence, which explained a lot of why the district operated like it was still in the previous century.

The origin of Cracker Jack's nickname is often discussed and disputed. Many believe it is from the amount of boxed treats and brown liquid he consumed and others thought it was because he seemed to always come out on top of a good deal. How he got the name seemed to have been lost to the ages, but everyone knew Cracker Jack for miles around and across two states.

The Waymor way is a proud cry throughout the community. Mainly because things were still done the way the parents and grandparents had done them growing up. There was nothing more upsetting than change. If the pony's running, ride it to the end, Billy had heard more than once. He still had no idea what it meant.

The powers that be in the community might have been a little more concerned had they taken notice that each year the town got smaller because their kiddos preferred to live in the modern era and moved off to Lubbock, Odessa, Fort Stockton, and some all the way to Sweetwater. But the Waymor way was the way things were done and would be done until Hell froze over or the Texas Rangers were brought to town. In Waymor it was "be and let be".

When Billy arrived at the pro shop, he loaded his clubs on the first cart by the curb. The country club was well maintained by the oil companies and included an 18 hole pro designed golf course, a clubhouse with a card room, and a small oval shaped pool for the kids so they didn't interfere with the drinking and gambling. He knew based on the time of day that Cracker Jack should be making the turn and would need to get a sandwich and refill his cooler. As he drove his cart over toward the 10th tee box, he saw the superintendent's group putting out on number 9. Billy parked under a shade tree next to the path where they would have to pass him on their way to the clubhouse. Cracker Jack had his regular group that consisted of two board members and a banker, but today he had added one of the biggest men Billy had ever seen. He was riding with Cracker Jack, which meant he must be a guest or a ringer brought in to help Cracker win a bet.

After whooping and hollering over a missed two-foot putt, the group walked toward their carts and started up the path to reload on supplies. Each man had his own cart, which was the Waymor Way, and each passed and waved as they went by. Billy had been in town long enough so that each man knew his name and since it was a small inbred town each made a comment about his previous days experience calling him Deadeye, Johnny Paycheck, or Bubba. Billy smiled and laughed good-naturedly with them, but realized he had lost the advantage of surprise.

Cracker Jack drove up with a smile on his face almost as big as the giant in his cart. Billy wasn't sure if it was a good day on the course, the case of beer he had consumed during the morning round, or the knowledge Billy was back to grovel for a job. When football season had ended back in November, another 1-9 campaign, he had turned in a resignation letter to Cracker Jack and walked out promising to never coach again. Cracker could take it to the bank! He was done! Finished!

Billy then applied for a pumper's job with the DownHole Drillers Oil Company, a wildcat group out of Midland. Their slogan was We Drill Deep, and their window stickers featured a scantily clad young woman of exotic proportions riding a length of pipe like it was a bronco at the rodeo. His college degree and the fact he could not only read the application, but also write the answers in cursive, placed him ahead of 95% of the applicant pool. The drug test eliminated everyone else but one older gentleman who walked with a cane. Billy was hired as the last man standing.

His experience in the oilfield had not been bad, though the crowd he worked with was considerably different than the educators he was used to. He had learned many new words and found himself cussing out answers that normally wouldn't require profanity. It just seemed to fit the nature of the work. Boredom finally got to him. Driving around looking at wells was great for a while. He enjoyed the outdoors and liked watching the animals, but a person had to be really competent in killing time to enjoy the day-to-day parts of the job. There are only so many cups of coffee a person could drink and so many books a person could read while hidden behind the only mesquite bush within a hundred miles. And then he had his melt down.

Billy was sure Cracker Jack was remembering every bit of his emphatic promise as he drove up with a grin on his face.

"Hey, Billy! You come to shoot some golf or the winders out of our carts?" he asked with a loud laugh.

"I guess most folks have heard about yesterday by now. Not my finest hour. " Billy replied trying to keep his emotions in check.

"Want to join us since you seem to have a lot of free time?" Cracker Jack asked with another beer-fueled laugh, enjoying himself immensely.

"I appreciate that, but actually I was here to see if you had any openings for this coming year. I'd like to come back to work. " Billy replied humbling himself before the Mighty Oz.

"You don't say?" Cracker Jack responded with fake surprise. "I thought you were through with education for good!"

"Obviously I made a foolish mistake, and I'm willing to admit it. I was upset with losing and . . . well it was impulsive I know. " Billy said groveling as low as he could go. "I'd like another chance if you are willing."

Cracker Jack looked thoughtfully into the distance as if he was trying recall if he had any openings at all. Billy had no doubt that Cracker Jack knew to the penny what the budget was and exactly what positions he still needed to fill, but this made it appear as if he was thoughtfully considering the situation.

"I tell you what Billy, if you can whip this feller's ass," he said pointing to the giant alongside him in the cart, "I'll hire you back!" He finished with an even look on his face and his eyebrows raised in questioning.

The giant next to him just grinned beneath his sunglasses and sunburned head.

"We'll sir, I guess that would be as good as a no because that's a pretty good sized man, and he doesn't look like he enjoys taking a beating," Billy responded politely and with a hint of disappointment in his voice.

Nothing was said for what seemed like several minutes. The giant smiled, Cracker Jack looked expectantly, and Billy sat mulling over whether he might could land a lucky punch before the giant could untangle himself from the cart knowing full well he hadn't hit anyone since junior high.

Cracker Jack finally broke the silence with a loud cackle of a laugh as if he had just told the funniest joke of all time.

"Billy I do believe you were considering giving it a go. You must want a job real bad. This here is the new Head Coach and Athletic director for Waymor High, Corliss Prescott Skinner, or Boomer, as he prefers to be called. He was just riding around this morning talking to me about staffing. Seems he's short a coach. Why don't you buy him a beer up at the clubhouse and take him off my hands. He ain't worth jack on the golf course, and he's draining my battery trying to tote him around."

The giant laughed, ease himself free of Cracker Jack's cart and stepped towards Billy with his hand stretched out. Looking at the size of the man and the hand coming at him, Billy realized how foolish he was to think about taking a swing.

"Hey Billy, let's get some beer," was all Boomer said as he shook hands and then swung into Billy's cart causing it to tilt dangerously to the right.

Billy turned slowly to keep from tipping over and drove back up the cart path.

4

Billy's interview with Boomer took place in the card room of the clubhouse while playing two-handed Gin Rummy and drinking beer. Billy learned that Corliss Prescott Skinner was the name that you would find on Boomer's service record and teacher certificate. It's the name his mother gave him at birth, but no one, including his mother, called him Corliss. If you think he might have been teased as a kid, think again. Boomer was 6'7" and weighed well over of 300 pounds. From what Billy gathered, he had been that large most of his life even though some of what was muscle in his younger days now resided closer to his middle. Regardless of the muscle to fat ratio, Boomer was a big man.

Boomer grew up in West Texas. He lived on a ranch and learned how to work at a very early age. He had the size to do manual labor and most folks thought he'd take up ranching, as he got older. Boomer, however, was an athlete like no one had ever seen especially in a 1-A school. His letter jacket had more letters than jacket and scholarship offers started pouring in while he was still a junior.

Boomer had his heart set on playing for the Aggies of Texas A&M. He wasn't sure exactly when his admiration for the Aggies began since everyone in town was a die-hard Red Raider fan. The expectation in the coffee shop and down at the barber was that he would go to Texas Tech so his family and friends could drive over and watch him play on Saturdays. It never really mattered because when Boomer went to take his SAT exam, it became obvious he should have been spending more time studying and less time throwing a ball or riding his horse. He could have flipped a coin and scored higher.

Now Boomer was not ignorant or even unintelligent. He just never really saw the need to worry about lessons out of books over things he didn't care for. He never had any problem getting passing grades all through high school. None of his teachers were going to keep Boomer off the field on Friday night; so, they designed lessons he could pass. His SATs were a bitter disappointment for the Aggie coaching staff as well as Boomer and his family. Everyone agreed he'd enroll down at Blinn Junior College long enough to get his grades up to passing and complete some remedial classes. The Aggie coaches promised to have a maroon jersey waiting for him in College Station when that happened.

Boomer worked hard and found that he like reading after all and his classes became easier as he spent time with his tutors. It seemed the plan to get him in Aggie maroon was well conceived and right on track until the Buccaneers homecoming game against Cisco. A chop block during the 3rd quarter by the right guard and center turned Boomer's left knee into pasta. By the time he had healed and rehabbed his knee, A&M had found ten more recruits with whole bodies and high SATs. Honestly, Boomer wasn't all that dejected. He found that he actually liked learning and all the practice time was cutting into his studies. He packed his bags and went back to Lubbock to enroll at Tech to become a teacher and coach.

Boomer listened to Billy's life story and his attempts to find himself. Boomer could see Billy had a passion for coaching although he had lost his focus during the struggles the last few years. They both saw someone in the other that they felt like they could trust. After a case of beer, with Boomer drinking it like it was lemonade, they shook hands and Billy became the new defensive coordinator of Waymor High School much to his delight and relief.

Over the course of the next few days, Billy was issued his regulation coaching gear which consisted of a couple of pairs of black double knit shorts, a pair of black game day slacks, and three gold double knit shirts. The school colors of black and gold reflected the oil influence in West Texas, black gold, which would have been seen as very creative other than the fact that eight of the ten schools on their schedule had the same colors for the same reason. This made it hard to tell teams apart during some games since gold could be considered a light color or a dark color so coaches had to agree ahead of time. The problem was that some coaches had their "lucky jerseys" and insisted on wearing them regardless of agreement. Some games wound up looking like inter squad scrimmages to the fans and resulted in more than one interception since quarterbacks under pressure looked for a familiar color and saw lots of players open. Unfortunately, half of them were the opposing team.

5

The first order of business prior to a new school year was the annual migration to Houston, Dallas, or Ft. Worth for coaching school. School is a loosely applied term for one last chance to get drunk and play golf before spending the next five months locked in the field house watching film and drawing plays six and half days a week when they weren't on the practice field.
Sunday mornings were always left open for church. Everyone knew if you weren't in church, you would surely suffer the wrath of God and lose because any work done on His time would come to no good.

Coaching school rotated annually through the big three cities,

20

and any coach that had been at it long enough had their favorite spots. The staff that Boomer assembled was made up of coaches from a variety of backgrounds, but to a man they preferred Ft. Worth if for no other reason that it took less driving time. Less driving time meant more time for golf and entertainment. That's not to say there weren't instructional sessions that could be attended to learn how last year's regional champs attacked a six man front, or how the new spread offense could stretch any defense to the point of breaking. The problem was that most of these ideas were based on having the horses in the stables to run them. In Waymor they already knew what their kids were capable of, which left very few options, so most of the time after registering and picking up gift bags was spent deciding on where to eat, scheduling the next tee time, and deciding the evenings entertainment.

Bonding as a staff was important and Boomer made sure there was plenty of bonding time. Joe T. Garcia's and Billy Bob's Texas were considered bonding Meccas, and Boomer and his staff made them office central. Billy Bob always felt like he and Billy Bob's Texas were kindred spirits and therefore a place he should bless with his presence as often as possible. Which is where they found themselves on a hot sweltering July night.

Cold beer was the only deterrent to the heat since just about every coach in Texas showed the first night, and it was standing room only. People danced in order to breathe a little and stretch. It was also a place for the local single women who turned out from TCU, North Texas State, and the many businesswomen that still were out there competing. There were also those that were married, but looking to stray. Everyone knew the coaches were in town for one last hurrah and the next three days would be a feeding frenzy.

Patrick "Paddy" McMahon was the offensive coordinator on the Waymor staff and was famous as being the "fastest white boy" in Texas. Each year he was in high school down at Cuero, he would line up at the state track meet to run the 100 and 200-meter dashes. Each year Black kids that ran like the wind flanked him. Each year he held his own right up to the finish line, but being 5' 6, he was always out leaned and had a drawer

21

full of bronze medals to show for it. His legs were so short that to keep pace he looked like a cartoon character where his legs appeared to be spinning in circles as he ran.

Paddy was a character. His Irish heritage blessed him with a head full of red hair, freckles, and sharp sense of humor. He was constantly joking, poking fun, and generally aggravating anyone near by. The only time he was sad was when he was alone. He thrived around people. Paddy sought out the party and made himself the center of attention. Paddy loved people and they loved him back.

Another passion of Paddy's was drinking. He claimed it as his birthright and felt obligated to set the pace. The heat and the excitement of their first night in town drove Paddy to effortlessly finish bottle after bottle of cold beer as he stood alongside Billy Bob talking to a couple of the locals.

Between his natural engaging personality and being fueled by a large amount of alcohol, Paddy located and enticed a couple of young ladies to join them. They had no chance of resisting. The smile alone would have done it. Beth Anne Howell was an accounts manager for a mobile home parts supply company in Watauga. She was twenty-six and single, living with her parents hoping to have her own place soon. Beth Anne had brought her friend, Charlene Parker, who was a clothing buyer for Dillard's over at the mall who took pride in her fashion sense.

Charlene had coordinated outfits for Beth Anne and herself for maximum effect knowing they would be competing with hundreds of other single ladies. She and Beth Anne had come in their sundresses accessorized with bangles and earrings along with their cowgirl boots. Their outfits emphasized their figures and highlighted their summer tans. Beth Anne was a blonde, at least she was this night, and wore white with turquoise accessories. Her boots were turquoise and black with silver piping. Charlene was a redhead decked out in green that matched her eyes and her boots. She had silver jingling from her ears and wrist. A silver metal belt cinched her dress up to a dangerous level of exposure. She felt like it provided an incentive to get to know her.

Paddy had spotted Charlene immediately and had been

22

talking her up non-stop for over an hour. Her laughter became louder the more alcohol that was consumed and Billy and Beth Anne had gone along for the ride. Each couple had taken several turns around the dance floor, two stepping to the music of a soon to be famous country western band. With sweat soaking through their clothes and their beer bottles empty, they returned to a table they had grabbed off in a corner to catch their breath.

Things were looking promising for both couples and everyone was heading in the same direction. A few more beers and then off to a quieter spot to have some late night fun that just might end with breakfast even though the girls had to be at work the next day. Breakfast was part of the incentive package the girls were offering. Right in the middle of one of Paddy's countless jokes he stopped mid sentence. His eyes were focused over Charlene's shoulder and as we waited for the punch line he shouted, "I HAVE to do that". We followed his finger as it pointed straight at the mechanical bull across the room.

"You can't be serious Paddy, " Billy said amused.

"No, I HAVE to do that! I have never ridden a bull, but I can ride that!" Paddy yelled convinced as he got out of his chair and started towards the menacing looking machine.

The sum total of common sense left in the group at that time was not enough to stop Paddy so they all grabbed their bottles and followed to cheer him on. When they found a spot along the rail that protected the padded area around the bull, they could see Paddy confidently handing over some cash while half listening to the instructions. Paddy mounted the beast, hooked his left hand in the grip, threw his right hand up over his head like he had seen rodeo cowboys do, pressed his knees against the metal bull's body as he had been instructed and nodded he was ready.

Although a mechanical bull doesn't have a head, it does have a neck that extends forward of the body, and it was the neck that moved back rapidly towards Paddy as soon as the operator pressed the button. Paddy's face and the bull's neck met with a sickening impact. When the neck went forward and Paddy when backward, it was evident that Paddy's nose was broken and looked like a smashed tomato. His two front teeth were lodged in his upper lip after being dislocated from his gums.

Beth Anne, standing beside Billy, turned away and threw up, right down Charlene's leg and into her boot. Charlene was hit hard and quick by the bloody mess before her, too much alcohol, and a boot full of squishy liquid. Her brain locked and a state of rigor mortis set in, but not before she was able to turn away from Paddy and the bull. She went rigid and comatose held upright by leaning on the railing. This was unfortunate because it allowed time for Beth Anne to reload and give her a matching pair of boots. The lights went out behind Charlene's eyes, and it was all Billy could do to catch her before she hit the floor.

Billy drug Charlene to the nearest booth and told the couple there to get her some help. He then grabbed Beth Anne and sat her down in an empty chair and helped her focus her aim away from him just before she launched for the third time. He turned to see about Paddy only to find him still in the saddle flailing back and forth, side to side as the bull continued to circle and buck.

What no one was in position to know was the Little Ronnie Rakestraw, the cowboy behind the bull's controls, had harbored a grudge against football players since high school. The players had their letter jackets, banquets, and trophies while people worshipped their every move. He was a cowboy. A real ranch working cowboy that no one noticed or cared about unless it was to call him a hick or snuff dipper.

Ronnie had looked forward to the night with a room full of drunken ex-jocks and was determined to punish as many as possible. He had managed a few laughs throughout the evening, tossing the heralded ex athletes aside one after the other. Until Paddy his amusement was short lived. Paddy was his masterpiece. He had maneuvered the bull with expert precision to keep him balanced and not letting him off. Paddy's cocky demeanor had set Ronnie off, and he intended to show Paddy that you couldn't pretend to be a rodeo cowboy. Being a cowboy was serious business, something you had to learn and earn. It was also tougher than being a dumb jock.

Ronnie toyed with Paddy like a cat with a mouse. Speeding up and slowing down, spinning to catch him, then smash him again.

Paddy was anesthetized with alcohol and had no idea his face was a bloody mess. He clung on waiting for his eight seconds to be up and the sound of the buzzer. Ronnie's game continued until people started gagging and screaming loud enough for a manger to notice. He rushed to Ronnie's side and shut the bull down fearing a lawsuit. Calling for a security guard to escort Ronnie out, the manager climbed in to the arena attempting to grab Paddy who was smiling a large gapped tooth smile while bleeding dramatically. When the bull stopped, he waved both hands in the air in triumph for having lasted "8 seconds" and immediately passed out falling backwards off the bull.

Billy rushed in fearing the worse. Paddy was still was unconscious, but still grinning. When the EMTs arrived to assess the damage, Billy went in search of Boomer. Billy found Boomer standing at the bar talking to the lead singer of the band about their new album. After a quick update, they ran back over to the bullpen where the EMTs pronounced Paddy alive, but in need of an all night emergency visit. Boomer and Billy carried Paddy out and laid him on the seat of the school van they were driving and followed the directions they had been given to find help. All the time the manger was reminding them Paddy had signed a waiver and couldn't sue. Nobody was listening.

The overworked doctor shook his head and mumbled as he worked on Billy. It never ceased to amaze him the lengths grown men went to be stupid. After some time and effort the doctor explained to Billy and Boomer that Paddy would need his nose fixed, a visit to his dentist to get replacements for the teeth he extracted from his upper lip before sewing up the holes, and lots of painkillers. He said all of that with a shake of his head and derision in his eyes.

Billy and Boomer managed to get Paddy back to the hotel and in bed with ice packed around his face and a couple of painkillers down his throat. They agreed to take turns making sure he was breathing throughout the night. Morning was going to be a surprise for the happy go lucky Paddy, a painful surprise. Billy took the first shift, promising to be attentive until relieved by Boomer at 3 A.M. Just before Billy fell fast asleep he suddenly wondered what had happened to Beth Anne and Charlene. The evening had been shaping up to be memorable, and they hadn't even exchanged phone numbers. The chance they might still be interested was a long shot. There might have been permanent trauma on their part. Something Billy decided was best left alone.

When Billy jerked himself awake he found Boomer fast asleep and Paddy gone. He immediately woke Boomer and after searching the room and hallway, they dressed and began searching the hotel grounds for their mangled friend. Paddy was sitting in the coffee shop, face swollen beyond recognition, entertaining a couple of waitresses with the story of his historic bull ride. He sipped coffee that drooled down his chin while eating a plate of greasy eggs and sausage. Some of the folks nearby weren't as happy to have him as scenery as they tried to eat without gagging, but the waitresses were convinced he was a PBR champion and were star gazing! They each had an autographed napkin tucked in their cleavage.

"Hey guys, where the hell have you been? We have a tee time over at Shadow Oaks in forty-five minutes. I thought you limp dicks might sleep right through it. "
Paddy greeted them as Billy and Boomer walked up to his table. Billy looked at Boomer, and they signaled for two coffees as they sat down.

6

Billy woke up Sunday morning in his apartment. The coaching staff had driven in late the night before and this would be the last day of rest for any of them before spending months locked up in the coach's office or on a practice field every waking minute they weren't in class teaching. His head ached more from the cumulative effect of the past few days than from anything specific. He downed some Advil and Aleve from the giant bottles kept nearby on the end table that he had gotten at Sam's the last time he had been in Odessa. He washed them down with a half empty bottle of stale beer he hoped was from last night instead of last week.

He started every Sunday the same way, singing to himself Kris Kristofferson's ***Sunday Morning Coming Down*** as he drank a couple of beers for breakfast, dressed in his wash day clothes, and started the first load of laundry. It's a song that both inspired and depressed him mainly because he felt he lived it more closely than he should. While the clothes were washing, he ate breakfast out of a cereal box since the milk had spoiled while he was out of town. Settling back in his recliner he tuned in Charles Stanley's religious program in hopes of finding inspiration and a way to maintain the little bit of sanity he was still working with.

After shifting a load from washer to dryer and bowing his head during the benediction on TV, he made a run to the local supermarket that stocked the basic staples and a few extravagances for the people of Waymor. He didn't need much at home since breakfast was about the only meal he'd eat there. Lunch would be at school and dinner in the field house, ordered in or brought by one of the more industrious wives. He threw a few things in his basket, and as he checked out, Wylie Tremain, the owner who acted as cashier and bagger on Sunday mornings so his staff could attend church, asked how the season looked for the Sand Crabs. Billy gave it his most positive spin by saying, "You can expect us to show up and play hard every game!" Which was code for "I don't know if we can win, but we hope so. " It wasn't actually code since it was something everyone knew. Wylie smiled and nodded as he rang up the sale and bagged Billy's groceries.

As Billy paid and started for the door, Wylie shouted after him, "Billy, I'm glad you're back at the school. I always thought you were good for the kids. They need someone like you. "

Billy smiled and thanked him promising again to do his best. He realized Wylie's words of encouragement had bolstered his mood more than anything lately, and he actually found himself bouncing along as he walked back to his apartment. This season was going to be better Billy said to himself, convicted and convinced.

49-6! Ft. Sam Hill over the Fighting Sand Crabs of Waymor. The two a day practices and prep work the weeks leading up to the first game had been great. The kids had come out in large numbers with the new giant of a coach which must have given them the idea Boomer could and would actually take the field with them. He was motivational and had them believing they could run through walls. Billy named his defensive game plan the Wall of China. Waymor was going to be bigger than any team they faced. They were also going to be slower than any team they faced. Billy's idea was simply to hold ground and spread as far across the field as possible with nine men leaving the two fastest players about twenty yards back. If a runner broke through the wall or a pass was completed, Billy hoped a twenty-yard head start might give them a chance to catch someone. In practice it was impressive against a junior varsity team made up of smaller slower guys. Spirits were high.

Fort Sam Hill was a small community nestled along the Pecos River further out in the middle of nowhere than Waymor. The town thrived because of the water and their main source of income was agriculture. This meant that about the time school started the migrant workers starting showing up for fall harvest and brought their children to enroll in school. The Hispanic kids were not big, but they were fast. As luck would have it, harvest season seemed to last about as long as football season, after which the migrants moved on down the road treasuring their awards from another championship season.

The Wall of China did its job during the first series of downs and the Waymor fans were encouraged as the quick little running backs from Ft. Sam Hill slammed into the Waymor kids and bounced back. The Sand Crabs first offensive series consisted of giving the ball to a running back who drug as many defenders as he could carry as far as he could carry them until like a pack of wolves bringing down a buffalo, the runner would succumb. Five plays took them over the goal line and the Crabs led 6-0. Having never scored much, kicking extra points was not practiced often and was never effective; so, the score remained 6-0.

The coaching staff at Ft. Sam Hill were not morons or new to football. They had their adjustments ready for the second go round and the track meet was on. Quick pitch sweeps wide,

28

passes lofted high in the air so a quick footed receiver could just run under it, and each time more points showed up on their side of the scoreboard. Billy had adjustments as well, he was just limited by the fact his kids were slow and there wasn't much he could do about that. He could teach a lot of things, but speed wasn't one of them.

At halftime he and Boomer tried their best to inspire and re-light a fire, but the Sand Crabs were happy to eat a package of powdered donuts and drink a Dr. Pepper before going back out for the second half. The kids accepted their role and their fate. Comfort food helped. Most of the stands were empty before the final buzzer sounded. The fans hadn't left angry; they were just resigned to another season of losses. They had hoped for the best, but were prepared for the usual. Boomer and his staff locked themselves in the office after they had gotten the kids showered, the laundry started, and the film sent off to Hobbs to be developed. It wouldn't be back for a couple of hours which would give them time to eat and figure out what they might be able to do different. Come Saturday morning they would need to meet with the team and convince them that winning was something they were capable of; they just had to convince themselves first!

7

"Billyee! Billy Bob Masters! You are just the man I am coming to see. " The voice of Cracker Jack Daniels echoed through the dark as he exited his pick up parked at the curb. Billy had come from the field house a block away where he had spent most of Sunday evening redesigning his defense to find a way to stop the Rocky Valley Kangaroos, their next opponent. The 'Roos had fewer migrants and more chicken fries and gravy boys like Waymor. He considered going toe to toe with them, but had to convince his guys they could meet them head on and come out okay.

Billy was carrying a change of clothes and intended to shower and dress in the gym before his first class which was early morning tutorials for those that showed up. By hosting the early tutorials Billy finished early and could be back at the field house shortly after lunch. He felt like this was a good trade off since sleep was never that important to him anyway. Cracker Jack caught up with him at the door Billy was holding open and followed him inside.

"What's up, sir?" Billy spoke with the deference afforded Cracker and his office.

"I'm here to make your day! You just get ready to thank me and I'd like a nice amber filled bottle for Christmas!" Cracker Jack said overly excited for a Monday morning.

"Okay. I guess I'm ready then?" Billy answered, though far from convinced. He'd been around Cracker long enough to know that there was only one winner in any situation he was involved in and that was Cracker. However, if you happened to be someone that helped provide the win, you benefitted handsomely for just be part of his scheme. He was determined to win, but not selfish with the spoils.

"Billy Boy, ol' Donnie C, The Rock himself, wound up in jail this weekend and we no longer have a high school principal!" Cracker crowed!

Donnie C was Donald Conway. He was called The Rock sarcastically because he was 5'7" in boots and weighed close to 300 pounds. He took it as a compliment thinking it referred to his solid stature. Most people used the term as a derogatory reference to the thickness of his head that prevented most thoughts and knowledge from penetrating. He had also been accused of having the personality of a rock. There were few that spoke nicely of Donnie C.

Donnie had been the high school principal until that very morning and a thorn in Cracker's side. Donnie had been the head football coach some years back and managed to have a two win season which through threats and innuendo with board members had parlayed the extra victory into the vacant principals job and what appeared to be a ride to retirement. He seemed to be the only person to ever get the best of Cracker, until now.

"What?" Billy exclaimed, "Jail?"

"Seems The Rock has been crossing over into Mexico down at Ojinaga to do some drinking and gambling on weekends. I have suspected he was using petty cash to bankroll himself, but could never catch him or prove it. He evidently won enough to replace what he may have spent and had a really good time using of school funds. His cash drawer still balances." Cracker explained.

"Well, that all came to a screeching halt Saturday night," Cracker continued. "It seems he was in a small bar down some alley when a young lady asked him to buy her a drink. When he pulled out his wallet to pay she grabbed his cash and tried to run. He grabbed her by the arm and was getting ready to give her what for when she begins yelling for help! She is telling everyone in Spanish that Donnie C was propositioning her and had threatened her. The authorities were called. He's locked up in general population until someone from the U. S. can get it straight. Everybody on both sides of the river knows it was a setup, a scam, but certain formalities have to take place and a fine will be paid. He probably won't be out for a couple of days! Couldn't happen to a nicer guy!" Cracker ended, laughing with his whole body.

"Either way, the morals clause in everyone's contract is all I need to remove him. The charges won't be dropped. He'll just be released and told not to come back. The Rock is either guilty of stupidity or banned from another country, which ought to do the trick finally and for good!" Cracker stated triumphantly. Still undefeated!

"Well, I appreciate you letting me know. Who is going to be the new principal?" Billy asked.

"Oh Billy Boy, why do you think I'm up this early tracking you down? You are! Congratulations!" Cracker said pumping Billy's hand like a politician at church.

Billy had only been half listening the last few minutes. He didn't care one way or other for Donnie and figured Cracker Jack was just looking for someone to celebrate with. This early, the choices were few. He had been more interested in getting a shower and dressed for the day so he would have time to stop by the snack bar in the cafeteria for a couple of Marbella's homemade breakfast tacos. She made her own green sauce as

31

well. A hot shower and spicy tacos was really what was occupying Billy's mind when it finally dawned on him what Cracker Jack had just said.

"What?" Billy exclaimed, "You have got to be kidding me! I have no idea how to be a principal! That's funny. Tell me you're kidding."

"Nope, not kidding" Said Cracker still smiling. "I've been thinking about this all night. You, my boy, are the perfect choice!"

Billy was a stunned as Paddy had been when the bull had rearranged his face. He was speechless.

Cracker gave it a minute and then in his most officious and serious tone he said, "Billy, look with me here. My choices to run this school are limited to those on staff here and at the junior high. If you go through each name you can understand there are few candidates to begin with. What you have going for you is that I've always thought you were blessed with intelligence and common sense. Not many get both and even though you choose to use only one or the other most of the time, you're young and will learn. Look, I've been leading this district for some time and it mainly comes down to using your head and thinking a little. I figure you can do that as well as anyone, and you always have cared about the kids. Best thing is, Ms. Dixie Lee sits right outside your door and will tell you anything you need to know. The only way you can screw up is to not ask or not listen. Other than that you take care of your kids and your teachers. You finish out this year and we'll see how it goes. We'll send you over to Alpine there at Sul Ross to get you a few hours and an emergency certificate. After that you can pick up the rest of the hours as you have time. Any questions?"

Overwhelmed, Billy was still struggling to wrap his mind around what was happening. It all began to sink in and not seeing any escape Billy asked, "So what happens next?"

"We'll, if I were you, I'd hop in that shower, get yourself dressed, cram down a couple of those tacos you've been dreaming about and get ready to meet your new faculty! Dixie has already sent out an all-call for an emergency faculty meeting and you'll be introduced in the library in about...forty-five minutes! Better get to it!" Cracker finished with a smile. This time more for encouragement that mirth.

"Congratulations Billy Boy! Someday you're going to thank me!"

8

Billy showered and dressed without thinking, skipped the tacos, and went straight to the office. Mrs. Dixie Lee was sitting behind her desk that guarded the entrance to the administrative area of the building. She was protector and sentinel for Waymor High School. No one passed with out checking in and getting her permission.

Dixie Lee's maiden name was Grant; so, since she got married, she legally was Dixie Grant Lee. You could make the jokes, she would tolerate it as she had thousands of times over the years, but more than a mention and a chuckle would be a disaster...for you. Dixie was born and raised in Waymor. She had been an outstanding student and athlete during her time in school as well as holding offices in as many clubs and organizations that she could fit into her schedule.

When Dixie graduated, she had numerous small scholarships, but still not enough to pay all the bills to go to college so she decided to work for a year to save money. She didn't want her parents to have to borrow. She started out as an aide in the Resource room, moved to Librarian, and then to principal's secretary all during a nine-month stretch. Obviously her abilities and intelligence helped, as did several bizarre twist of fate. Between fate and luck she found herself that June being asked by the principal at the time to stay on one more year and then to go to college. And she stayed. Then she fell in love with Kenneth Lee, a roustabout with manners and a way about him that inspired trust and devotion. They got married, had two kids, a girl and a boy, and fifteen years later she was still running Waymor High School.

Dixie had never looked back or wondered what might have been. She loved her school, her town, and her family. She protected each with a fierceness that was unmatched by the

33

common man. She was a force to be reckoned with if you showed up in the office with some petty complaint or a desire to bad mouth the school. You told her your business and she told you to have a seat and wait or she told you to get over yourself and get out. This applied to anyone, from the toughest tool pusher to the Mayor himself. School board members were deferential to her as well.

Dixie's job was safe. She was the only one that knew where everything was stored and all the bodies were buried. She was the closest thing to J. Edgar Hoover that Waymor had. She had a dossier on file in her brain on every individual in town. She knew where the skeletons were and how much dirt was there. Too many men now in the age range of leadership in the community had grown up with Dixie and made the mistake thinking she might want them to grope or grab the body the good Lord blessed her with. "No" was usually explained with a knee to the groin or a right handed slap to the face that caused the head to turn just in time to catch the left coming back the other way.

Only one person was known to make the mistake twice, and many believe it was the alcohol and that he was too drunk to realize who she was until he gave her a slobbery kiss at a party one night. As her knee landed square in his groin and the light began to fade in his eyes, his memory kicked in just long enough to register the mistake and then the right hand landed. He never felt the left. Dixie was devoted to Ken and Ken to Dixie. Unless you were a stranger in town, you knew it, too.

The fierce protection Dixie had for the school included protecting the principal's office. Protecting the office was not the same as protecting the principal. She felt like it was her job, among others to make sure whoever was sitting behind the desk did not bring shame or embarrassment on the school with their behavior or decisions. She had learned over the years how to coax, push, and demand to the point that most who had served there were able to come close to meeting her expectations. The Rock, Donnie C, had been one of her biggest challenges. He was a an uncouth man that laughed way too loud, passed gas at any time regardless of who was present, showed up late, and left early. His greatest sin was when she put a folder of forms on his desk that required his signature, and he didn't sign them. Usually she had to remind him two or three times, which threw her schedule off. That was unacceptable.

Dixie was thrilled to find out that Donnie C was languishing in a Mexican jail. She didn't wish him harm, but she was glad he was out and Billy was in. But Billy would never know either of those things.

"Good Morning, Mrs. Lee" Billy started timidly. "I guess you may have heard by now, I'm supposed to be the new principal starting here in about fifteen minutes. "

"Congratulations, Mr. Masters. Have you had anything to eat?" Dixie asked.

"No Ma'am, I decided to skip breakfast since I'm kind of nervous to be honest. " Billy said with a smile hoping to appear more confident that he was.

"Wrong choice on your first decision! You aren't starting off great, but I suspect you'll get better. " Dixie said as she took a package of peanut butter crackers out of her desk and slid them across to him. "Now go over there and get some coffee, I don't serve you coffee. I'm not a waitress. You'll get your own coffee, sit at that desk and get some food in you so dry heaving is not the first impression you make on your faculty. Got it?"

Dixie didn't wait for an answer, but plowed right ahead, "When the meeting is over and the day has started, you and I will go over what you need to know to live through today, okay? You don't need anything right now other than to stand up straight, speak clearly, act like you know what you're doing, and make them believe everything is fine and will continue to be fine. Tell them to have a nice day and dismiss them. There will be one or two teachers that see this as opportunity to get something they have been wanting and will immediately ask you for decisions. You simply say let's talk about that this afternoon after school. They won't come back because they don't do after school. That will end that. Got it?"

Billy was waiting for her to go on. The silence hung heavy for a few seconds until he realized he was supposed to speak. "Yes Ma'am."

"One last thing for now. You are Mr. Masters to the staff and me. You are the leader, the boss. Don't give anyone permission to call you Billy. They might any way, but don't encourage it. And you may call me Ms. Lee or Ms. Dixie, I don't answer to Dixie or sweetheart because I am to be respected as well. So far your manners are impeccable, and I appreciate your mother for teaching you correctly. Good luck. You'll be fine. " She winked and shooed him away towards the coffee. "I'll let you know when it's time. "

9

The faculty meeting was mostly anticlimactic. Most had already heard about Donnie C and really didn't mind Billy being the principal. Most had carved out their niche and knew they were here when a new principal came and would be here long after that principal left. The only thing that might cause them interest was if there might be an attempt to "bring about change" for some odd reason. Billy didn't stir up any feelings since he stuck with the script Dixie had given him once Cracker Jack made the introduction. He said this was a surprise, and he'd need a little time to get his feet on the ground, but was determined to do a good job. They all applauded and grabbed an extra donut on the way out. The donuts were a nice touch only Ms. Dixie would have thought of. Billy was already indebted to her, and he hadn't even seen his desk yet.

There were two teachers who lingered after the rest left for class. They had concerns about the "promise" that The Rock had made just the previous week about providing them some extra funds so they could take their biology classes on a field trip over to Monahans to visit the sand dunes and then come back by Balmorhea for a swim. They assured Billy of the relevant learning opportunities of the trip and wondered if they should schedule the bus. Billy's first thought was that it sounded like a fun day and was fixing to say sure go ahead when Ms. Dixie's words came back to him to beware of lingering teachers. He apologized and asked them to hold off until he had time to get with Ms. Dixie and see where the funds might come from. Then he asked if they could come by after school for an answer. They both smiled with their lips, but not with happy eyes, turned and left abruptly.

Okay, thought Billy, so far so good. Now I guess I go and find out what else I might need to know.

The bell had rung, students had trooped in as they did each morning, and Billy stood in the hall saying hello to those that chose to look his way. Then the halls cleared, classroom doors closed, and learning began. He turned and went back to the office for his lesson.

Ms. Dixie was on the phone when he came through the door and motioned him to go sit in his office until she was through. He went in and sat in the chair that Donnie C had used and realized is was way too short. The back spring had broken from him leaning back too far and the base was loose from holding his weight. To say it smelled like a feedlot was an understatement. He must have lived on Marbella's bean burritos and green sauce. This wasn't going to do at all. He was in the process of hauling the chair from around his desk when Ms. Dixie came in.

"I'll have the custodian throw that in the trash. I wouldn't expect anyone to use it. I have a chair stored in a closet down the hall that will do just fine. The custodian can bring that back on his way from the dumpster. For now sit here. " Ms. Dixie said as she pointed to one of the armchairs in front of the desk.

"Here's a pad and a pen, write down as much as you need in order to remember these things. We'll start slow and add to your list as the days go by. You will find that at some point things begin to repeat themselves and the answers will already be here. That is until something unexpected happens, then we deal with it. Okay?" she asked, handing him a legal pad and a nice pen.

"First of all, don't let anyone borrow your pen. There are several old pens in your desk you leave out for others to use. People have germs. They stick the pens in their mouths and chew on them, but mainly walk off and keep them. The adults are as bad as the kids. Next, keep this little notebook in your pocket at all times along with your pen. When you're down the hall and someone asks you something, write it down. They think

37

your interested and it reminds you to give them an answer. Speaking of answers - the only ones you need are yes, no, and let me check on that and get back to you. Never get in a hurry to respond unless there is smoke or blood. The biggest mistake rookies make is to answer too quickly, have to change their mind, and then they look wishy-washy. Nobody wants a wishy-washy leader...especially me." Ms. Dixie paused while Billy caught up taking notes. She smiled to herself as she saw he was starring and highlighting the right things. She thought again, there might be hope for this one.

"Alright, if you want to be good at this job, get here early. You should be the first one in the office. Turn on the lights, start the coffee, and have your door open. Most business gets done between the time you walk in the door and when the first bell rings. If the teachers think they have someone that they can turn to, you've won half the battle. You don't have to stay all that late because most people bail out of here at four and those that stay are usually the English teachers that live here. Never try and out stay those folks. Next, return your phone calls regardless of how bad it may be. That keeps people from calling back, and if you make them mad they call Cracker Jack. He doesn't like that to happen. He has his own phone calls to answer. Give a teacher an answer within forty-eight hours, even if it's 'I don't know yet', so they know you haven't forgotten. One last thing for today. If I put a folder on your desk for signatures, you sign them. You can read them if you want, but know I've checked every form, I wrote half of them, and they are ready to go except for the campus principal's signature. I'll do that for you. You sign them and get them back to me by the time specified on the sticky note on the front of the folder. Deal?" Ms. Dixie asked with one eyebrow arched anticipating an answer.

"Yes ma'am," replied Billy, not sure if he had another option. One thing he was learning quickly was that keeping Ms. Dixie happy seemed to be the most critical part of his job, and this seemed to be something that would make her happy.

"Good, then. Any of what we've covered seem to be beyond your ability?" she asked.

"No Ma'am. I believe I can handle it. I'll need to study my notes, but I'll be ready," replied Billy, almost believing what he said.

"Your first meeting is at the start of Activity Period. The Cheerleaders want your approval for the theme of this Friday's pep rally and game. They want to either white out the Kangaroos by wearing all white or black them out which requires turning the lights off during the pep rally. Which seems to appeal to you?" Ms. Dixie asked as a form of pop quiz.

"My first thought is I'm not fond of a dark room with hundreds of high school kids present, " Billy answered, wondering if he passed.

"I'd go with the my instincts on this one then...that usually works best. Trust yourself. " She said as she stood up. "Take a walk around the halls and be visible. Nothing is pressing right now, and by the time you get back your chair will be ready. Here's your radio. If something comes up I'll call you. " Ms. Dixie winked and was gone.

Billy walked out into the hall as if it was new territory never explored even though he had walked these halls for years. He heard a voice behind him as he started off, "Look confident, be confident!", so he straightened up and walked as if he owned the place.

10

As Billy walked the halls during class he began to realize he had never considered the administrative side of education. He hadn't even thought about what went on behind the scenes when schedules were made, classes assigned, and countless other things that caused him to hyperventilate. He shook off the feeling of panic as a couple of students he had taught came walking up the hall towards him. He tried to give his most confident look as they passed and high fived him. It seemed they were happy about his promotion. Knowing them, it would last until the next time they were sent to the office. Billy turned and walked back. Advisory period would be starting in five minutes.

39

Laci, Staci, and Kaci were sitting in front of Ms. Dixie's desk waiting for their meeting. They were the senior captains of the cheerleading squad. As he walked through the office door, they all stood and said is unison, "Hello, Mr. Masters" as if Ms. Dixie held a training session in his absence. It did make him feel good and he waved them into his office where he noticed a brand new executive chair had been placed behind his desk and surprisingly adjusted perfectly. It fit like a glove. He also noticed a third guest chair had been placed in front of his desk as each of the girls plopped down making themselves comfortable. He grew more impressed and intimidated with Ms. Dixie as the day went on.

"Alright," said Billy, "what is it that I can help you with?"

"Well," said Laci, "we come in each Monday to get approval for the week's theme for the pep rally and the football game. This week we have two choices, and you can tell us which you like the best. Okay?"

"Yes Ma'am, I can do that. What are the choices?" Billy said as if he did this everyday.

"Well," said Staci, "Our first thought was to black out the Kangaroos which would include having black lights and glow in the dark paint in the gym for pep rally. We'd cover all the windows and turn out the lights so all you could see would be like skeletons dancing and things like that! Then we wear all black to the game!" she had finished with a flourish and was obviously excited about this choice.

"And choice number two?" asked Billy.

"Well," said Kaci, "Our other choice is to white out the Kangaroos. Everyone wears all white and we decorate the gym like a winter wonderland and use canned snow, which we of course clean up and then we all wear white to the game." She finished not quite as strong as Staci and I'm sure that had been coordinated to leave the emphasis on the black out. Why did high school students like to turn out lights and be in the dark? Billy thought, and then face palmed himself mentally because he knew exactly what the attraction was.

"Well, ladies," Billy began sounding as official as he could muster, "as my first act as principal of Waymor High, an act that

40

I'm sure will go down in history, I've always been partial to white. I choose to white out those Kangaroos. Let's change that gym into a winter wonderland," Billy finished with a smile on his face as if he had just pleased everyone, knowing full well he had pleased only himself...and Ms. Dixie of course.

The girls smiled bravely, thanked him, and promised they'd do their best as they went back to class.

Ms. Dixie watched them leave before poking her head in his door. "I take it from the looks on their faces you went with white."

"Why yes I did. I gave it thoughtful consideration and followed your advice. My gut was very clear!" said Billy.

"Just so you know, the cheerleaders have been trying for about five years to do the black out theme and haven't had much luck. Their last hope they thought was you. They thought you were either gullible or not so old as to be intimidated by students in the dark. Guess they were wrong." She winked and left

11

The first couple of days had gone remarkably smooth while everyone settled in and waited an appropriate amount of time for the honeymoon to be over. Although the days had been business as usual, Billy had snored himself awake each night in his recliner well after midnight with his dinner tray still in his lap. He would trudge to bed in time to hear the alarm go off in what seemed like mere minutes.

Wednesday morning found him in high spirits, which wasn't unusual. He was always more upbeat on Wednesdays. It went back to his coaching days where all school activities ceased by 6 P.M. to allow students to attend church if they chose. For coaches it meant a rare night off early and a trip across the state line to grab a case of beer at the liquor store built in exactly that location for that exact purpose. The mission of Pablo's Cantina was to supply the good citizens from the Texas side of the desert with beer since they refused to vote their own county wet in order to maintain a proper environment for the children. Both sides benefitted and were perfectly happy with the arrangement.

The coaches took turns making the drive, but regardless of who went, the first beer can hit the pavement with the ping of aluminum while they were still within the shadow of the billboard announcing great deals on booze and beef jerky. The reward for being the mule was getting to start early.

The rest of the night was spent at the weekly poker game that moved from one house to the other on a rotating basis depending on whose wife was out of sorts. The longer the season went and the more time husbands were away from the raising of kids, fixing squeaky doors, and broken dishwashers, the fewer wives were willing to put up with a bunch of drunken coaches letting off steam while smoking cigars and playing cards. By the mid point of the season, it was up to the single coaches with apartments or their own rent house to host. Being only the second week of the season, there would still be sandwiches made, chips, homemade cookies, and the desire to maintain the appearance of a "coaching family". Wednesday night beer and poker was why there was a smile on Billy's face when Ms. Dixie walked into her office.

She noticed the coffee made, Billy smiling, the lights on and the door open. So far so good she thought. Hopefully the rest of the lessons would stick as well.

"Good morning, Ms. Dixie!" Billy called out as she placed her purse in the filing cabinet. "How are you this morning?"

Ms. Dixie made her way around her desk and stepped into Billy's office. "Good morning, Mr. Masters, you seem extra chipper today. Did you finally get some rest?" She asked returning his smile with one of her own that looked a little less sure and somewhat curious.

"Yes Ma'am, I did. I slept about four hours in my recliner and about two hours in my bed, plus tonight is Wednesday!" Billy said with a half way fist pump not sure how appropriate Ms. Dixie would find fist pumping in the administrative area.

"And is this Wednesday a special day that I am not aware of?" Ms. Dixie asked knowing full well all the sordid details of past Wednesdays that resulted in many Thursday morning

42

headaches, hangovers, and discreet apologies. It didn't hurt that her husband Ken was an auxiliary sheriff's deputy and had a police ban radio on at all time listening for calls. Some of the more outrageous ones were usually made late at night on Wednesdays and mainly involved school personnel. A lot of escorting people home took place for their protection and the protection of the rest of Waymor and the surrounding county.

"Why Ms. Dixie, for someone that knows everything, surely you know that school shuts down at 6 P. M. on Wednesdays, and that's the one night we can get together and play cards. " Billy explained to her as if she was clueless.

"Play cards...like hearts and spades?" she asked more mocking than naïve.

"You're kidding me now, aren't you?" He saw in her demeanor another lesson coming.

"Mr. Masters, do you remember that you are now these people's boss, and tomorrow you may just have to fire one or all of the people you have hung out with before. Considering past behavior, you could easily fire the entire coaching staff if you had the mind to. Do you think sitting side by side with them matching them drink for drink and raise for raise would make that job harder or easier?" she asked.

Billy's smile had long since faded from his face and fighting against what he had suspected already, he still hesitated before stating the obvious, hoping for some last minute pardon. Ms. Dixie never blinked or moved, prepared to wait as long as it took for him to confirm out loud what he needed to do. Finally, he nodded and said, "So my social life is now over if I want to be the principal?"

"Not over, just changed. You will need to find new friends that aren't your employees, have kids in school, or are related to someone that works here," she said with the twinkle returning to her eyes.

"And who in Waymor might fit that description?" Billy asked now fully depressed, but curious as to where he might be able to make new friends.

"Donnie C was a horrible excuse for a person and did everything he could to irritate me. He acted completely unprofessional the majority of the time, but he did one thing right. He took his party on the road. He left town when he felt the need to blow off steam. I would caution against using school funds and going to Mexico, but leave town. Oh, and don't drive home drunk. That wouldn't help matters."

Dixie was not sure how detailed she needed to be. Based on her experience with men, both good and bad, there were never enough details to cover every situation they might run into and given one loophole, they usually managed to completely screw up.

Billy sat there mulling over everything she had said, trying desperately to salvage some resemblance of fun that had gotten him up for another day of work, but every word she had uttered was like another nail in the coffin of his personal life. Finally he asked, "So I'm supposed to drive away from Waymor to places where I'm not known, have a great evening with people I don't know, not drive home drunk, and be back in time for work tomorrow?"

"That's one option. Or you can go down to the First Baptist Church for prayer meeting and the social that is held afterwards for those that wish to have cake and coffee. You just might meet a nice girl and have fun the old fashion way by talking, smiling, and laughing...sober. " Ms. Dixie said the last words as she spun on her heels and left having made the point needing to be made and now the rest would be up to Billy.

She poked her head back in the office as Billy was still staring at his desk and said, "That's where I met Kenneth. And we have lived happily ever afterwards...so far!" She smiled and winked for encouragement and went to work.

The rest of the day passed in a daze as Billy's brain fog continued. He felt trapped and torn. There was nothing that said he couldn't associate with employees, have a beer, or play poker as long as he didn't get arrested. He knew Ms. Dixie was looking out for his best interest, but there were some things that were sacred and Wednesday night poker was one of those. He thought he would like being a principal, but at what cost. Sure he needed to set an example, but couldn't it be one that was fun loving and fair?

Billy had not figured out the best thing to do by the time school was over and decided he could table it for this week so as not to make a mistake. He remembered not to be hasty making decisions as one of his rules on the yellow tablet. How funny that came back to him. When he left school Billy stopped by the pizza place and ordered a large with everything on it. Why not? He took himself home where he spent the evening drinking his last two beers and a couple of Dr. Peppers as he finished off his pizza. Around eleven he awoke in his recliner, the pizza gone, and the empty soda cans intermingled with the beer cans. He flipped off the TV, brushed his teeth and went to bed.

Surprisingly enough, Billy woke up before the alarm on Thursday with no headache. He bypassed his usual medical regime of aspirin and Rolaids for a green sauce taco Marbella put together especially for him. A spicy taco was not something Thursday mornings in the past would allow. The smell of any cooked food had created waves of nausea after the usual Wednesday night carousing. Today, he added extra sauce and momentarily considered prayer meeting.

12

The week ended uneventfully including the whiteout pep rally although it was touch and go for a few minutes. All was going according to the pre-approved script. The band was playing the fight song, the cheerleaders had oversized bows in their hair that were flying and flopping as they twirled and step toed in front of the adoring student body, pompoms secured in each hand alternately thrust into the air to match the beat of the bass drum. What would school be like without bow headed twirly girls?

The skit, which came after some half-hearted cheers and a dance routine that highlighted the cheerleaders' pompoms and skirt flipping, had a Kangaroo come waltzing across the floor only to be met by the Sand Crab mascot. The young man that volunteered to dress as a Kangaroo had evidently studied up on his part. Having learned that kangaroos appear to box, he decided to go all Muhammad Ali on the Sand Crab who took offense and went into Joe Frazier mode backing the Kangaroo up against the pep squad. After landing several blows to the Kangaroo's pouch, wiser heads prevailed, and the two were separated.

Billy felt that someone should have known that the two mascots were trying to date the same girl and had chosen to settle it in front of the entire student body. Maybe it ought to have been him, but he really thought the cheerleaders had a more direct line into the social lives of the students. No injuries were reported with their baggy suits and oversized heads taking the brunt of the blows. Since it was a skit, the crowd assumed it was supposed to be funny. Billy just gathered them in the corner of the gym and warned them sternly. After agreeing to shake hands, Billy sent the love struck boys back to the pep rally. The cheerleaders had gone right into their high-energy dance routine with hair flipping and leg kicking. Then the crowd fully embraced the drum line and their percussion routine clapping along with the beat. The first notes of the school song brought everyone back to attention and then it was a mad dash out of the gym.

As Billy walked back to the office, he decided he would speak to the cheer sponsor about vetting their volunteers a little better in the future. Ms. Dixie seemed to approve of his overall handling of the situation after he reported back when everyone had left for the football field in preparation for the night's game. He watched as she got her purse out of the filing cabinet and was holding the door for her to leave when the phone rang. He motioned for her to go on and he'd get it.

"No!" She stated almost emphatically, more urgently than he had heard her speak all week. "Go get your legal pad and write this down under rules. Never answer the phone after 4 P.M. on Friday. It's always bad news. Nobody calls at four on Friday to thank you. If they are happy they go about their business for the weekend with a note to call on Monday and praise us. Only unhappy people call after 4 P.M. on Friday. Their kid just came home with a note from a teacher or told them something that's got'em all fired up. They're calling to light into someone. If you answer the phone on Friday, you get the brunt of an end of the week tired, already into the first bottle of booze angry, and they

46

need someone's butt to chew on. If it's still important on Monday, they'll call back, but with less anger. If it's no longer important, you dodged a bullet!" She finished as Billy sat there wide-eyed with his hand still hovering over the ringing phone. And then it went to voicemail.

"And don't listen to the voicemail until Monday so it doesn't wear on you all weekend or you have a weak moment and decide to call back earlier. It also gives you deniability. Don't do it!" She emphasized with a shake of her head.

Billy agreed and went to get his notepad as Ms. Dixie started for the door.

"Will I see you tonight at the game, Ms. Dixie?" Billy asked.

"I haven't missed one since my youngest was born and only then because they chose Friday afternoon to enter the world. My husband still caught the second half!" she replied proudly.

"Alright. Ms. Dixie, I cant thank you enough for this week and all the help you've been. Obviously, I would have screwed this whole thing up if it were left up to me. I hope I've always remembered to say thank you, but in case I haven't just know how much I appreciate you." Billy said to the woman he saw as his guardian angel.

A wink and a wave was all that Billy got in return as Ms. Dixie headed to her car. He thought he might have seen just the slightest moistening of her eyes, but wasn't willing to place any bets on it being more than allergies or relief the week had ended.

There was an advantage to being the principal at a game instead of a coach Billy realized almost immediately. As he walked across the parking lot to the stadium, he saw he could enjoy the food booths setup to sell grilled burgers, turkey legs, desserts, or a variety of other choices prior to the game instead of warming up the players. He decided he deserved a couple of plates of food and took pride in supporting the fundraising efforts of the various clubs. As principal, he couldn't favor one group over another; so, he found himself overly stuffed by game time. He would need a new approach for the next game. He would need an Alka-Seltzer for this one.

As he finished off his grilled corn on the cob slathered in butter, paprika, lime juice, salt, and pepper, he noticed a cloud

47

back in the southwest. Clouds weren't unheard of in the desert, but ones that looked like rain were rare. You got to know the small ones that packed some punch and usually carried a downburst that lasted about five minutes and were gone. This one had potential. Rain wouldn't affect the game, but lightening would. The trainer had a gizmo that measured lightening strikes and distance, so he felt like that was under control and went back to picking the kernel husk out from his teeth and wiping his mouth. He had an umbrella in his car that had been a wedding present. It had been missed during the sorting of possessions and stayed under the seat all these years, still unopened. If it started to sprinkle, which was about all anyone out here ever expected, he could at least stay dry.

The teams took the field, the students filled the students section all wearing white t-shirts, effectively whiting out the dastardly Kangaroos, and the band marched into the stands playing the fight song. The stadium was rocking with everyone expecting great things. The slow-footed Rocky Valley boys looked like an even match for the slow-footed Waymor Sand Crabs. A real possibility for a win fueled the enthusiasm of students and adults alike.

Prior to the playing of the national anthem, Billy made a pit stop at the men's room and walked out to his car to get the umbrella. He noticed it was decorated with pictures of kittens in rain boots. The cloud was still there looking more ominous than before. His manhood could handle the kittens and staying dry seemed important.

When he returned to the stadium, he caught the trainer on the sidelines to make sure the spark meter was calibrated and working. After being assured all was safe, Billy took his place on the track in front of the student section and right next to the cheerleaders. He felt this would be the best place to see and be seen. Hoping all the enthusiasm would be directed towards the field in a positive manner and no one would do something silly or foolish, Billy expected to be able to watch the game undisturbed.

As the captains of each team met at midfield and shook hands, the small cloud moved above the stadium. As the Sand Crabs kicked off defending the north goal the cloud unleashed a downpour not dissimilar to the bucket scene in *Flashdance,* a movie he recently seen. The water came down not in drops, but as if it was poured from a bucket. Billy managed to get his umbrella opened and leaned against the stands to protect himself as much as possible from the deluge. It was over as quickly as it started and the closest thing to a flash flood Billy had ever witnessed. As he shook out his umbrella, the kittens no worse for the wear, he turned to see how the fans had fared. To his horror he quickly realized that he had created the world's largest wet t-shirt contest...with mostly under aged minors at that. All his students in white t-shirts were sopping wet. Their shirts were sticking to their skin and had become transparent. The guys were not a problem. It was the 15-18 year old girls that concerned him and specifically those further along in development than others. He was trying to take an assessment of the situation, but at the same time felt uncomfortable staring up in the stands at his female students that basically were standing there in their undergarments. Billy did give thanks they were almost all wearing undergarments.

As he struggled for what to do next, the game continued amidst cheers from both sides and the students were unfazed by being wet and half naked. It appeared he was the only one that felt the situation needed a solution, and that it was up to him to find one. Only as he peeked upwards once again did he see Ms. Dixie making her way down the stairs from the reserved seating section where she and her family had sat each game for years.

Ms. Dixie stopped at the rail and motioned for him to come over. Billy made his way to her and stood as tall as possible as she squatted down and spoke to him through the chain linked fence separating the field and stands.

"What are you thinking there, Mr. Masters?" she asked. "You seem to be very concerned and distressed."

Billy's first thought was whether his distress was that obvious to everyone or just to Ms. Dixie who had super powers.

"My choice of white t-shirts seems to have back fired, and it appears I approved a wet t-shirt contest for underage girls of varying development. I was just thinking maybe I ought to fix it

49

before it goes much further," Billy responded resignedly having no idea what to do next.

"I kind of thought that," Ms. Dixie replied. "Don't trouble yourself. This is what is known as an act of God. If you start thinking you can solve every problem in every situation, you will have a very short and painful career," Ms. Dixie assured Billy. "You will undoubtedly catch any blame and the grief from those that want to cause a stink, but it's an act of God remember, and there's nothing you can do. You take the heat and move on. This will resolve itself by halftime and then nobody will care. Trust me."

The last two words were unnecessary since Billy had already committed to being a follower of Ms. Dixie regardless of where she went or what she said. She obviously was the wisest of them all. Between her and Billy there was no contest.

Billy thanked her and went back over on the track to watch the game. He took one quick look into the stands and saw the girls were still there, still wet, and still unconcerned. As the second quarter began and the sun went down, the desert starting cooling as deserts do. The hoodies and jackets came out and as promised, the situation resolved itself by halftime. Billy just shook his head and wondered how much worse could a blacked out gym be?

The Kangaroos hung another *L* on the Sand Crabs; Billy got everyone out of the stadium and then he headed home. He had now been a principal for one week. Billy decided he was battered, but not beaten, possibly wiser and better off. Maybe he'd try it again next week.

13

Boomer stood outside Billy's office waiting respectfully for Ms. Dixie to get off the phone and allow him entrance. It was amazing to Billy how someone commanded such respect and authority that everyone recognized and knew better than to flaunt. Billy smiled to himself as he sat there and offered Boomer a half wave and a nod that he understood the delay, but protocol was everything. When Boomer finally was given the green light, he walked across the office, extended his right hand and said,

"Hey Boss, how they hanging?"

"Right now they're hanging just fine, but I'll let you know as the day goes on," replied Billy amused that just a couple of weeks ago he was working for Boomer and now Boomer was calling him boss.

In reality they were peers and fellow administrators, but Boomer needed Billy to help with teaching assignments for his coaches and when the always-present problem of his athletes running afoul of the discipline policy or grade issues, they would have to work together. Mostly Billy assumed Boomer was being polite.

"How are we looking for this Friday night?" Billy asked as a way of making small talk.

"Any given night any team can beat another team, so that's our game plan for this week," Boomer answered honestly.

Boomer and the Sand Crabs next opponent had championship trophies stacked in closets since they had run out of trophy case space years ago. Save the uniforms and hopefully not get anyone hurt was usually the plan when the Pronghorns showed up. This year would be no different so Billy didn't ask any follow up questions.

"We need to fill your coaching spot. I've been short handed for the last couple of weeks since you moved up to the big time," Boomer informed Billy. "I assume you've been using a sub to cover your classes."

To be honest Billy had been so overwhelmed it never occurred to him that he had left a vacancy behind. Boomer had been handling the football side of it and he guessed Ms. Dixie had been making sure his class load was covered. In reality as the second ranked coach on the staff he had the lightest load as far as the classroom was concerned. He had a couple of study halls and a P. E. class where the students mostly threw balls at each other or sat in groups and talked. As long as they didn't create problems he didn't create grief. Both sides had been happy with the arrangement.

"What do you want to do for a coach?" asked Billy.

"To be honest, I've been talking to Johnny B, and he'd like to return from the dark side. I think he could run the defense for the rest of this year. If we move him into your teaching slot, we could find us a coach to teach Johnny's history classes," suggested Boomer.

Johnny B or Johnny B Good, officially known as John Baldwin, was the girls' basketball and softball coach. He had started out like most guys to win football championships, but after too many 1-9 seasons had decided that he liked winning more than he liked football, so he applied and was hired as the girls' coach. Over the years he had actually been successful. In high school Johnny B had played a little round ball and was part of the intramural championship basketball team in college three out of four years. He also could use his baseball background on the softball field. The principles of the two sports seem similar. Hit, throw, and catch. Score more runs than your opponent.

Johnny B's basketball girls had come the closest of anyone in Waymor to real success since Cracker Jack was winning district football championships decades ago. The girls finished their season in second place and made the playoffs the year the UIL expanded the number of eligible teams. Their play-off streak ended at one, but the excitement that accompanied the days leading up to the game was unbelievable. Monahans was chosen as a neutral site and most of the win starved town drove over to watch. The parade behind the bus strung out for over a mile.

Johnny B had the same problem as the football team. His girls were big, but slow, which describes almost everyone in Waymor. He had tried to exploit what he had and did better on a basketball court than Billy had on a football field. When you pack five large girls into a zone, you can force a team to shoot over you each game. For the teams that relied on driving the basket or offensive rebounds, the Sand Crabs dominated. If a team showed up with a sharp shooter from outside...more than likely another victory was in doubt. The girls' offense was to stack high and low, passing the ball above the heads of their opponent, making a move to the basket while leaping an inch or two off the ground.

To make matters better, a new field superintendent was brought in at the gas plant and happened to have a daughter that not only could dribble, but shoot as well. During the regular season the girls packed the zone with four, chased the ball with one, and had a shooter/passer on offense. Dreams were created each night about how far they might go. Monahans was the answer. They would go as far as Monahans. When the new gas plant supe found his daughter in a car with a boy he deemed less worthy, both partially undressed, she was sent back to Houston to live with an aunt. Pleas by the community to wait until after the season fell on deaf ears of the man protecting his daughter's virginity. He wasn't aware he closed the barn door long after that horse had galloped away. Along with the contrails of the airplane heading east, the fantasy of having a state champion in Waymor slowly faded, and then disappeared.

Over the years, Johnny B Good won more than he lost and folks were pleased to have him coaching. He had made the transition and was enjoying the semi popularity that came with being a cult hero; a winning coach in Waymor. Working with girls and their hormones each day had taken its toll on Johnny. He had long ago decided the girls taunted and teased him when he came into the locker room each day for practice or for a game. The girls were given a set number of minutes to be "decent" and have their business taken care of then he knocked and went in. Regardless of day or time as soon as he walked in a girl flushed and came out of a stall pulling up her shorts. The more he turned red the better the girls liked it and were encouraged to do it again. His planned to wait them out until they got tired of the game. He was still waiting.

Another game they played was to not wear a bra during practice and see if he would say anything. He waited for three days until half his team was flopping around the court to set them down and give them the minimum required amount of undergarments each girl was required to wear. It had been an effective talk, but the girls giggled the whole time asking questions just to make him more uncomfortable.

The rest of the eye rolling he did had to do with girls that needed to sit out of practice because of cramps. He had talked to one of the junior high coaches that was a player herself who told him not to put up with that crap. She suggested putting them all on the baseline and run them until everyone was cramping. He had chosen not to do that. The winning season and play off run had energized him as much as the town, but those days were a couple seasons past and the wear and tear was once again getting him down. He needed to be around guys who were popping towels and playing grab ass so he could yell and put them on their face in push up position and make them think twice about acting the fool. He knew what guys needed. Girls crying. Lord have mercy! How could any man be expected to deal with that at home and then at work as well?

"If Johnny B wants to come back over, we should be able to find a social studies teaching coach," Billy told Boomer.

In reality, Billy had no idea what it took to find teachers much less hire them and after the school year had started to boot. He and Boomer agreed to meet back the next day and finalize their plan and approach...after he conferred with Ms. Dixie, which was left unsaid, but understood by both.

Billy got up to walk Boomer to the door when Boomer asked, "So what do you think about being the guy with the desk and the tie?"

Billy really hadn't dwelled too much on the difference, but now that Boomer had mentioned it, he realized he kind of liked the idea if not the everyday problems and responsibilities that went with it.

"Boomer to be honest, I don't think I want to go back to coaching or the classroom. I like the flexibility and that offsets some of the down sides," replied Billy.

"You know, I've been thinking about getting my Masters and an administrative certification," Boomer said catching Billy off guard.

"Seriously?" Billy asked.

"Having the papers opens up a lot more opportunities. Bigger schools like their athletic director to be certified administrators. Who knows, I might want to do what your doing one day. There are only so many losing seasons a man can take...as you well know," Boomer said and smiled. "Maybe we can ride over to

Alpine and take some of those classes together. Think about it," Boomer said as he patted Billy on the back and walked out of the office.

Surprised, Billy stood in his doorway wondering where that had come from. Then he noticed the woman sitting in the visitor's chair across from Ms. Dixie.

The woman was looking straight at Billy with some of the darkest eyes he had ever seen. The look on her face was neither angry nor happy. She had a smile that might be considered a smirk just curling her lips. Her hair was dark and short, shorter than most, but she wore it well. She was relaxed and exuded an air of confidence. She was in control.

Billy also noticed she had on leathers and riding boots; her jacket thrown over the arm of her chair. He had to assume she had a motorcycle near by or was into strange behavior. Then again it could be both. The tank top she was wearing was white and had the globe and anchor of the Marine Corp emblazoned across the front, stretched taunt and displayed proudly.

Ms. Dixie cleared her throat in an attempt to remind Billy that he wasn't at a bar, and that she was sitting right there watching him undress the woman with his eyes.

"Mr. Masters, I would like you to meet my sister Dallas," Ms. Dixie said.

"Dallas, this is Mr. Masters the principal of Waymor High and my boss."

It registered with Billy that Ms. Dixie had said sister and as he looked and compared them, he realized that Ms. Dixie had chosen to grow her hair long and lighten it over the years until she was almost blond. Dallas had stayed with the almost jet black hair they were born with. When he looked close enough he realized that their cheekbones were identical and unmistakable...a compliment to their heritage that went back well before the Europeans even thought about taking a boat ride. Their frames were similar with Ms. Dixie carrying a just few more pounds due to a couple of child births and Dallas looking more like a MMA cage fighter, but both were well shaped and blessed by God in all ways possible.

Realizing he basically had been ogling both women with his mouth open, Billy gathered himself and walked over and extended his hand to Dallas.

"Ma'am, it's a pleasure to meet you for sure!" Billy said with more enthusiasm that really had been necessary.

Dallas took his hand, smiled and said, "Dixie told me you had manners. I can see that," letting him off the hook for his primal instincts that had been on display.

"Are you here on family business or may I help you in some way?" Billy asked hopefully and gallantly.

"I came to invite you to prayer meeting tonight. Dixie, my loving, caring older sister seems to think it might be good for you to have a social life outside of school. Maybe I can help with that," Dallas said with her smile becoming a little more mischievous.

Billy struggled with his reply. He didn't want to seem over eager. Billy knew it was for church, and he revisited his initial evaluation of Dallas as a very attractive woman that rode a motorcycle. The good Lord was extending an invitation and the devil was daring him to take it.

Once more Ms. Dixie broke into his mental debate by stating flatly that it was Wednesday, and he had no official obligations after school. So unless he had personal plans, he was free to attend should he choose to do so.

Billy thought for a minute and realized the last time he had even been close to a woman in a social setting was at Billy Bob Texas in July. That poor girl may still be in therapy. He more than wanted to spend time with Dallas, and if that meant prayer meeting, then he'd go and pray with the best of them.

"Thank you. I would love to go to prayer meeting this evening, and my calendar is clear. What time should I pick you up, and what do I need to bring?" Billy asked recovering his composure.

"Prayer meeting starts at 7. The refreshments and social are right afterwards. We usually have cake and coffee by 7:45 unless there is a longer than normal list of needs. Business is good, most people are healthy, and no parole hearings are coming up so it should be a short night. Plus, it's my week to cook, so you

56

can bet the dessert will be delicious." Dallas explained without the slightest bit of bragging in her voice. Simply stating facts.

"All this and you cook, too?" Billy forgot once again he was in an office with Ms. Dixie sitting at her desk as he waved his hand across her at her body.

"I can bake a cherry pie as fast as a cat can wink its eye, Billy Boy, Billy Boy!" Dallas recited the children's nursery rhyme.

"I am impressed," said Billy with lustful infatuation already setting in.

"You have no idea... Charming Billy," Dallas said leaving that thought lingering as she strode out of the office with her jacket over her shoulder.

"I'll meet you at the church before 7. Just bring yourself and a repentant spirit," she said without looking back, but laughing to herself.

Billy just stood and stared with all kinds of thoughts racing through his mind. He would have gladly watched her walk all the way down the hall if Ms. Dixie hadn't spoken.

"Do you think you can focus long enough to sign these forms or should we just call it a day?" The smile on her face was insincere and the sarcasm was obvious.

Billy knew Ms. Dixie was always professional, but imagined that the last few minutes had tested her ability to not slap him. He figured he had pushed his luck as far as he needed today, so he took the folder from her, thanked her for thinking of having her sister take him to prayer meeting, and retreated back in his office to sign.... and to relive what had just happened.

The day could not end quickly enough, and Ms. Dixie evidently was harboring some sort of grudge because she left without so much as a goodnight. Straight up four she turned off her computer, took her purse from the filing cabinet, and walked out as she turned out her light.

Billy knew Ms. Dixie was critical to his success and not someone to antagonize, but dang, her sister was smoking hot and looked like she could hold her own. Was it too much to ask that he have one night of fun and pleasure while doing this job? Surely a principal's life had to be at least one step better than a monk's. As he sat at his desk and looked out the window towards the football stadium, it came rushing back to him as he re-imagined the leather pants, the sculpted arms, the short cropped hair, and of course the tight tank top, that it had been months since he had even thought about a woman much less been close to one. He realized that any further work for this day was out of the question as his focus was on his date . . . .to church that very night. He packed his briefcase with papers he would never look at tonight and walked out of the building without the slightest memory of doing so. His thoughts were far away and in the gutter.

14

Billy had showered and dressed hoping for the right amount of reverence while remaining casual. He went with jeans, boots, a blue button down, and sports coat with no tie. He hoped he would not be too dressed for Waymor or underdressed for God. As it turned out, he had it just right for the people that showed up on Wednesday night. The faithful that go to prayer meeting are the committed ones, the true believers that take time out of a weeknight to attend church for the third time each week. How Dallas fit into this group he wasn't sure, but if she was going to be here, then, by God, he would as well.

Dallas drove a jeep instead of her motorcycle so she could transport the dessert for the evening. It was a carrot cake as opposed to cherry pie as Billy had expected, but it was a first date and maybe cherry pie was for committed relationships. She had also managed to find the happy medium between formal and casual as she showed up in an oversized sweater that covered her assets and hung almost to her knees and was matched with jeans and boots as well.

As promised the prayer meeting had few topics and was proceeding fairly well. The pastor had offered words of wisdom and encouragement to open the service, the list of prayer request were read and the praying began. Most folks focused on one or two of the needs and then Deacon Jones, an eighty something pillar of the Baptist faith and life long resident of Waymor who had been chosen the designated closer, began to pray. He covered the requests one by one, and then sensing the evening had been brief and would finish early, started in on the military, naming each Waymorite who was currently serving at home or abroad. He shifted next to the government starting at the local level and worked his way up to Washington, D.C., and finished strong by covering the weather and surprisingly the educators that taught the children of our nation.

Although heavy breathing could be heard a few rows up from someone that was having a hard time staying awake like the disciples in the Garden, Billy kept his eyes closed and only peeked at Dallas' legs a couple of times as he bowed his head and felt some how caught off guard when educators were mentioned. With the final amen, most stirred and moved in their seats to restart the circulation that had been lost during the time of reverence. The pastor had some closing thoughts and then invited everyone to stay for coffee and cake supplied "by our very own pastry chef, Dallas Grant." It was exactly 7:49.

After visiting with a few of the members that introduced themselves and invited him to return, Billy walked with Dallas to the serving line and helped himself to a large piece of cake and a cup of coffee. Dallas stood beside him looking amazing and smelling of fresh soap and lotion more than any perfume. The church folk made their way one at a time over to tell Dallas how marvelous the cake was and what a talent she had.

"My talents are varied and abundant and few have seen them all...just so you know," Dallas informed Billy under her breath when they were semi alone.

Billy, remembering he was in church, in the presence of God, tried really hard not to try and guess what other talents she might have besides baking.

"Do you have any plans for the rest of the evening?" Dallas asked as they cleared away the last crumbs on the serving table and rinsed out the empty pan.

"Well, actually, no," said Billy. "I haven't had plans in months to be honest however desperate that might sound. "

"Why don't you follow me home. I'll show you my house and gym and then we can sit out by the fire pit and you can tell me your life story," Dallas added as she smiled. A smile that seemed inviting and devious at the same time.

Billy swallowed rather hard and said, "That would be great."

He followed Dallas' taillights as she meandered through the streets of Waymor and out on the highway until she turned into the driveway of a nice size house on the outskirts of town. It was close enough to see the lights of Main Street, but far enough away to allow for some privacy. They had passed her nearest neighbor a half mile back. Billy parked and walked up to the door she was holding open.

The cold noses of two Doberman Pinchers greeted him. They had growls rumbling deep in their throats and stood as taunt as a bowstring. The fact their master was inviting the intruder in seemed to be the only barrier keeping them from ripping his throat out. Billy extended his folded hand in an offer of friendship, but wasn't sure he would get it back in one piece.

Dallas shooed the "pups" away as Billy thought 85 pounds wasn't a pup regardless of age, but he let it pass as an affectionate term for the killers in front of him.

Dallas led him into a nicely appointed living room and offered him a chair while she changed out of her "church clothes". She handed him a beer while he waited without asking his preference. As she disappeared down the hall, he looked around and decided the house was furnished as minimally as possible to meet the task at hand. He decided he liked her taste, the amount of space, and lack of doodads. This was not a frilly house and probably reflected Dallas' personality. Simple, strong, no extra frills, what you see is what you get, but perfectly functional. As he sipped from the cold bottle he was painfully aware of the two beasts that sat across the room from him just waiting for an excuse to dismember him for fun if nothing else.

In a few minutes, after Billy's bottle had been empty long enough that he was twirling it on his finger; Dallas reappeared wearing a white t-shirt and black stretch pants. Her toned muscles were highlighted by the snugness of the material and it became even more apparent that she was one fine, chiseled, athletic woman. Billy felt self-conscious as his own lack of muscle tone and months of physical neglect. He would have felt embarrassed had he not been a guy and the feelings he had at the moment had more to do with Dallas than himself.

"Why don't you take off your coat and stay a while?" Dallas asked as she breezed into the room.

The Dobermans immediately relaxed their guard and lay down on the floor without taking their eyes off of Billy regardless of how much their master seemed all right having him in their house.

Billy realized he still had his sports coat on and made the effort to remove it while she took his empty and came back with two fresh cold beers. They sat opposite each other on the two chairs available; an accommodation that plainly announced only one other person was welcome or expected here at any one time. He was fine with that since tonight he was the one that had the pleasure.

After a few casual comments about prayer meeting, a few of the people he had met tonight, and her carrot cake, Dallas offered to give him the tour of her home. Billy followed thinking this is the part where they go to the bedroom and immediately began to feel excited and a little intimidated. It had been a while and he was painfully aware of how he didn't measure up physically for sure.

To his surprise she opened the door that led to the garage and showed him her home gym. It included several machines for exertion, exercise, and weight lifting. In the middle of the floor was a silhouette punching bag that she explained was for boxing and kickboxing. It appeared to be a man in an aggressive stance and there were several places that had been abused so badly that they were repaired with duct tape. Most notably was the groin area where stuffing leaked out despite the tape. The area around the head and throat was only slightly better. Dallas suddenly used her foot to smack the dummy to explain how it was used. Her swiftness and the power of the blow sent chills down Billy's spine. He felt like there was a message being sent that he received loud and clear. The sheer force of the blow was filed away between the notation of the two killer dogs and her powerful foot to the groin and throat of the dummy in less time than it would take Billy to raise his arms.

Dallas noticed Billy's unease. Having accomplished her goal, she offered to show him the patio where the fire pit was located. As they went out the back through the kitchen, Dallas picked up a bottle of wine and two glasses. She motioned for Billy to have a seat on the glider and lit the propane flame that heated the lava rocks scattered around sending warmth and light into the night sky. She sat down next to Billy close enough to make him very happy and uncomfortable at the same time.

As Dallas uncorked the wine and poured she laughed and said, "I just like men to know what they're up against. I don't want to be seen as a pushover or someone that can be taken advantage of. If you choose to hurt me or in any way do something I'm opposed to, it will be painful. And while we're at it, that includes hurting my sister as well."

Billy would have moved further away had he been able to but since he had sat right up against the armrest to begin with, he had no place to go, so he feebly said, "I understand."

"Do you?" Dallas asked. "Do you understand that you and I can have a great time together.... as long as... well...my first responsibility is to my sister and protecting myself. I work in the oilfield, and I've had too many guys come along looking to get in my pants for a good time and the intention of being gone before breakfast. That's not going to happen. If you want to be with me, you have to be with me." She finished almost frustrated in trying to explain. "I want someone who is willing to invest the time."

It was quiet for some time. The flames flickered in the fire pit and each of them sipped from their glass. Billy fumbling in his mind for something to say finally broke the silence by saying, "So you work in the oilfield? I was thinking I might have seen you before. Don't you have a crew?"

Dallas shook her head in exasperation, but answered, "Yeah. I've had a pulling crew for several years now. I worked my way up from roughneck to tool pusher. I've had to put up with a lot of crap and more than a few guys have been kneed in the groin or flat out punched for their behavior, but now my guys look out for me. They know I'll take good care of them and don't want to see me hurt.

"Wow," said Billy, "I thought I had seen you before. I was in the oilfield for a while and I'm pretty sure I had heard about you a few times. "

"I know. My crew cleaned up the area around the pump jack after your melt down. I have to say I'm impressed based on the number of empty beer cans and shell casings left behind that you didn't kill yourself or do damage to something near by," replied Dallas with that smirky smile.

Embarrassed, Billy said, "That wasn't my finest hour. "

"Hour, you did all that in an hour? I heard it was an all day event. " Dallas goaded him.

"That's funny. Look, I'd had enough," Billy explained lamely. "When we get to the part where I tell you my life story, you might understand. I just needed a fresh start."

After several minutes of silence, interrupted only by the breeze and a pump jack squeaking in the distance, Dallas said, "I'm glad you got your fresh start. It's turned out for the best. My sister thinks a lot of you and has placed her hopes and dreams on you succeeding. That's why we're here. You can be something special for her.... and me, if you just don't screw it up."

Billy wasn't quite following. "What do you mean?" he asked.

"Look numb nuts, Waymor is a rough place to live and my sister and I aren't exactly ugly which means we've had our share of being hit on. Our daddy knew early on from working in the oilfield himself that we needed to be able to take care of ourselves. He taught us well and we've managed to have each other's back, so we've survived. That doesn't mean we aren't unscathed. We've let people into our lives that have hurt us emotionally and a couple that tried to hurt us physically. We are older, wiser, and more cautious. We both think you're a good man and could be good for both of us if you play your cards right. I just want to make sure you know the ground rules before we start. If you're willing to put in the time with me I'll make it worth your while. I don't put up with cheating, and if you do anything to hurt Dixie you just as well pack up and leave town. " Dallas finished looking him straight in the eye for the longest time without blinking, and then she smiled.

Billy wasn't sure how to respond. He was happy and terrified at the same time. He was stymied as he tried to through his emotions and may have stayed that way had one of the Dobermans not chosen that minute to stick it's cold nose on the small of his back that was exposed where his shirt had ridden up. Billy jumped forward right into Dallas' arms. They both were surprised at his sudden movement.

As Dallas slid her arms around him she said, "I take it you're interested."

At the touch of her warm body, Billy's hesitation and uneasiness disappeared. He forgot about the killer dogs, the stuffing falling out of the groin of the dummy, and Dallas' direct manner. He was a guy that hadn't felt the touch of a woman in months and resolved that for the pleasure that could lie ahead, death was acceptable as payment.

Dallas turned out the burner in the fire pit, finished the bottle of wine by refilling both their glasses, and then took his hand leading him to her bedroom. Billy couldn't take his eyes off Dallas as they undressed in the moonlight that streamed through the windows. She had the most amazing body Billy had ever seen. For someone that had demonstrated and bragged about toughness, she turned out to be kind, gentle, and very loving. Billy realized from the beginning he would be hard pressed to hold his own with her physically, but she seemed to move at his pace and showed a very considerate and compassionate side. Billy thought that had made her even more desirable.

Sometime late into the night Billy lay exhausted on the bed with Dallas' head resting on his chest. He could tell that he was much more winded than she was, but he was too satisfied to care. He just hoped this was real and he hadn't been dreaming or hallucinating.

Billy was too wide awake to sleep and too exhausted to suggest another round of lovemaking so he asked Dallas about her Marine Corps tank top she had been wearing. She waited a few minutes and then told him about a guy she had dated her senior year that was the son of the most senior oilfield executive in the area. He had been raised in wealth and privilege and had come to Waymor from somewhere in Louisiana. She put up with some of his arrogant ways because he was handsome and he bought her nice gifts. However, one night when their group of friends was gathered in the grocery store parking lot laughing and drinking, he held Dallas' hands behind her back and he lifted her t-shirt exposing her boobs for all to see. He had been bragging at school to his buddies about how big they were and that she let him do with them as he pleased. It was all talk, but they challenged him. Peer pressure finally won out, and he put her on display as his buddies circled around for the show.

Shocked at first, Dallas really didn't immediately grasp what was happening. When the realization set in that someone she thought she loved had betrayed her to impress his friends by treating her like a piece of meat, she lost it. The stories varied from the witnesses, but all ended the same way with her ex boyfriend unconscious with several broken bones in his face and possibly damage to his reproductive system. Those who had been enjoying the view just seconds before quickly left at the sight of someone completely unhinged vowing to rip the balls off of everyone present while she continued to kick the unconscious figure on the ground.

Charges were filed. When the case came before the judge, he was aware of the circumstances, but was under extreme pressure from the family to lock her away. She was seen as a hooligan and a menace to society. Trying to find a middle course, the judge offered to let Dallas join the military instead of going to jail. The next day she drove over to Odessa and signed on with the Marine Corps. She decided if she was going to do it, she wanted to do it right. She wanted to be the best and see the world. She stayed in for four years learning everything there was to know about hand-to-hand combat, weapons, leadership, technical skills involving machinery, while circling the globe twice.

When she returned to Waymor, her ex boyfriend and his family had moved on and she settled into a job in the oilfield making a name for herself and convincing others to spread the word. Look but don't touch.

The uneasiness Billy had been feeling earlier in the evening quickly returned as he listened to the destruction she brought when betrayed. Dallas sensed she had freaked him out again, so she took his face in her hands, kissed his lips, and climbed back on top of his very tense body.

Just before dawn she nudged him and said, "Better head home. The sun will be coming up in a little while, and you need to go to work. Besides your truck in front of my house overnight might have some people talking not the least of which is your boss, Cracker Jack."

Billy wearily slid his legs off the bed and began to dress. He was half asleep as he leaned over and kissed Dallas, told her he loved her, and turned to leave. The dogs escorted him to the door to make sure he didn't change his mind. Billy walked out into the fog and darkness that surrounded the desert just before sunrise.

He was halfway down Main Street when it dawned on him.

"I told her I loved her! Holy Hell!"

15

When Billy walked into the office, Ms. Dixie was already at her desk. He glanced at his watch to make sure he wasn't late which would have been almost impossible. The adrenaline that had surged through his body on the way home had kept him wired until he finally showered, dressed, and decided to come on into work.

"Good morning Ms. Dixie. You're in early this morning." Billy said with cheerfulness he actually felt. He somehow was more excited and buoyant than he had been in weeks, maybe years. As a matter of fact he was downright happy.

"How was prayer meeting?" asked Ms. Dixie without looking up.

"Well it was nice to be able to spend the evening with a lot of good folks and Dallas's Carrot Cake was amazing," said Billy vaguely.

"Hmmmm," was all Ms. Dixie said.

When Billy saw she hadn't raised her head from her work and that no further conversation seemed forthcoming he started through his door. As he turned he heard her say, "Be careful."

Billy stopped and faced Ms. Dixie. "Dallas and I had a long talk last night and I think I understand how you look out for each other. I promised Dallas and I'll promise you, that I'll do my best not to do something stupid and hurt either of you. You don't have to worry," he said as sincerely as he felt.

Ms. Dixie finally looked up and with out the slightest trace of a smile she said, "Its not Dallas that I'm worried about. Men who hang around Dallas very long wind up in the emergency room or leaving town. Things seldom end well."

"Be careful," she said again softly, lowering her head back to her work and dismissing him.

The giddiness and cheerfulness he had felt moments ago had dissipated. Once again there seemed to be danger signs coming at him from ever direction, but every time he thought back on the night before, he couldn't help but find himself smiling. He vowed to start working out again to make a better accounting of himself and not have her waiting for him to catch up. Billy was past deciding. He planned on giving it a try. He'd put in the time and show Ms. Dixie and Dallas he was the man they thought he was.

Billy had a stupid grin on his face staring blankly at the wall when Boomer knocked and made his way to a chair.

"Wow, that must be some thought you're having. I've knocked and spoken a couple of times and finally Ms. Dixie told me to come on in and shake you out of your reverie. Was it that good?" Boomer asked.

"Was what that good?" Billy asked back thinking how could Boomer know about last night already?

"Whatever it was that had you transfixed. It had to be something special," replied Boomer not indicating he actually knew anything.

"Oh, I was just fantasizing about being on a beach somewhere, you know how that is when you feel the need to be faraway without worries or responsibilities." Billy downplayed his moment.

"Sure do buddy, but not today. We need to hire us another coach. Remember?" Boomer asked.

"Sure, I'm good, just a little sleepy. What do you have?" asked Billy now back to reality and focused.

"As I told you yesterday I'd like to move Johnny B Good back over to the guy's side and let him take over your defensive duties and help with baseball. I also think he should get your class schedule since it fits with the athletic periods he would have. That would leave us needing someone to coach girls' basketball and softball as well as teach Social Studies," Said Boomer.

"Okay. I talked to Ms. Dixie yesterday after we visited. There shouldn't be a problem as long as we can find a girls coach this far into the school year with basketball season coming up fairly soon," Billy said. He couldn't help thinking that he might have his work cut out for him over the next several weeks beating the bushes to fill the spot especially with Waymor located so far out of the way.

"Funny thing about that is I happen to have a niece, my older brother's kid that will graduate in December from Texas Tech. She's a semester off because of a case of Mono last year. She wants to coach and was All-State in high school in both basketball and softball. She's doing her student teaching right now, but we found out if she has a job, that could count as her classroom hours. She is willing to help us out the remainder of the year if you're interested," Boomer finished smiling like someone that had won the lottery.

"Wow, do you think she could do the job and would she be willing to come to Waymor?" asked Billy.

"She can and she will. I've already quizzed her pretty thoroughly, but of course the final say will be yours. She's an extremely mature young lady and is confident in her ability," emphasized Boomer as he continued to convince Billy.

"Well okay then. Let's see when we can get her down here and talk to her," said Billy.

"She drove in last night and is sitting outside the office as we speak. I took the liberty of having her come spend the night with my wife and me, so we can get this thing done if you approve. No pressure buddy, but I think you'll like her. If you don't, that's okay and we'll start over," smiled Boomer.

Billy was a little surprised that he was minutes away from his first interview, but also proud of how quickly Boomer had worked to solve a problem Billy didn't need. He pictured a woman that was related to Boomer and his older brother and had been an All State athlete to look something like one of the Russian weightlifters that may or may not have been a steroid user. That was probably unfair. He felt she was probably a sweet girl, but the gene pool dictated someone big and powerful which aren't the best traits for a young lady...as far as he was concerned. He needed a coach and someone to teach classes so if she intimidated the kids into behaving, managed to get the girls to games on time, and they performed decently, then so much the better. What she looked like really wasn't the main issue he decided.

"Well, I guess let's meet her Boomer. I don't really have any questions ready, but we can wing it right?" Billy said.

"It's okay, don't worry about it. I'm sure you'll like her. Her name is Savannah Skinner. I'll go get her and make sure she's ready. I left her talking to Ms. Dixie so I'm sure she's been lined out by now," said Boomer as he got up and crossed the room.

Billy was a little unsettled, but told himself he wasn't the one needing a job and it was he that got to decide someone else's fate this time. And then Boomer walked back into the room followed by his niece.

Billy had been leaning back in his chair rocking when Boomer started back in; he got up and walked around his desk to greet the young lady. Boomer had blocked any view of her until he stopped and stepped aside. Billy's knew his face showed surprise because before him was a young lady that was maybe 5'5", slender, and.... well...lovely. She smiled the most pleasant smile he could remember, offered her hand to be shaken while introducing herself as Savannah Skinner and finally Billy pulled himself together, reached out and introduced himself.

Everyone was all smiles while they stood around looking at each other before Billy finally asked Savannah to have a seat across from him. Boomer took the chair off to the right.

"So Savannah, you want to be a coach?" asked Billy.

"Oh, yes sir, I do," responded Savannah with sincere enthusiasm.

"I understand you were an outstanding athlete in high school," continued Billy not having a clue what he should be asking. He figured he do the same thing he did at bars when he tried to meet women. Just keep asking questions until something good happened.

"Oh, yes sir, I was fortunate to be on some good basketball teams and softball teams. We were able to win a lot of games," she answered modestly.

"They won a lot of games because Savannah was on the team," Boomer added proudly.

"So basketball.... what position did you play?" asked Billy not sure how that had worked considering her size.

"Oh, I was the point guard. I was the one that brought the ball up the floor and called the plays," she answered.

"And averaged 27 points a game, I might add," added Boomer. "She was a shooting machine!"

"And softball?" asked Billy.

"I played shortstop and was a slapper. My job was to get on base and score runs. " She answered and smiled.

Billy looked at Boomer who could hardly contain himself and said, "And I suppose you did that prolifically as well?"

"Oh, yes sir. We set a few records for runs scored and things like that," she answered somewhat embarrassed talking about herself.

"Well, it seems you are more than qualified to help us with our coaching. How do you feel about the classroom side of this job?" Billy moved on starting to find a rhythm to his interviewing approach.

"From what I understand it would be a couple of history classes and a couple of government classes. Is that right?" Savannah asked Billy.

Billy took a minute to check the master schedule since it was Johnny B Good's classes, and he really wasn't sure.

"Yes, that's right. Sorry. We're moving some things around and I'm haven't committed it to memory yet," Billy said finally.

"That's perfect then," Savannah said. "When I went off to college my dream was actually to work in government. I had hopes of moving to Washington, D.C. and making a difference. I took a lot of political science classes and had planned on going to law school. I served an internship in Austin and then one in Washington so I was able to see how the government works at the state level and the national level. I've also worked in a meat packing plant growing up during the summer months and to be honest it was the most honest and pleasant job of the three. When I saw how the day to day business of government worked, completely discarding the concerns of the people while simply serving the interest of the elected officials and I saw myself on Judgment day telling my Jesus I had used the precious life he had given me to work in politics.... well I just couldn't. I just couldn't. To be able to face Him I had to do something that would make the world better. I switched to education with the hope of making a difference in the lives of students so they too could make this world a better place. I know history and government inside out. I may just need some help as far as designing lessons and maybe classroom management, but to be honest I think I'll be alright. " Savannah was the picture of confidence and sincerity.

Billy had been listening intently, mesmerized in fact, as she covered her abilities and experience and, to be honest, when she finished, he didn't know whether to applaud or propose. He seriously considered both.

Billy sat in silence spellbound.

Boomer finally spoke up.

"She would have a mentor for the classroom right?"

"Oh, of course. There would be a couple of the ladies in the department that could help her with lessons to get started and offer support until she felt confident enough to go on her own," replied Billy rejoining the conversation.

Wanting to spend more time visiting with Savannah just for the pure pleasure of it, Billy searched for anything else he might be able to add. He felt he was in the presence of a pure soul and simply blurted out, "Are you actually related to Boomer?"

"Oh, yes sir. I know what your thinking. My dad calls me runt. My brothers are 6'6" and 6'7", but I'm the baby and…. I guess the runt. My mom is 6'1", but I believe God made me special for a reason. " Savannah ended with a smile.

"Amen" was all Billy could think of to say. Then he laughed to lighten the mood, but knew he was simply in awe of the person sitting across from him. How could anyone so talented and so grounded wind up in his office in Waymor, Texas?

"So if this works out, when do you think you could start?" asked Billy trying to regain some sort of dignity.

"Tomorrow would be fine it that's okay with you. I brought a suitcase full of clothes just in case, and I'm staying with Uncle Corliss and Aunt Bev. I'm good to go if you are," Savannah answered with eagerness.

Uncle Corliss? He was sure he had seen Boomer winch at the name. Even though Corliss was Boomer's Christian name, Billy had never heard anyone actually say it out loud…until now. He wasn't sure anyone could get away with saying it without serious regrets later…except for the sweet young lady sitting directly across from Billy.

Billy stood and assured her that tomorrow would be just fine and that Uncle Corliss would take her by the superintendent's office to meet Cracker Jack Daniels for the final approval and to fill in the all consuming paperwork. He had no doubts that Cracker would be thrilled to death.

Billy walked them to the door and promised to see them back soon. As he watched them walk down the hall he heard Ms. Dixie say once again, "Be careful."

16

When Billy went back to his desk he realized that Ms. Dixie had placed a folder of forms to be signed on his desk. He wasn't sure how she had done that without him noticing as he had either been in his office or standing in front of her desk…unless it had been when he watched Savannah walk down the hall. He definitely had to be more discreet in his distractions.

Billy had been very diligent about signing Ms. Dixie's forms in a timely manner. He intended to maintain his spotless record and stay on her good side even though he seemed to have stumbled a couple of times lately.

As he opened the folder, on top was a telephone message from Albert Duncan who had asked to have his call returned at once. The time the call was received according to Ms. Dixie's very efficient notation was just as his interview with Savannah and Boomer had started. Billy decided he was already late in calling back so he picked up the phone and dialed. Albert answered on the first ring, which made Billy think he was sitting by the phone.

"Mr. Duncan, this is Billy Masters. I'm the principal over at the high school and I have a message to call you back. What can I do for you?" Billy asked sounding his most officious self.

"Well, I called about an hour ago, and I needed your help then. I thought having a new principal over there that things might be different. I see nothing's changed, and I can't get any help," replied Albert very frustrated.

"Mr. Duncan, I am new, but why don't you at least tell me what the problem is. Maybe I can help," Billy said without a lot of conviction.

"I sure as hell think this will be another waste of my time and what breath I have left, but I guess it can't hurt to try," Albert said. "I live across the street from the high school. Every morning when its time for the news, that darn band starts beating their drums, and I can't even hear my program. Why can't they go somewhere else and make noise? I've asked everyone I can think of and still, bam, bam, bam. So can you fix that?"

"So is this every morning?" Billy asked not knowing what else to say.

"Seems like every morning," Albert responded still miffed about missing the weather.

"Let me talk to the band director and see if we can help you in any way. What's your address or in which direction from the school do you live?" asked Billy.

73

"If you walk to the front door of your school and look straight down the sidewalk, you'll see me looking right back at you," explained Albert very precisely.

"Okay, got it. Let me see what I can find out, and I'll call you back," promised Billy.

Billy set the note aside and signed Ms. Dixie's forms. He walked out to lay them on her desk and asked, "Uh…Ms. Dixie do you know Albert Duncan? He lives across the street."

"Sure. Mr. Duncan was born in that house and has lived there his whole life. Why?" Ms. Dixie asked innocently.

"It seems that our band interferes with him watching the news each morning. Has that been a problem before?" Billy wondered.

"Only from August until November and only Monday through Wednesday since he retired," replied Ms. Dixie with a smile on her face that indicated this might have been a practical joke or at least her having some fun with him.

"So this isn't anything new? Is this a running joke or is there anything that can be done to make it better?" Billy asked hoping for at least something to work with. He felt like he owed Albert some relief.

"As you can imagine Donnie The Rock did what rocks do and just sat there. Before Donnie, I believe the band director tried to adjust his outdoor marching some, but during Donnie the Rocks time everything was neglected and we have fallen back into our old habits," Ms. Dixie said with a little less smile on her face, but still amused as she watched Billy struggle. "Why don't you go talk to T-Bone Reeves and see if he has any ideas. The good news is that we are only a few weeks away from the end of football season and then the band moves inside for concert season."

Billy thought about it and decided he could use some fresh air and a little walking. He looked at his watch and knew T-Bone would be at the junior high for sixth grade band so the walk down the block would do him some good. It would also give him a chance to reflect on the previous night…and his interview this morning. Both events were very prominent in his mind.

"I think that's a great idea. I'll just walk over there and see if there is any solution. Call me on the radio if anything comes up...and thanks," he said.

"You might be thinking about the trash that gets into his yard as well. That also bothers him pretty regularly," Ms. Dixie said with that same smirky smile he had seen somewhere else.

"Like how regularly?" asked Billy stopping and turning back around.

"Oh, I'd say everyday after lunch and maybe most afternoons after school lets out," said Ms. Dixie. That same smirky smile.

"Huh," said Billy. "Maybe one battle at a time? I'll try to see about this band thing for now how about?"

"Sounds like a plan," Ms. Dixie said.

17

Billy took a radio and hooked it to his belt. He had learned never to leave the office without one. He didn't necessarily like people being able to get in touch with him, but he did like being able to reach the office when he needed to ask a question. He also thought that if he was ever in a bind like being attacked or held hostage, it might be a good thing to have. Hopefully it never came to that, but he imagined worse case scenarios when he had free time or a few beers.

Billy knew the way to the junior high by heart since he had walked down that block for years to help with their athletic periods during his coaching days. He allowed his mind to wander as his feet followed the familiar path. He replayed the interview in his head. He could still see those brown eyes as they flamed with passion and conviction while Savannah extolled the virtues of teaching over the nefarious life of a politician. He smiled just thinking about it.

Savannah was a beautiful young lady with poise and confidence. She obviously was talented and according to her resume just a few years younger than Billy himself. Five years younger, but as adults that's not really a major difference he convinced himself. She was legal and they were both single. The sound of the motorcycle pulling up along side of him cut short his daydreaming.

He turned and watched as Dallas came to a stop and cut the engine. She didn't make the effort to park the bike. She simply straddled it and kept it balanced between her legs. She did remove her helmet revealing her short-cropped hair tied back underneath a red bandana. She took off her sunglasses, folded them, and slid one of the earpieces down the front of her v-neck t-shirt. Billy watched with interest.

"Hey, Dallas, I was just thinking about you and how great last night was," Billy sort of lied. He was planning on thinking about Dallas and last night and would have been had she come along a few minutes later.

"Good to know," Dallas said. "I wasn't sure since no flowers have been delivered this morning or a card describing your feelings."

"What?" asked Billy temporarily stunned. "I didn't take you for a flowers kind of girl, I'm sorry. I told you I'm a little rusty at this dating thing."

Dallas laughed a lot harder than Billy thought necessary. "You are way too easy and this is going to be so much fun. No flowers. No cards. Not necessary. If you're with me you're with me. If you ever need a gift I prefer tequila. 100% agave. None of that half sugar crap. If I wanted sugar, I'd drink rum.

"Okay then. Good to know," said Billy. "You did have me going there. I definitely had a great time, but I've had a few things going on this morning. I have been distracted. So what are you doing out today?"

"Billy Boy, I am on days off. My crew is working ten and four and I am not due back until Sunday. So I thought maybe you might like to come over tomorrow night and we could cook out and maybe look at the stars. How about it?" Dallas asked.

"That would be great," said Billy, "but it should be my turn to take you out."

"I don't suppose you do a lot of cooking on that stove in your apartment and my steaks are better than anything you'll get in any restaurant this side of San Angelo. You can take me out some other time when we need a road trip," offered Dallas.

"At least let me bring something. I feel like I'm just along for the ride," Billy said.

"Bring your toothbrush, and I'll pick you up at six so your truck wont be parked in front of my house. That'll make life simpler and less of a rush. " Dallas replied with a smile.

"All that sounds great for sure, but just remember this puts you up two," Billy laughed.

"Are we keeping score?" Dallas replied with her smile fading which Billy didn't catch.

"How else are we going to know who wins," replied Billy being flirty, witty, and charming. He quickly realized he was none of those when he looked back at Dallas' icy stare and the silence hung very heavy in the air. Billy had learned long ago that when he stepped on a landmine it was best to stay very still and be very quiet. He thought he had grown past such self-inflicted danger. He had not.

"We're supposed to be on the same team, dumbass. " was all Dallas said as she put on her sunglasses and helmet, started the engine, and sped off in a matter of seconds.

"See you tomorrow?" Billy called lamely after her knowing she would neither hear nor respond. "Well, that went well. "

18

Frustrated at himself, Billy continued on to the junior high band hall where he found T-Bone Reeves in front of dozens of screeching horns playing different notes in a rhythm best described as random. The percussion group that resembled four year olds whose aunt had given them a drum for Christmas was enthusiastically supporting the horns. T-Bone was the district band director responsible for all bands from 6th grade through high school. Which meant he had three bands, the largest being the 6th graders.

With each passing year fewer kids wanted to put in the time to practice and march. The idea of becoming a quality musician faded and the cold nights marching at football games proved too much to bear in spite of the trips to Odessa for contest. And contest meant eating at McDonalds and riding home on a dark bus where getting in a few kisses and squeezes were always possible. But in sixth grade the dream was alive and the evidence was there in front of Billy. Every chair was filled and every face was red from exertion and enthusiastic participation. How T-Bone stood it, Billy would never know. It was rumored he drank regularly during the day. Billy couldn't fault him.

People often assumed that T-Bone got his name from playing the trombone, but others say it has to do with his capacity for steaks. Considering his size and girth, the steaks seemed most logical. The best way to describe him was the average of Donnie the Rock's short and very wide and Boomer's tall and very wide. He would have been the stair step in between those guys. He was large, but very agile as he moved about the room correcting, encouraging, and adjusting.

At some point the screeching had reached the end of a song, and T-Bone made his way back to the director's stand, where he waved his baton, and brought the chaos to a halt. After a few instructions he told the kids to put up their instruments and get ready for the bell. Chaos in a different form. T-Bone waded through the mass of sweaty prepubescent towards Billy as the students scrambled in the opposite direction.

"Well, Principal Masters! What do I owe the honor of your visit to my humble kingdom?" T-Bone asked as he waved a hand across the room. He then pulled out his secret weapon. Earplugs in both ears, winked, and smiled a conspiratorial smile.

"I was wondering how on earth you were able to put up with that everyday for an hour," Billy said as he shook T-Bones hand.

"One of the first lessons taught to wannabe band directors. These kids think they're monitors, but in fact they're just plugs that cut the sound in half. Otherwise insanity or alcoholism would ensue," T-Bone explained and then added, "Sometimes those happen anyway. "

Billy wasn't sure he was talking rhetorically or from personal experience, but after just five minutes of the symphonic overture he could understand and sympathize.

"So what can I do for you? Surely you aren't here for pleasure, and I'm hoping this isn't an unannounced evaluation of myself or my program," T-Bone said with the confidence of a man who knows his job is secure for life since the district would be hard pressed to find a replacement. He was like a tenured professor that had a job for better or worse even if it included drinking a little to get through the day. He was safe as long as he kept his hands off the students. So far that hadn't been an issue. He had swapped out wives about every five years for the last twenty years. That seemed to be the limit of their affection for him, his profession, or Waymor in general. Once again this made perfect sense to Billy.

"Albert Duncan called and has a hard time hearing his news program in the morning when the high school band is out marching. Have you ever had an issue with him before?" asked Billy already knowing the answer.

"Albert and I are old friends.... acquaintances might be a better word. We've had this discussion a few times over the last few years since he retired," explained T-Bone. "When he worked he was gone by the time we started our practices, but now that he's home everyday, well, it's just a problem. We usually march on the parking lot behind the school where the sound is shielded by the building some, but on days when the wind is whipping up and the dirt is blowing out of the west we move to the parking lot on the north side of the building so we are shielded by the vocational building and field house. When we do that we are practically blowing our horns and beating our drums right in his living room. Now I hate it for Albert. He's a decent guy, but honestly I'm not going to put my kids or my program in a bind so he can watch TV," T-Bone explained.

"Other than moving behind the building, have you found any other solution that might makes things better?" Billy asked hoping for an answer.

"I got Sasquatch the Rock to move our band period once, but it screwed up everyone else's schedule and Albert still complained because he couldn't hear **Price is Right.** So the next year we moved it back and said screw it." T-Bone shrugged.

"So there's really not an answer that doesn't involve doing away with band?" Billy asked.

"Sure there is. Albert can move, he can die, or he can get over it." T-Bone answered like a man that had little sympathy for things that got in his way. "But I'll tell you what I'm going to do Billy. Since you seem to be a decent sort of person and I'd like to see you hang around for a while, but mainly because you would owe me a huge favor, I will cancel marching practice for the rest of the year. Problem solved! You'll be the promised messiah as far as Albert is concerned." T-Bone spread his arms wide and had a very big grin on his face. Billy's first thought was to wonder how early he started drinking.

"I'm really not asking you to do something that drastic. I don't want to hurt your program. Surely we can find a compromise that would help," Billy said.

"It's really not a problem. I would have done the same thing anyway even if you hadn't shown up this morning. It's just that your timing makes you the new genius. See, we have two games left in our typically miserable one win football season plus an open date. Both our games are out of town and I am out of travel money. So we won't be going to the games. In essence our marching season is over. Time to save the uniforms and start practicing inside. Problem solved, you're a hero and owe me big time, bucko." T-Bone laughed a deep and maniacal laugh.

"Do you need a bigger budget for travel?" asked Billy somewhat concerned since he knew nothing about budgeting.

"Don't ever let Cracker Jack hear you say something like that. He'll run you out of town personally! An administrator's first rule is never offer more money to anyone. Make them ask and then make them beg. Those that really need it will plead their case in desperation! Just some advice from a long time program director that knows how the system works. Hell, I get more money than all your core subjects combined. Horns are expensive and my program keeps a lot of kids off the streets. I just spend big early to keep my kids interested enough to finish out the year. I'm perfectly happy not making those last two trips and nobody even misses us since most people aren't even there," T-Bone said.

"Okay then. Thanks for the tip and thanks for the help. I'll let Albert know his problem is solved, but what about next year? Do we just wait and do it all over again?" asked Billy.

"Well Albert is getting older and...well next year is a long ways off so all we can do is just wait and see," T-Bone said with a little bit of crazy in his eyes.

After a moment to ponder this last statement, Billy reached out to shake T-Bone's hand and thank him again. Billy turned towards the door to make his way back to the high school. He was pretty sure he caught the sight of a flask in T-Bone's hand, but decided it was best not to look closer. Today he was batting 2 for 3, which were hall of fame numbers. Thanks to Boomer he had a new coach, with T-Bone's help he solved the noise problem, but he'd definitely struck out swinging with Dallas. That he'd have to make up for.

Billy was humming **A Good Hearted Woman** as he walked back into Ms. Dixie's office still distracted by Dallas' reaction to what he still considered a funny and acceptable response. All he was trying to do was to be generous and pay his way. Women. He knew he'd never understand.

"You seem to be in a good mood. Did you solve the band problem?" Ms. Dixie asked.

"As a matter of fact we did. T-Bone and I figured out a way to make Albert happy," Billy said proudly.

"And what did you two decide?" Ms. Dixie asked.

"To cancel band for the rest of the year. " Billy said triumphantly.

"Cancel band or just marching practice?" Ms. Dixie asked.

"Marching practice. It seems that the band will not be traveling to the last two out of town games," explained Billy. "So no need to practice marching."

"He spent all his travel money on food for the first few trips again," she said shaking her head.

"As a matter of fact that is exactly what happened. How did you know?" Billy asked somewhat puzzled.

"It's happened just about every other year for the last ten years once T-Bone realized he was bulletproof. He has side deals with the restaurants where he takes his kids to eat in the different towns. T-Bone will feed the kids hamburger steaks, which they're thrilled about and he gets the biggest t-bone, rib eye, or New York strip they have. It never shows up on his ticket, but they add about six or eight meals to off set the expense. Cracker Jack has known about his little scheme from the beginning, but doesn't want to have to find another band director. To be honest T-Bone does a good job with his kids and program. Everyone just looks the other way and considers it a bonus for him staying in Waymor," Ms. Dixie explained.

"So if Albert had waited one more day this would have all been over?" Billy asked.

"It seems so, but now this makes you look good and you'll have made a new friend," she said with a smile. "I'd go and call him with the good news."

"I believe I'll do just that," Billy said feeling a little like he had been setup, but it was a win he'd take.

Billy dialed Albert and leaned back in his chair. When Albert answered, Billy identified himself and explained that the problem with the band had been solved.

"Great!" Albert said. "Now about the trash…"

19

The rest of the day was uneventful and Billy found himself bouncing between thoughts of his interview and thoughts of his conversation with Dallas. He wasn't sure if he should call and apologize or if his date was still on. He wasn't sure if he should even be thinking about Savannah other than as one of his staff members that he was supposed to support and evaluate on a professional basis, but her smile, brown eyes, and intensity kept overcoming any professionalism he might have had. Billy finally decided that after school he needed to make a flying trip across the border. Tequila made a nice gift he remembered her saying and if everything blew up in his face, it would be of some solace to him.

About 2:30 the phone rang and he answered.

"Mr. Masters?" a voice that sounded sweet as syrup asked.

"Yes it is. May I help you?" he replied.

"This is Savannah Skinner. We met this morning in your office. Well, if you still want to hire me I've gotten all the paperwork filled out and Mr. Daniels said I was good to go. He let me borrow a phone and thought you might like to hear it from me personally," Savannah explained.

"That's great. Absolutely. I'm thrilled to hear it!" Billy heard himself babbling. Reining in his enthusiasm he asked, "Tomorrow's Friday. Do you still want to start or wait until Monday?"

"I think starting tomorrow would be best so I can get an idea what's going on and then have the weekend to plan and get ready," she answered having obviously given it some thought.

"Alright then. I'll have the lady who's been subbing come in as well so she can show you what the classes have been doing. I'll also have Mrs. Daniels, the department head, available to work with you and be your mentor," Billy informed her. "We're excited to have you helping us out. Why don't you come to my office about 7:30 tomorrow morning and I'll show you around." Billy once again caught himself acting like a complete fool as he tripped over himself trying to make her feel welcome.

"Thank you so much. I'm excited and Uncle Corliss and Aunt Bev are excited for me. I can't believe I'm going to be a teacher and a coach," Savannah replied, overjoyed to be part of the Waymor High School staff.

Billy could have drawn out the conversation a little longer by telling her again how excited he was, but decided she had gotten the message. He promised to meet her in the morning, thanked her, and said goodbye.

Billy walked out to Ms. Dixie's desk to let her know they had a new coach and staff member only to find that Ms. Dixie had a new teacher folder already made up with keys and a name badge.

"I see you know about Savannah," Billy stated a little perplexed.

"They faxed me her information from the central office so I could have it on file. From your side of the conversation I just heard it sound like you're happy she's coming?" Ms. Dixie asked.

Billy realized he might have been even more enthusiastic than he imagined.

"I'm just glad we have a full staff and a permanent teacher in that classroom. Her being Boomer's niece doesn't hurt. He's good people so I have a feeling about this working out." Billy replied.

"Yes. Good for us," Ms. Dixie replied and went back to typing an invoice.

"Ms. Dixie, I need to run an errand. I think I'm going to call it a day." Billy said as he went back into his office to pick up his briefcase and jacket.

As he turned out his light and closed his door Ms. Dixie said, "Be careful" for the third time that day.

Billy pointed his truck west towards the desert then north. His path led him to New Mexico and Pablo's Cantina. Billy bought two bottles of Añejo and was back in his apartment in time to open one bottle to wash down a TV dinner of enchiladas, beans and rice. He turned on the TV just for the noise, but it wasn't enough to distract him from wondering about what tomorrow might hold; Savannah in the morning and Dallas tomorrow night. When he woke up it was 2 A. M. and he was still in his recliner with a crick in his neck. He brushed his teeth and put himself to bed for what would be a very short night.

20

Billy was sitting at his desk looking out the window across the football field watching the sunrise. The throbbing in his head was minimal and he counted himself lucky. He had fallen asleep before he could do any real damage and three Advil would make him a new man by the time he finished his second cup of coffee. He had showered in semi cold water to clear his head and then dressed in his best button down instead of his usual Friday attire, which consisted of the same black knit coaching shirt with a sand crab embroidered on the collar tab, and black knit pants. He also opted for creased jeans and his boots were polished.

All of his preparations, he realized too late, had been driven by a subconscious need to be presentable above and beyond to impress his new teacher. He really wasn't sure why and wondered if anyone else would notice. Ms. Dixie came in and remarked how nice he looked and asked if he had a meeting she wasn't aware of.

"It's actually kind of embarrassing," Billy said. "I didn't get around to doing laundry and when I got up this morning these clothes were all that were clean." He lied. Right to her face.

"Umm Huh. That happens," Ms. Dixie agreed skeptically. "Hopefully the cologne isn't because you didn't have time to bathe." Her left eyebrow was cocked in a questioning manner.

"Oh no, I showered,'" Billy responded way too quickly before he realized she was toying with him.

Hoping to redirect the conversation and get back on safe ground Billy said, "Did I mention I have another date with your sister?"

"She mentioned something about that. Maybe that's why you're all cleaned up and spiffy. " Ms. Dixie offered even though she and Billy both knew better.

It was at that moment that Savannah Skinner walked into the office. She was dressed for church with her brown hair pulled back in a ponytail and her brown eyes sparkling with excitement. She had a change of clothes for her athletic periods on a hanger hooked over her shoulder.

"Good morning," she said with a little wave of her hand. "I am just so excited. I think I'm a little early, but I couldn't wait to get started. I wasn't sure what to wear to make a good first impression so I went with this," Savannah gestured at her clothes. "Do you think this is okay?"

Billy was willing to make an appraisal of her overall appearance and gave her a thumbs up. He turned to Ms. Dixie and asked if she agreed that Savannah looked nice.

"Yes, sweetheart you look lovely. You'll put the rest of us to shame. Why don't you sit over here and I'll walk you through this folder and get you some keys. We'll let Mr. Masters get ready for his day while I get you settled," Ms. Dixie said as she gestured Savannah to the chair beside her desk and dismissed Billy.

Billy didn't really have anything he needed or even wanted to do except stand out in the office and be part of the conversation, but he had been dismissed. He did his best to listen in as Ms. Dixie went over a few instructions and asked a few questions. He heard Savannah speak a couple of times and there were some laughter from both the ladies and then they got up and left. When Ms. Dixie returned, she was alone.

"I took Savannah down to meet Betty Daniels who said she would get her started in the classroom and pointed in the right direction to the gym when the time comes. I think she'll be in good hands and do just fine," reported Ms. Dixie when she stuck her head in Billy's door. "It's a good thing Uncle Boomer is close by. Someone as lovely as that and single will attract all kinds of interest. I'm sure we all can look out for her since we want her to have a good experience here at Waymor High. Who knows, she might even want to stay."

Yes, we can, and maybe she will, Billy thought.

Chastised, Billy mentally kicked himself for being such a guy. He was the principal, and it was his job to look after Savannah's welfare and best interest. He had to think like a professional and not like some half drunk cowboy at a bar trying to get her alone and in bed. He reminded himself that she was the niece to a giant man who was fast becoming one his best friends.

Finally, he reminded himself that he had a date that very evening with a woman he had spent the night with just two days ago and actually said he loved her before leaving. That of course had been more of a spontaneous response than a serious vow of devotion, but he had said it just the same and women that he had known didn't shrug off expressions like that easily. Her sister also had been sitting outside his door watching his overly involved behavior the last couple of days and it seemed she was doing her best to shield Savannah from him or at least protect him from himself. Either way it was time for him to get his crap together before he made a mess of everything.

The rest of the day went smoothly with just a few Friday behavior issues that resulted from teachers being tired and ready for the weekend. Some had shown movies that may or may not have anything to do with their subject matter and some let the kids bring snacks. By the afternoon the number of students bouncing off the wall increased exponentially. Billy would learn that this was normal for this time of year when the holidays were close, but not close enough.

When the last bus pulled away from the school, Billy went back to his office to clear his desk.

Ms. Dixie stuck her head in his door and said, "Savannah stopped by to let you know that she had an awesome day, she can't be anymore excited, and can't wait until Monday," Ms. Dixie pretended to read off a message pad. "I think she had a good day. Now you, Mr. Masters, should have a good weekend. Enjoy your date."

She turned, took her purse out of the filing cabinet, and turned out the lights.

"Thank you, Ms. Dixie for all your help! You know I appreciate you!" Billy hollered across the office trying to catch her before she was gone. "Have a nice weekend!"

"You're welcome, and I will. The kids are staying at their grandma's house. It should be nice indeed," Ms. Dixie said as she smiled and then winked before walking down the hall.

21

To be honest Billy wasn't even sure he still had a date. The way Dallas had left in a huff made him wonder if she still wanted to see him. He debated whether or not to call and changed his mind several times, but in the end he thought if he didn't give her the chance to cancel, she might still show up. He hoped so.

He also wasn't sure what to wear. It was unseasonably warm so he could go with shorts, but then it might look like he was being too casual and taking her for granted. He had worn creased jeans for the meeting with Savannah, which Ms. Dixie was aware of and if word got back then there would be the comparison issue. That discussion wouldn't go well. He also couldn't wear the same clothes he had worn to meet Savannah. That was another ambush waiting to happen. He wished women weren't so hard to figure out. If it had been a group of guys nobody would even know the next day what anyone had worn the night before. He figured he might be over thinking, but since he was already in the doghouse, it would be best to at least try not to start another fire. He finally opted for a different pair of creased jeans, short sleeve polo, and a different pair of boots he quickly polished in case anyone was keeping score. He felt like a teenage girl getting ready to go on her first date. Half his clothes were scattered across his bed. He should slap himself.

Billy was sitting in his recliner with the tequila bottle, his penance, sitting on the counter nearby. Right at 6 P. M. he heard the pipes of a motorcycle as it made its way into the parking lot outside his window. A few minutes later there was a knock on his door and as he opened it there stood Dallas...wearing shorts, a tank top, and her rubber soled hiking boots.

"My, aren't you dressed up," Dallas said as she gave him the once over. "It's summer time you know. Shorts weather. Haven't you even been outside today?"

"I felt like I needed to make a good impression since I offended you yesterday so I went with... well this," Billy explained. "And I bought you a bottle of tequila," he added hurriedly and pointed towards the counter as she simply half smiled and half smirked at the whole situation.

"Okay. I appreciate the effort. I can tell you're sincere. Let's just agree you're a guy and you are going to do stupid stuff on a pretty regular basis, so you don't have to go overboard every time. As often as I expect this to happen, you can't afford the tequila, and I don't want to waste my time while you grovel and prostrate yourself. Now go put on some shorts and wear lace up tennis shoes. We're going to be on the bike," Dallas said with a smile and an almost invisible shaking of her head.

Billy smiled, leaned over and kissed her, and went to change. When he was dressed again for the fifth time that afternoon he grabbed the bottle of tequila off the counter, and they walked out to the parking lot. He took her hand, which was warm and surprisingly soft since she definitely labored manually in her job.

When they got to Dallas' motorcycle she put the bottle in one of the saddlebags and handed him an extra helmet. She folded down the back foot pegs for him to use, slid her leg over the saddle, and pushed the bike off the kickstand, balancing the machine between her legs.

"Have you ever ridden before?" Dallas asked.

"Not since I was a kid, and then it was mini bikes, and we crashed a lot," Billy confessed.

"Good to know. Here's what you do. Make yourself comfortable in the seat and keep your weight balanced in the center. When we turn, just look over my inside shoulder. Don't try shifting your weight or leaning. Just look. That'll be enough. Hop on," Dallas instructed.

When Billy managed to get settled he asked, "Where do I hold on?"

"You can lean forward and put your arms around my waist, but that looks like a girl and probably not the best look for you. You can hang on to that strap you see across the seat, or you can trust that you will be fine balancing with your feet and leaning forward a little. If you must, you can hang on to my shorts. Just don't give me a wedgie," Dallas listed his options without any hint of frustration or amusement. She seemed to have been prepared for his lack of skill in this area.

Billy looked at the strap, moved back and forth getting the feel for just balancing, and then looked at the waistband of her shorts. Her tank top had ridden up when she had leaned forward and he had a nice view of the tan line that separated her back and her bottom. He decided this was where he would like his hands. He slid the fingers of both his hands inside her shorts and grabbed a handful of cloth. Her skin, once again, was remarkably soft and he could feel her body heat on the backside of his fingers.

"Ready!" Billy said over the noise of the engine.

Dallas turned her head in his direction enough that Billy could see her smile and she winked at him. "Good choice," was all she said before she tapped the bike into gear and slowly accelerated out of the parking lot and onto the street.

The feeling of Dallas' body heat on his hands along with the power beneath him as they flew along the highway, was more than enough to relax and excite him at the same time. He found that all the tension he had been feeling for days had disappeared and had been replaced with outright joy. Dallas was obviously an expert when it came to controlling the motorcycle and soon all thoughts of crashing were distant memories. He was somewhat disappointed when she slowed and turned into her driveway. He thought maybe someday they could go for a longer ride and suggested just that when they had stopped and removed their helmets.

"Sure," said Dallas. "There's nothing better than taking off across the desert and making your way up the mountains just to get lunch. I have to do that occasionally just to stay sane. Riding is the best therapy there is. You come back a different person and are good for a few weeks until you can do it again. I've ridden north to the mountains, south through Big Bend, and west all the way to Phoenix."

"Therapy is something I could use on a regular basis. Just on the ride over it felt like a weight was lifted. I can't imagine how much better I would feel after a whole day," Billy explained.

"It's like having sex with me," Dallas said with absolute conviction. "When its over you're exhausted, sore, but extremely gratified. Right?"

"Well Ms. Modesty I can say with my limited knowledge that I tend to agree with you as far as the sex part. I will, however, reserve judgment on the riding until I can see if it actually measures up," Billy replied knowing he once again had been led into a minefield and his words were triggers. He felt he had diffused them for now.

"Nicely done," she smiled and took the tequila out of the saddlebag. With a bottle in one hand she looped her other arm inside his and walked him to her door where they were met by the two killer dogs he had forgotten about. The dogs seemed not to remember he was just there a couple of days ago. That or they didn't like him then and now he was back. Either way they weren't very inviting as he slid inside the door as Dallas reached down and patted them both.

"I didn't ask you last time what their names are. I guess that was rude and they seem to remember my lack of manners," Billy said as he tentatively held out his hand so they could get a good sniff.

"This one is Chesty Puller named after the most decorated Marine of all time, and this one is Gunny after my Gunnery Sergeant that took the time to train me properly and also had my back on more than one occasion. Both were short on words and long on action. They were the kind of people that would run

90

toward the fight. You'll find my dogs are like that. They'll run towards a fight and let their actions speak for them," she said. "I prefer actions over words."

"So your saying I won't hear them coming when they go for my throat?" asked Billy only half kidding.

"That's right," answered Dallas without even hesitating or offering some other encouragement. "If they feel you're a threat, well... it's over. So don't be threatening and everything will be fine."

"None of that reassures me," Billy said feeling the tension creep back into his body. "What if our definition of threatening is different?"

"You'll be fine as long as you don't try to hit me or hurt me. Raising your voice in anger is not a good idea, and if you ever pull a weapon on me, well...it's all over. No one will ever find your body because after I have mangled you and rendered you unconscious, I'll let the dogs eat you," Dallas finished with a laugh. "Seriously, just relax and be the good guy I know you are, and we will all get along fine. Quit worrying about the dogs, and let's get this party started. Beer?"

After nodding affirmative that a beer would be ideal for the moment, Billy took his hand and gently rubbed the heads and scruff of each dog calling them by name. Trying to convince himself as much as them that they were all friends. He managed to squeeze past their focused eyes and clinched jaws into the kitchen as Dallas produced two bottles of Lone Star and popped the top off of each. She motioned for him to sit at the bar while she flipped a switch on a reel to reel that sprang to life with country music.

After she started two potatoes baking in the oven and lit the grill, they went through a six-pack while she seasoned the steak with what was described as her own special recipe. She demonstrated her proficiency at handling a knife while quickly cutting up vegetables for a salad. Billy was content to watch as she moved efficiently around the kitchen. Billy had learned she had skills in many different areas and now found that she was just as capable in the kitchen. He offered to help more than once, but each time she just smiled and encouraged him to stay seated...and stay out of the way.

When the potatoes had cooked and were wrapped in foil resting on the cabinet, Billy followed Dallas out to the grill with two steaks that were the size of the plate.

"How do you like your steak cooked?" she asked.

"Medium rare," replied Billy. "Hot pink in the center."

"I knew I liked you for some reason," Dallas said. "Two medium rare coming right up. I never understood people that cooked steaks to death and pretended eating shoe leather was enjoyable. Why don't you open the wine on the counter so it can breathe and we should be ready in just a few minutes."

Billy went into the kitchen only to come face to face once again with Chesty and Gunny. He immediately betrayed himself by giving off whatever scent fear smelled like and tried to convince the dogs that he hadn't carried Dallas off and buried her somewhere. He explained that she was just outside. He evidently was amusing to them, as they looked for a minute, growled slowly and lowly in their throats and lay back on their beds.

Billy let out an audible breath and found the corkscrew. He managed to get the bottle opened and the glasses down from the rack when Dallas came in with the steaks. He honestly wasn't sure he could eat a piece of meat that size, but Dallas solved the problem for him. She cut one in half and put a portion in each of the dogs' bowl, and then cut the other steak in half and placed a portion on plates for her and Billy. Surprisingly enough, the dogs didn't run over each other to get to the food, but slow walked over to their respective bowls where they gulped down the meat with hardly any effort. Afterwards, eyeing Billy, they returned to their beds, circled twice, and plopped down with half opened eyes ever vigilant.

"My dogs eat as well as I do. We look after each other," was all Dallas said in way of explanation.

The meal was better than advertised. Not only was it the best steak west of San Angelo, but also the best one Billy had ever eaten. When he asked what made it special, all Dallas would say was the secret was in her spices…and, of course, a good cut of meat.

For dessert she had made a cherry pie.

Dallas and Billy sat at the bar and ate until they were stuffed. The food was delicious, and he had already decided he couldn't take one more bite when she slid off her chair and fetched the pie. Oh Lord, thought Billy. I can't go on, but I can't stop now. He manned up and ate the large serving she had placed on a plate for him. She matched him bite for bite, and he had no idea how she could hold that much food and still be as slender and ripped as she was. He guessed it had to do with metabolism or the amount of calories she burned working out. Rubbing his stretched belly, a three-hour napped seemed appealing, but then he'd miss all the fun.

Dallas washed; Billy dried and put away the dishes. After they had cleared the counter and wiped away the crumbs, Dallas took two shot glasses, the bottle of tequila, and motioned for him to follow. The sun had set, but its red glow was still dazzling in the west and it matched the flames of the fire pit when she lit it. It was late fall so even though it had been unseasonably warm; a chill had begun to set in when the sun went down.

Billy was tasked with opening the bottle and pouring each a serving. He had splurged to show true repentance and bought sipping tequila. Quality Añejo was a drink to be savored, not thrown back and covered with lemon and salt. Sipping, savoring, and snuggling on the glider, Dallas and Billy made the most of the Indian summer night. Chesty and Gunny made themselves at home behind them on the deck. They appeared to be half asleep, but always watchful.

When the last embers had burned low and the bottle was less than half full, Dallas stood and took Billy's hand leading him to the bedroom. Thankfully, the door was closed leaving the dogs on the outside. Billy removed Dallas' tank top then kissed her softly on the lips while unhooking the black lacy bra that had been underneath. He unbuckled her belt and slipped the fastener of her shorts loose dropping them to the floor. He noticed she was wearing one of the new thongs that he had heard about. It was black and lacy as well. He slid his hands inside the band and slowly rolled it to the floor. The moonlight was shining through the windows again and he couldn't help but look at her perfect body that stood before him. Perfect in every way.

As Billy stood enjoying the view he said, "You do know the thong was originally made for men?"

Dallas was very much in the mood and barely answered that she did not know that.

"Yeah. It was called the jockstrap. The only difference is it has two straps in back. That's because the load in front on men is bigger and the straps act like the stabilizer bars on trailers. They keep the load in front from swaying back and forth and getting out of control. The women's version doesn't need the stabilizer bars since the load is not likely to shift so they just put that one little string that runs up the back. Sure enough," Billy finished amused and entertained. He gave himself an A for creative conversation.

"Billy," Dallas whispered as she moved in close pushing her body against his. "Do you remember what I said about my heroes?"

"Sure. A lot of action and few words," replied Billy satisfied he had paid attention.

"Billy," she said as she took her arms from around his neck and slid into bed. "Be my hero."

Billy had consumed a fair amount of alcohol and was overloaded on carbs and fats, but her words sank in. Stand up comedy wasn't what she was interested in. He began ripping his clothes off, letting them lie where they were tossed. Billy looked down at his body that was neither ripped nor toned. He swore he would do something about it later then quickly slid into the bed next to Dallas. Drawing her close to him, he held her tightly. She smelled of charcoal, body soap, and the slightest spritz of perfume. The combination was intoxicating.

"You are beautiful and smell delicious," Billy whispered close to her ear.

"There you go talking again," was all that Dallas said.

No words were spoken for the next six hours. There were sounds of pleasure, ecstasy, exhaustion, elation, and later on

Billy woke himself snoring, but no words passed between them the rest of the night. Only actions.

22

The cold nose touched Billy's arm that had fallen off the bed as he lay on his stomach depleted and exhausted. It took a moment for Billy to realize what it was. Dragging himself back to consciousness, he turned his face out and looked Gunny right in the eye. His first instinct was to yell, but thought better of it since that might trigger threat mode. He stared and Gunny stared back. Finally Billy spoke and asked what he wanted. When Billy spoke, Gunny must have felt that his job was complete; so, he had turned and walked out of the bedroom. Billy rubbed his eyes and looked over on the other side of the bed. There was no lump and as he reached across, the sheets were cold. He realized Dallas was up and left the door open.

Billy sat up and dropped his feet to the floor. Getting his bearings, he stood and wobbled a little as he made his way to the bathroom. He took care of his business, then washed his face and hands with cold water trying to cut through the layer of fog that seemed to be hanging around his head. After splashing water on his hair, he mashed down the spiked clumps that spread in various directions. Using a brush he borrowed from Dallas, he worked until he looked somewhat presentable. Billy redressed in his clothes he found scattered about the floor and furniture. By now he smelled bacon frying and coffee.

When Billy staggered into the kitchen half asleep, Dallas congratulated Gunny on being a good boy and getting Billy up. Billy was hoping for some accolades himself, but got a mug of coffee instead. He was all right with that. He looked out of the window and realized the sun wasn't even up. The clock on the stove said 6:05.

"It is Saturday right? Do you always get up with the sun?" Billy asked confused.

"Big day, big boy. We've got to get moving, so sit down, eat your breakfast, and then we are hitting the road," Dallas explained as she stirred the eggs in the skillet and checked the bacon at the same time.

"Road trip?' Billy asked.

"You asked for it so you got it. You earned it last night...once you quit talking," the accolades finally coming put a smile on Billy's face. "I work ten days on and get four days off, so I go back to work tomorrow. This will be the last chance we'll have decent weather until spring, so we're going to take the motorcycle up to Ruidoso and have lunch. Just be thinking about this. You'll be feasting on Carne Adovada, beans, and a bowl of posole in just a few hours. You'll need at least three beers to put out the fire in your throat. Wicked Felina's. No place on Earth like it. You'll thank me for the rest of your life. So eat up, gas up, and away we go," Dallas explained.

Dallas was obviously excited and more animated than Billy had ever seen her. Her enthusiasm had started to rub off on him. He remembered the feel of the motorcycle for just the short ride from his apartment and Dallas's description of what a road trip was like. Having just survived a most gratifying night with her, he found himself getting energized as well.

They finished their breakfast, washed up the dishes, and put the dogs outside for the day. They had shade, water, room to roam, and Dallas assured him they could come through the back door should the need arise. Evidently that had happened in the past. His respect or fear for them grew each day.

"It's going to be a warm day, but it still gets cool on the bike. We need to go by and get you some jeans and a coat of some kind," Dallas explained as she slid on her leathers and grabbed the helmets. "Rubber soled boots would help and a pair of gloves if you have them.

"I can put together something that will work," Billy assured her as they mounted the motorcycle and started out the driveway.

Dallas reminded him about his weight shifting and turning again in hopes of not scattering their broken bodies across hot pavement. Billy hadn't thought about it since the night before, but felt sure it would have come back to him. He felt a lot more comfortable on the back of the bike, but was still not sure about how high speed and long distances might affect his opinion. He knew he was about to find out. On the way to Billy's apartment, they pulled into a convenience store and topped off the tank of gas.

Once again Billy ripped clothes out of his closet that represented different phases of his life from college student to should be lawyer to oil field worker to coach to principal. He wasn't exactly a pack rat. He just never knew when his current job would implode and he would be forced to go back to something he had done before...and he would need clothes.

As it turned out he found his old steel toed, rubber soled work boots from his recent job as a pumper, his leather jacket from college, and a pair of gloves he had bought the first time he had gone skiing. Coupled with a flannel shirt and a pair of jeans he felt ready to ride. When he looked in the mirror he decided he was only a football helmet away from being Jack Nicholson in *Easy Rider.* There was nothing he could do about it and other than Dallas, who would even know the difference?

"I need to stop by Dixie's on the way out of town to drop off some paperwork she needs. We have some joint investments and Dixie is the paperwork partner that keeps us straight. I'm sure you can imagine," Dallas explained, as she looked him up and down before she smiled and motioned for him to climb on.

Billy thought seeing Dixie might be interesting.

When they pulled into Dixie and Ken's drive, Dixie came out the front door to meet them. She had her hair pulled back, no make-up on, and was wearing her robe. Billy was surprised since he had never seen her at any time where she wasn't perfectly put together. He decided he liked the casual look.

"Good Morning Mr. Masters," Dixie said as if they met like this everyday. "Road trip?"

"Do you think since I'm dressed like I just came from the Salvation Army store and you have on your robe, we might could just go with Dixie and Billy?" he asked.

"I think that would be alright...Billy," Dixie managed to say although it was a little awkward.

"Well...Dixie...from where I sit on what I believe is called the bitch seat, you look quite refreshed and lovely in you casualness," Billy offered what he thought was compliment.

"Hmmm. Thank you. Let me just say you look quite content and happy this morning perched up there behind Dallas. I would say that look works for you," Dixie said with the slightest trace of a smile.

"I thank you as well," replied Billy.

"Are we done here, or do I need to kill the bike so y'all can have more time," Dallas asked obviously uninterested in their mutual admiration party.

"I'm good," laughed Dixie. "Ken is cooking us breakfast and I'm sure it's about ready. You two kids have fun now." And she turned and walked back toward the house raising a hand in a backward wave as she went.

Billy's natural reaction was to wave back, which he did and almost fell off the bike as Dallas gunned the engine and pointed them west. In a matter of minutes Billy was able to see over Dallas' shoulder that they were cruising at 90 mph. He quickly realized why the jacket and gloves were necessary and why leather pants or chaps might work better than the blue jeans he had on. He was concerned what it might be like when they got to the mountains. He also wondered about Dixie and how much different she looked when she wasn't in the office and not all professional. He wondered about how much she and Dallas looked alike even with the hair length and color different. He had a lot on his mind as they sped across the desert.

As the miles flew past and he adjusted to the rhythm of the road, which in this part of the country was a straight line for the most part, he leaned in a little more to Dallas' back and felt the warmth from her body. He also spent time reliving the night before and found himself quite content.

Along the way they stopped a couple of times to stretch and get something to drink. The morning had been sunny and the wind was almost non-existent. A rare day indeed. They crossed into New Mexico and ran parallel to the Pecos River all the way to Roswell. Turning west, they started the climb to Ruidoso where the ride became more interesting as the road wound through the trees. The temperature dropped, but not enough to be uncomfortable. Billy watched as fruit stands and cabins passed. After an hour of weaving in and out of shadows and winding up hill, he caught sight of the racetrack that guarded the east side of town.

Billy had been to Ruidoso a few times in college to ski and once in the summer for the horse races. It had been a few years, and there had been some improvements made to the town, but for the most part it still looked like he remembered it. He realized when a person lived in the desert and became accustomed to the flat and barren stretches of earth, they forgot what mountains and trees looked like and to him this was almost like an exotic vacation. The smell of pine in the air was intoxicating to someone that smelled wellhead gas and dust each day.

The trip had taken about four hours and since they had gained an hour, there was time to kill before the restaurants opened for lunch. Dallas found a place to park the bike and they stored their helmets and shed some of their clothes. The walk up and down the streets was a way for Billy to get circulation back into his legs and stretch.

Dallas and Billy held hands as they walked the sidewalk occasionally peeking in stores that sold souvenirs that ranged from imitation Indian paraphernalia to handcrafted pottery. They also found clothing stores and since the ski season was just days away pending the next big snow storm, they had clearance sales to get rid of last year's inventory and make room for the new more expensive items needed by every ski bum that came through. After debating about buying a pair of bib ski pants for the ride home, he decided it would be a waste of money. If he was going to be a permanent fixture on the back of Dallas' bike, maybe she could help him find some riding gear that looked more like Peter Fonda and less like Jack Nicholson. Either way, the ski gear was left behind.

It was then that he entertained the idea of having his own bike for the first time and not having to ride like a girl the rest of his life. The devil on his shoulder reminded him how warm and good Dallas felt with his arms around her or holding on to her pants, but his ego said his place was in control. He was still mulling this over when Dallas announced they had arrived at Wicked Felina's.

They found a corner table where they could look out on the street and see the mountains above the tree line. Their waitress was eager and willing to serve them since they were the first ones through the door. Most folks that lived in Ruidoso or New Mexico in general were still moving slowly during the last days of "off season" and were an hour away from being hungry. Being first meant being blessed with immediate attentiveness. Two bottles of cold beer that weren't Lone Star, but still refreshing were placed in front of them as they scanned the menu. Billy did it out of curiosity since this was his first time and Dallas was looking to see if any new items had been added since her last trip a few months past.

When it was evident that she saw no challengers to her favorites and Billy was willing to let her be the guide, Dallas ordered them both a plate of the Carne Adovada with a side of beans and a bowl of vegetable posole. She asked for extra flour tortillas and for them to come out first along with butter. The waitress who was a young girl and probably a member of the family that owned the cafe had long dark hair and eyes as dark as Dallas'. Her white teeth were dazzling in contrast. She was probably a high school student based on Billy's experience and more than likely not the wicked Felina that was the café's namesake.

When she reappeared to take their order, she said her name was Catalina and her friends called her Cat. They could call her Cat as well. She smiled and nodded as she and Dallas worked out the order then made her way back to the kitchen to hang it on the clip in front of the cook. In no time there was a basket of homemade tortillas in front of them and a platter of butter. The steam that rose from the basket erased all doubts as to their freshness. After slathering butter across one and devouring half of it in one bite, Billy was able to guarantee they had just come off the grill. He and Dallas did their best to eat sparingly knowing the best was yet to come, but had a hard time resisting the tortillas in front of them or the salsa and chips Cat slid across the table on her next trip by. She also placed a fresh beer in front of them both even though neither had asked for one. She cleared away the empty bottles and smiled. She was getting a nice tip Billy was certain.

As they took turns dipping chips into the hot sauce, which was indeed hot, they looked out the window at the mountains that had the first hints of snow covering the peaks. Billy and Dallas talked about everything and nothing. It was one of those days when you finally felt comfortable around someone that even the most mundane things were up for discussion. Billy hadn't been happier since...he was a kid at Christmas.

The large plate of Carne Adovada arrived and was placed center table to be eaten family style. The bowls of beans and posole were placed to the side while an empty plate that covered half the table was given to each of them to be used as they saw fit. For those that liked their food mixed together or those that didn't like their food touching, it was their choice as to how to proceed. Billy was happy to see Dallas go for the casserole style of meal where she piled her plate high with all three ingredients and then splashed extra hot sauce on top of what would prove to be very spicy meat. As if on cue, two more beers appeared as the two empty bottles disappeared. He followed Dallas' example, piled his plate high, and they spent the next twenty minutes in silence except for an occasional moan of pleasure or a whooshing sound as they blew through their mouths trying to extinguish the fire.

When they could eat no more, Billy was astounded once again that Dallas had matched him bite for bite and might have even had more tortillas. He sat back stuffed and amazed, but very satisfied. He lifted his finger in Cat's direction to ask for the check and made sure Dallas knew it would be his treat. She smiled and didn't argue. If anyone were keeping score this would put Billy within one of tying the game. But then they were on the same team he reminded himself!

Billy slid a twenty under the edge of his plate as they left. He had always had a soft spot for waitresses that worked hard for tips especially when it was high school kids he knew were balancing their study time and working. He also appreciated good service. Billy knew they had been the only ones in the café for most of the time, but he felt like Cat would have done just as well with ten busy tables. There was no substitute for initiative, and he had decided to reward it as often as possible with the means he had available. They made their way back out to the street leaving behind few clues as to the amount of food that had been placed on the table. Once again Dallas had been right. He had never eaten food that even compared. He vowed to come back...soon.

They would lose an hour going back across the border and with the days getting shorter they needed to leave soon to get back to Waymor before dark. They also needed to walk off the meal and alcohol before straddling a motor that would propel them across asphalt at close to a hundred miles an hour. They decided it was best to be a little late and safe than be another horror story on the morning news. Dallas hooked her hand under his arm and they made their way back up Main Street, which had come alive with people that were finally moving about on a lazy Saturday morning.

After an hour of people watching and window-shopping Dallas felt like they were good to go, so they walked back to her motorcycle and suited up for the road. Backtracking down Main Street, Dallas turned left onto the highway and Billy soon realized going down mountains was completely different than climbing them. He reminded himself to do his part on the turns. A little over an hour later they rolled into Roswell and turned south without so much as a pit stop.

The miles passed by and as Billy became more relaxed and comfortable he leaned into Dallas a little more and reached around her waist. Her body felt good and he enjoyed the combination of the open road and the feel of her in his arms. He decided he'd slip off a glove in order to feel her skin against his hand and as he did so the glove was swept immediately into the jet stream and lost forever. He decided not to mention this to Dallas and maybe confirm her belief that he just might be a dork. He thought that he had made great strides lately to distance him from those opinions.

Since the temperature of his hand had dropped dramatically during the few minutes of indecision and placing it on Dallas' bare skin might result in catastrophe, Billy chose to hold on one handed for the rest of the trip with his bare hand stuffed in his coat pocket forever useless for gripping or affection. And the weekend had almost been perfect.

Dallas pulled her bike into his parking lot with time to spare before dark, and they got off to stretch and for Billy to hand back his helmet.

"Would you like to come in for a night cap or something?" Billy asked. "It's early."

"I need to get home and check on the dogs. I also work tomorrow. It'll be an early night for me," she reminded Billy. " I probably won't be around much the next ten days. My crew starts early and works hard. I hit the sack each night as soon as I can. Just don't think I'm ignoring you if you don't see me around. I had a great weekend. Thank you," She said as she leaned in and kissed him. Her lips were soft and they lingered on his lips for a long time.

"I had a great time. Believe me this may have been to most memorable weekend of my life," Billy told her trying too hard. "It was remarkable!"

"Easy big fella. I believe you," Dallas assured him with a laugh. " We should do it again. Soon. I always make time for Wednesday night prayer meeting unless we have a call out. You can meet me there when you're free."

"Count on it," Billy said with confidence. "I'll be there."

"Prayer and cake is all that's on the menu this week. Just know. Early bedtime. Okay?" She asked.

"Sure. I'm good with that. I understand," Billy assured her.

"See you Wednesday then," Dallas said as she cranked up the bike, kissed him once again quickly, and then drove off up the street and out of sight.

Billy became aware that he was standing in the middle of his parking lot staring at the road in the direction she had gone. He realized he already missed her and that might be a warning sign. He smiled to himself and walked through the door of his cold dark apartment. On the plus side it was only Saturday night and

103

he had Sunday to rest up and catch a few games on TV. What a whirlwind of events.

Billy spent the first hour re-hanging all the clothes he had scattered around the room like a schoolgirl and then sat in his recliner to watch what he could find on TV. Food never entered his mind since he had eaten enough at lunch for a week. He still had the remainder of the first bottle of Tequila. A glass to take the edge off sounded like the best idea. Two would work even better. This time he didn't have to take himself to bed in the middle of the night. He awoke in his recliner stiff and sore well after sunrise and in time for a breakfast of cold cereal and almost sour milk.

23

The days passed quickly for Billy since their road trip. He decided that being out on the open road on a motorcycle had been a rush, and the only thing Dallas had been wrong about was comparing it to sex with her. The trip had been great, but not even close to a night with Dallas. When he mentioned that fact to Dallas at prayer meeting the following Wednesday she had actually blushed and then shushed him with a reminder they were in church among fine Christian people who were within earshot.

School had disintegrated into the Thanksgiving holidays. It came down to simple survival the last couple of days before the break, as everyone got excited about the first major holiday of the year. Billy spent most of those days shaking his head in disbelief at some of the things the grown ups did to enflame the insanity and decided the teachers should know better which made it hard for him to really discipline the student offenders. Either way, they survived and moved on to giving thanks and watching football.

Billy had gone so far as to call his parents and promise to come home for a couple days before Ms. Dixie reminded him that the basketball teams played in a tournament during the holidays. As principal, he would need to be there as an administrator. Silently swearing under his breath, he wondered who had been the idiot to decide that four days off was too much free time and that basketball teams would lose their edge with that kind of break so they scheduled tournaments. To make matters worse the tournament his teams were going to was in Rainwater, Home of the Roughnecks.

The first settlers of Rainwater had to have been pissed because of the promise the town name brought and had attracted them to settle. It was only after they moved in did they learn that it never rained in Rainwater, and the name had actually come from their founder, Dewey P. Rainwater, a land man and speculator from back east. Fortunately, he had died years ago or they probably would have strung him up on one of the gas lamps he had installed on both sides of Main Street to celebrate the discovery of oil and gas.

What had once been a boomtown was now just a town of angry people, a disposition passed down through the generations. The citizens took their anger out on each other and anyone that ventured into their miserable lives. Going to Rainwater for any school event usually ended up with a fight or someone being assaulted, and it wasn't always the kids. The Roughnecks were less likely to brawl if they won, but were guaranteed to dispute any score that found them on the short end. Most schools avoided Rainwater as often as they could.

When Billy had the complete agenda for his Thanksgiving holiday, he vowed to find whoever did the scheduling for basketball and thoroughly blast them for such poor judgment. His only compensation for this terrible turn of events was that he could sit behind the bench and watch Savannah coach, up close and personal.

Savannah had done a remarkable job. She had never missed a beat in the classroom or on the court. Her basketball girls had known success under Johnny B Good, so she had a higher starting point than most. With her enthusiasm and determination, the team had early success and looked as though they could contend for a district title.

Billy called his parents and canceled, apologizing and empathizing as they wondered why anyone would schedule games during a break. It was unchristian they said and he needed to make that right before next fall. He promised he'd do just that. He also promised that he would be home for Christmas and to make sure his stocking was hung over the fireplace.

Billy spent a quiet Thursday in his apartment since Dallas' schedule had been rotated again and she had to work. It seemed pump jacks broke rods on holidays just like they did on any other day. The oilfield never closed...until the oil ran out, and everyone hoped that didn't happen...in their lifetime. The horses had to be rocking to bring up the oil to make the money to pay the people so they could feed their kids and buy booze.

He fixed himself a hamburger since cooking turkey wasn't even a consideration. He did have the coconut crème pie Dallas had brought over after prayer meeting the night before. Billy had been so despondent about working the holiday and feeling sorry for himself, he forgot to go. She had finally asked what his favorite dessert was and he actually had the nerve to tell her it wasn't cherry pie or Carrot cake, but coconut crème. She didn't seem to be the least bit put out and made it a point to bake him one. She even delivered it without reproach for his failure to show for prayer meeting.

The pie was there on his counter sitting like a trophy and he intended to eat every last bite of it. After all he was going to be watching basketball for the next two days in Rainwater instead of eating turkey and gravy with his family or sleeping in Dallas' arms. Until then he would eat his pie and watch the Oklahoma and Nebraska game. The game should be another classic and the last regular season game once again to decide the Big 8 Conference Championship and who would go to the Orange Bowl.

24

The trip over to Rainwater had given Billy plenty of time to think while he drove and listened to a Neil Diamond tape since the radio station signals gave out long before they could reach this part of the state. At night the stations out of Del Rio, that had antennas across the river in Mexico, cranked up the power, and the folks in the desert had something to listen to. Border blasters were good for country music and that worked for just about everyone in the area. If a person had more refined taste, other solutions had to be sought out. George Jones worked just fine for Billy.

Billy had sated his hunger the day before by eating almost his whole pie and the football game had been as advertised. He put himself to bed early since the girls team was playing the tournament opener and was scheduled to start at 9 A. M. He left at 7 to allow plenty of time. He cursed Rainwater again. They had scheduled the team with the longest bus ride to play the earliest game. Rainwater's team, which would sleep in their own beds, would play the last of the opening games making for a leisurely day to adjust from the gorging on Thanksgiving Day. Home cooking in more ways than one, but not unexpected.

Billy was selfishly hoping both the boys and girls team would get in their two games, be eliminated, and they would all be home before Saturday lunch and not have to even deal with the fans of Rainwater. The brackets were set for both the Rainwater teams to make it to the finals. He, of course, would never say that out loud and felt ashamed for wishing his kids ill, but it was Thanksgiving. These games wouldn't count toward district and...he wanted a break.

He cursed Rainwater for the twentieth time when he parked his car and showed his district pass to the lady manning the cash box out front. An Administrator's pass of any kind was usually good enough to get in any game as a courtesy each school showed for visiting administrators who everyone knew showed up to work and not to watch. Not Rainwater. No Passes accepted. $4. Per session. $10 for a tournament pass. Not even a smile or an apology. Billy refused to take the bait and argue. He knew the Roughnecks, students and fans alike, loved to provoke and engage. He simply bet on losing and decided to pay for one session at a time.

Billy bought a cup of coffee at the snack bar and sprinkled in some powdered creamer. He used two extra spoonfuls to recoup some of his entrance fee and felt smug about doing it. Taking his seat on the visitor's side, he found himself alone with the exception of a couple of Waymor parents who had loyally followed the bus over earlier that morning. The first game would be against Van Horn, one that attracted no interest from either town this early on the Friday after Thanksgiving. The gym sounded more like a mausoleum with echoes reverberating with each thump of a ball on the floor.

The game was as lackluster as the fan support and none of the girls seemed that into to it. Lethargy won the first quarter and then Savannah showed why she was a winner. She circled her girls up, got in their face, and for the next two minutes alternated between motivating and intimidating. The five girls that returned to the floor for the second quarter had a different demeanor about them and were definitely more focused. The first half ended with Waymor scoring twenty unanswered points and they ended up winning by a comfortable margin.

Billy walked down to the court to congratulate Savannah on her inspiring coaching and resulting victory. She apologized for the slow start and promised they would do better in the morning when they played their second game on the winner's side of the bracket. Billy had no doubt they would be ready at tip off. She thanked him for coming and went to get her girls back on the bus for the trip home.

Billy walked down the hallway to the larger boys gym to catch the last of the guys game that had started at the same time. The boy's team was playing Socorro and was holding their own until a couple of late turnovers down the stretch cost them the game. They would have to wait around until 4 P. M. to play their second game on the loser side of the bracket. Billy was stuck for the rest of the day, but avoiding direct contact with Rainwater was still possible.

Billy killed the next few hours by picking up a hamburger basket with extra fries and a large Dr. Pepper from arguably the best hamburger joint in West Texas. The shame was it represented the only positive thing the town had to offer; so few outsiders ever had the good fortune of tasting the Roughneck burger. Billy took advantage when he had to travel west, but would sneak into town and stay only long enough to get his order and leave.

Today he drove out into the desert to a rise that provided the only break in the flat landscape that cursed Rainwater as it did Waymor. He topped what was known as Victory Hill and parked his truck facing west so he could see Guadalupe Peak in the distance. He thought there might be a covering of snow on the top, but then it could be fog or haze. He was still a good distance away.

Billy parked away from the charred remains of the last bonfire that the locals burned on football Friday nights. It was meant to intimidate. As soon as it appeared the Roughnecks had control of the game, the boosters lit the fire that could be seen from the stadium below and fans on both sides had a clear view. The visiting teams knew as long as the fire was dark they still had a chance, but as soon as they saw flames shoot skyward, most teams simply gave in. It was quite dramatic and evidently demoralizing. Rumor had it that more than once the flame was lit after a first possession touchdown. Regardless of when they saw the flames, the locals became "fired up" in the literal sense and many times were on the point of being out of control. Intimidation was their not so secret weapon. Victory Hill. Thus the name.

On more than one occasion, advance parties from visiting schools tried to sneak up and burn the fire the night before. Every time they found it guarded by heavily armed Roughneck boosters that doubled as real roughnecks during the day. No one had the courage to take them on. One group tried the flaming arrow approach, but only got off one shot before a barrage of bullets was unleashed in their direction. They retreated as rapidly as they could. The arrow fell harmlessly short of the mark. The visitors found the half burned shaft dipped in the blood of an animal displayed in their dressing room the following night. The fire was lit when they ran out on the field for warm up.

The frenzy in the crowd made everyone from the visiting town that showed up want to simply turn around and go home. The only positive to the beating they took on the field was no one died. Broken and beaten, they gave thanks they all survived and slipped out of town without a post-game meal.

Billy savored his burger and used every one of the extra catsups he had asked for. When he finished eating, he read a book he had brought with him and occasionally scanned the horizon. He could see Guadalupe Peak now covered by clouds and to the south, Mexico was visible as a rugged stretch of land across a very narrow ribbon of water he assumed was the Rio Grande. When it was almost time for the game, he got out and walked over to the burn site looking around to make sure no armed guards were near by and pissed on the ashes. When he was done he dropped his trash, turned, and left. Billy felt the satisfaction alone was worth the trip over.

The boy's game was never close. Waymor was good in games where it came down to playing zone defense, getting rebounds, and walking the ball up the floor to run a set offense. They struggled with faster teams and teams that had gunners. Pecos liked to fast break, and if they ever had to shoot from outside, they rarely missed. As good as Pecos looked against Waymor, they had earned their way into the loser's game by being beaten by the Rainwater boys only an hour earlier. They still had enough gas in their tanks to outrun and out shoot the Sand Crabs. Friday came to a close. The boys' team had taken care of their part of the deal and were done until the following Tuesday, but Billy would be back on Saturday to support Savannah and the girls. After he had made sure the bus was loaded and homeward bound, Billy cranked up Golden Country from Del Rio and cruised back home as the night closed in around him.

The tournament bracket had a couple of losers' games to open the day on Saturday so Billy was able to sleep a little later. He finished up the coconut pie for breakfast and started back down the highway for the 1P. M. tipoff. Waymor was scheduled to take on Monahans, a larger school that was a volleyball powerhouse, but could still play basketball. Their volleyball team had failed to qualify for state this year, so they probably had a practice or two prior to the tournament, which was unusual and not encouraging for Waymor.

Billy spitefully pulled out his pass at the front desk and showed it to the same lady that must have sucked on lemons as a hobby only to have her explain again that no passes were

110

accepted and he could pay $4 per session or buy a tournament pass for $10. Billy defiantly slid four dollars across the table and picked up his orange ticket she had torn off of a roll and shoved it in his pocket. He was going to be out $12 at the most, which wasn't the problem. It was the principle. It was Rainwater.

Billy ordered a Frito pie with onions and jalapeños that was served in the Frito sack that was slit down the side. It made for tricky eating, but evidently saved the group running the concession stand about $.02 each time they sold one. Over the course of the tournament they probably had made an extra $1.50...money Billy would have gladly given them if they would simply give him a paper bowl strong enough to keep the grease from leaking out and staining the crotch of his pants as he sat and ate his lunch.

At tip off, he noticed once again that he and a couple of parents occupied the raised visitor side of the gym. There was still no one in Waymor that was willing to commit to the trip thinking anything good would come of it. It was also Saturday and football games were scheduled for the afternoon. He didn't mind. He would be able to watch the game without having to worry about kids acting up or a parent getting loud and obnoxious. The two parents present were silent supporters. Always there but rarely heard from. He liked that kind.

True to her word, Savannah evidently had a come to Jesus meeting with her girls sometime prior to the game. They came out and pressured Monahans all over the court. The Waymor girls caused a multitude of turnovers from a Monahans team that was still was thinking about dig, set, kill. Their ball handling gave the Lady Crabs many opportunities to take the ball the other way for easy layups and by the time their coach called his first time out, Waymor led by 16 points. Waymor increased their lead before halftime and although Monahans tried to rally to start the third quarter, the game had been over as soon as it started. Savannah and her girls had played their way into the finals and a match most likely against the Rainwater Roughneckettes. Billy was less than thrilled, but couldn't fault the girls who had really played an outstanding game or their coach who had prepared them.

With the other semi-final game and the consolation games still to be played, the final was scheduled to start at 7:30, but Billy knew tournaments usually ran late so most likely it would be closer to 8 P.M. or later when the game actually started.

Billy had a nagging feeling that he couldn't shake, one of foreboding. He wasn't a basketball fan because of the loud noises, big crowds packed close together, and the high intensity and emotional involvement. All taking place within arms reach of the players, coaches, and officials. It was great from a fans perspective, but few knew what it was like to be responsible for controlling that kind of atmosphere to keep it from exploding into a riot. He was more of a fan of empty gyms and echoes bouncing off the walls. Those games were past he knew and tonight...Lord help him.

With about five hours to kill before the next game, which would cost him another $4 making him the loser of the bet between him and lemon lady, Billy seriously considered driving back up to Victory Hill just to piss on it one more time. He calmed his emotions down and decided there might be boosters that had noticed his previous desecration and were lying in wait for him to return. As his namesake, Billy Shakespeare, had cautioned years before, discretion is the better part of valor. Being discreet, he opted to go to a roadside park about a mile south of town and read instead of fanning the flames of hostilities prior to the game. With any luck Rainwater would win and be so self absorbed in themselves they wouldn't notice him and the team slipping out of town afterwards. One could only hope.

The first clue to the direction the night would take came when Billy drove back to the gym and noticed the parking lot was full with a line of people winding out of the door. Taking deep breaths, Billy calmed himself enough to park down the street and get in line trying to be as innocuous as possible. When his time came, he simply threw down $4, picked up a red ticket, and made his way to the concession stand. The line was four deep and after a quick assessment, Billy decided he could wait for a bag of popcorn and some coffee until after the game started. The third place game was finishing up, and he hoped a large part of the crowd that blocked his way to food would be leaving to take their seats inside. Open seating provided the right amount of motivation to leave food behind he had found.

Billy wandered over to the stairs that led up to the raised visitor section. Climbing the stairs, he was surprised to find he would not be alone tonight. Aside from a few fans that were preparing to leave after the buzzer sounded in the third place game, Billy recognized over two dozen adults and at least ten guys from Waymor High that were probably boyfriends or brothers to the girls that would be playing. It seemed Waymor would have its own cheering section for the finals. Good for them, he thought, and made his way to the front row in the far corner nearest the girl's bench. This placed him between the fans that opted for the prime seats in the middle and the stairway to the floor. It also gave him the ability to hear anything that might be said towards the court that might need to be addressed before an official asked him to. Billy settled in for what he hoped would be a fast and non-confrontational night. It was not to be.

As the third place game ended, the Rainwater faithful began to flood the court and bleachers like ants. Scrambling for the best seats in the pull out section that put them right on the court and in the middle of the action, they pushed and shoved each other as if it were a mass game of musical chairs. As Billy watched awestruck, the people kept coming until almost the entire home side was filled, the pull out section on the floor first and then each row on the upper section until fans were touching the rafters at the top. Billy thought for a minute that the overflow might decide to sit on the Waymor side and that was last thing he wanted, but as it turned out that was the last thing they wanted as well. Being able to be part of the mob and see the faces of their girls across the court in the seats set up underneath the raised section of visitors was more important than a better seat. Billy was perfectly fine with that.

Billy's uneasiness grew with each passing minute and when the teams took the floor, the roar that thundered across the gym at them was deafening. The Waymor girls came out of the dressing room and began their warm up drills and more than a

113

few boos rained down on them. Most of the players had expected it evidently and went about their business, but it was a little unsettling for Billy. He searched out Savannah to see how his young coach would react and found that she was extremely focused and if the look in her eye was an indicator; Waymor wasn't going to be intimidated. It seemed she had played in places like this before.

He watched as the officials came out and received their share of boos as they stood by the scorer's table and took note of the crowd and their mood. After a brief conversation, one walked over to Savannah and spoke to her while the other official made their way to the Rainwater bench. After a minute, Savannah turned and pointed directly at Billy and motioned for him to come to the floor. He walked down the nearest stairs that led to the court and extended his hand to the official and confirmed he was the administrator on duty. The official explained that because of the "hostile environment" that seemed to be present, they wanted the administrators to sit on the floor behind their respective benches so the officials could contact them quickly if needed. It was only then that Billy realized it wasn't his imagination and others recognized a dangerous situation developing. Then he got scared.

Billy took one of the empty chairs that was setup for the visiting team and placed it behind the row for players and coaches. He sat close enough that he could hear Savannah giving her last minute pep talk about how much she admired their effort and how proud she was of them. She finished by promising they were going to win this game and take that trophy home! "No, No, No!" thought Billy. Winning is a very bad idea. Play hard, win the moral victory, and then try and save the uniforms while sneaking out of town.

Right from the opening tip it was bad. Waymor's guard grabbed the tip, but when a Rainwater player cut her legs out from under her, she was whistled for traveling. The first sounds of dissention rose from the small, but increasingly vocal visitors. They weren't happy being pushed back and elevated away from the court while their host sat right on top of the court, the players, and officials. They tried to compensate by yelling louder.

114

Billy wasn't happy about the first call, but didn't feel getting into a war of words with the other side that had a tremendous numerical advantage was the best course of action.

The officials appeared to be intimidated by the home crowd, but had some measure of conscience and credibility as they struggled mightily to be impartial without causing a riot. Throughout the first quarter, girls from Waymor were slammed to the floor by over aggressive defense, undercut when they went up for a rebound, and hacked when they shot. The officials found a compromise they were comfortable with by calling one foul for every three infractions. They hoped that might be acceptable to the mob and still retain a semblance of fairness and control. History has shown appeasement never works and after the third Waymor girl came out bleeding from her lip and sat beside the two bloodied noses, Savannah stood up and called a time out. She motioned for the officials to meet her and the Rainwater coach at the scorer's table.

Billy sitting behind the bench was close enough to hear her comments despite the razing and hooting that came from the vulgar people sitting across the gym.

"We came to play basketball! I Do NOT want my girls hurt!" Savannah said with her finger stuck right in the face of the lead official, but with her eyes focused directly on the opposing coach. "Back it down and call it right. I mean NOW!"

Savannah whirled around and marched back to her girls who were huddled up in front of the bench. She didn't wait to see the officials look at each other and roll their eyes, nor did she see the smirk on the face of the opposing coach as he went back to his bench to rally his girls.

In the huddle, before she sent her five back on the floor, Billy heard Savannah adamantly explain that there would be no retaliation or push back at any point. Their job was to play ball and let the officials deal with the rest. All she expected from them was their best effort, and she would have it, or they could sit by her. They would overcome by winning. She promised them if they would stick to their game and listen to her as she called out the plays, they could beat these girls and then they would take their trophy home and celebrate!

"Hands in...1,2,3...TEAM!" Savannah yelled and sent her players back out to do battle.

Maybe it was Billy's wishful thinking, but he thought maybe the rest of the first half wasn't quite as brutal as the opening minutes. It could have been that Savannah was doing a masterful job of switching up defenses and her offensives play to take advantage of the Roughneckettes or "Roettes" as the home crowd chanted evidently having a hard time with the number of syllables in the whole team name.

When the half ended the Roettes held a three-point lead and received a standing ovation from the home crowd who began to push their way across the floor to the concession stand for refills on soda pop and hot dogs. The Waymor girls slipped around the corner to their dressing room looking confident, but battered and bruised. Billy went down the hallway past the girls' dressing room and found a restroom and water fountain. He took advantage of each, but only taking a small sip of water fearful it was the contamination from the chemicals in the oilfield that caused the brain damage he had witnessed during the first half. He had no hopes for a peaceful ending to this day and simply prayed for no broken bones or hospital visits. Despite what Savannah had told the girls, hoisting the trophy would not be necessary for him to consider this a successful day. Making it home in one piece would be fine.

The buzzer sounded to call the teams back to the floor. Rainwater had already been on the floor flinging balls towards their goal and visiting with family and friends who walked back across the floor to their ringside seat holding barrels of popcorn and buckets of Coke. The Waymor girls stayed in the dressing room until the warning buzzer and simply walked to their bench without fanfare or warm up. Their eyes told Billy that Savannah had once again motivated them to the point of intensity that would carry them through the next half and back onto the bus with a trophy. No shouting or screaming was necessary. It was time to go to work.

Both teams came out and picked up where they left off. The number of fouls began to mount and when the Waymor girls tried to fast break, many times they were called for charging even though the defender was throwing a body block as they went by. Savannah changed tactics and her long-range shooters began to chip away at the Roettes' lead and by the fourth quarter the game was tied.

The game of attrition began when Rainwater's coach put in his hatchet man to take out Waymor's gunners. Hatchet head picked up three quick fouls, but the damage was evident as the shooters started focusing more on getting hammered than the rim, and their shoots began to bounce off. Free throws kept them close until finally hatchet head fouled out, but only after Waymor's best shooter was on the bench with ice on a sprained knee. The crowd had given the goonette a standing ovation reserved for a hero. Billy could only shake his head and look over his shoulder as his fans made their way to the railing to launch their verbal assaults on the referees and the crowd across the way. They were small in number, but overachieving.

One referee had the audacity to come over during a timeout and ask Billy to get his fans under control and off the railing. Billy almost laughed in his face. "When you can come over here and say that with some sort of dignity, I'll consider it. Friend...you've got a lot of nerve," was all Billy said as he pointed at the triage at the end of their bench filled with ice bags and bloody towels. He turned his back on the ref and walked away taking deep breaths.

With ten seconds to play, Rainwater held a one-point lead and the ball. The last of Waymor's starters had fouled out when she was called for charging giving the Roettes the ball out of bounds and setting off a roar from both sides of the gymnasium. Profanities flew from the Waymor side and gestures were returned from the home crowd. The officials had decided that their own survival was more important than a game. Waymor had their last five players on the court including 4'6" Pam Logan who was affectionately called Pumpkin or punkin' depending on the person.

Pam was a defensive specialist because of her size and her nickname came from her "stocky" body. She was low to the ground, wide as she was tall, but surprisingly quick so she could cut off a player driving to the basket, hold her ground, and many

117

times took the ball from them before they realized it. She wasn't much for shooting or rebounding, which limited her to a few minutes a game when a stop was needed or in situation such as now when all other choices were eliminated.

Savannah had her girls ready and focused even though Rainwater's strategy became evident as soon as their players walked back onto the floor. Each opposing player was taller than her counterpart from Waymor and the Roettes intended to utilize their height by throwing the ball in over the top of the defense. Rainwater intended to play the remainder of the game above the heads of the Lady Crabs. Waymor knew if the ball came in, they would have to foul just to have a chance; so, Savannah was shouting out numbers to let her girls know who the weakest free throw shooters were. Not that it mattered. If the free throw missed, Waymor had no chance of a rebound, but Savannah refused to give up or be denied.

The Roettes simply lined up along the half court line and when the ball was handed to the inbounding player, the Rainwater girls all broke to the basket except the one that was guarded by Pumpkin and she broke backcourt. The girl was a foot taller and the mismatch was obvious from the start. When Pam had gone with the girl to be ready to foul and had her momentum going towards the backcourt, the Rainwater girl broke forward towards half court prepared to catch the ball that had been lofted in her direction.

What happened next was simply karma. It may have happened before, but Billy had never seen it. The ball floated to the girl breaking from backcourt and it was simply a given she would catch it and throw it towards her basket to one of her two teammates who had made camp under the basket just waiting to throw in the clinching basket. From out of nowhere another of Rainwater's tall girls who rarely played and was redlining adrenaline, came rushing back from down court thinking the in bounder was in trouble, leaped for the ball, and touched it just before the first girl collided with her in mid-air. In what could have been a vacuum, the gym went completely silent as the ball was punched back towards Pam who was still trying to catch up to her girl. It landed square in her arms and without a thought

118

she turned and launched the ball towards the Waymor goal. No one spoke or moved during the seconds it took for the ball to arc high towards the gym ceiling and then begin it's descent towards the goal. Nothing but net. Swoosh. Waymor wins! The referees signaled good, motioned game over, and sprinted for the door to their dressing room before the Roughnecks could mobilize.

From complete silence, the gym exploded. Behind him Billy heard shouts of elation and taunts flung towards the home crowd who had gathered themselves and realized they had lost. The Rainwater coach grabbed the trophy he had stashed behind his bench as a foregone conclusion, walked over to Savannah who was jumping up and down with her girls, and the entirety of the presentation ceremony amounted to thrusting it in her direction and one word, "Here. "

Billy's level of concerned had risen considerably while the "trophy ceremony" was taking place as he noticed that mob mentality had taken over and a large number of students and adults alike moved towards the referees running off the court. Unable to catch them, and finding the officials door locked and unbreachable, the mob turned their attention to the opposition which were the fans and the girls of Waymor holding the trophy like a lightening rod above their heads.

Billy's survival instincts kicked in, and he rushed up to Savannah in the midst of the celebration and told her to get her girls off the court and into the dressing room immediately. As an afterthought he added, "Lock the door!" He began pushing the girls in the direction of the hallway in the corner of the gym. Savannah looked a little confused at first still reveling in the hard fought victory. When she saw the wild look in Billy's eyes and turned in the direction of the crowd, she understood the situation was disintegrating rapidly.

Savannah pulled and tugged on the girls until each grabbed their bag and trotted off the court. Savannah gathered up her purse and equipment bag in one hand and the trophy in the other. She moved with purpose, but not with fear. She had no intention of letting anyone intimidate her. It had never happened before and it wouldn't happen now.

Billy stayed between her and the crowd holding Savannah's elbow while guiding her to the dressing room. He was desperately trying to cover the distance to the hallway quicker than the crowd that was moving steadily in their direction. He thought Savannah could have moved faster and it would have helped, but she was not interested in showing fear. Billy had no such reservations as he was in full fight or flight mode with the fight part simply being part of the expression and never an actual consideration.

Billy arrived with Savannah at the entrance to the hall as the last of the Lady Crab players went through the dressing room door. He was turning Savannah towards the door and safety when a hand reached out and grabbed one of the aluminum pillars of the trophy. Savannah was holding the trophy by another of the aluminum pillars with her right hand. Billy placed himself in the middle of the doorway and in between Savannah and the mob as he grabbed onto a third pillar creating a three-way tug of war.

"This is OUR trophy! You cheated and stole it from us and we're taking it back. Our girls won that game. We're the winners, so let go!" demanded the man that was evidently the leader of the pack. He was a human fireplug. His body was thick and solid and his neck tapered up to his head, which was topped with stubble that matched his face. His face was weathered which made him look older than he was and on second glance appeared to look similar to the hatchet head that had been sent into the game to wreak havoc. Billy thought that would not be surprising. The scar tissue around his eyes indicated he was not a stranger to fist fights, and his lip that was filled to overflowing with Copenhagen was also scarred. Anger contorted his features to match the demented look in his eyes. The sun faded black t-shirt he wore was stretched to its limits trying to cover his chest as well as his biceps. Billy was at least six inches taller than him and did not consider this an advantage in the least.

Savannah looked the man squarely in the eye. Tugged on her portion of the trophy and said, "My girls won this trophy fair and square and had to beat everyone in this gym to do it. This is our trophy, and it will go home with us!"

Billy was both proud and surprised by her demeanor, but recognized they were outnumbered and no amount of bravado was going to back this crowd down. While he pulled, the man pulled, and Savannah pulled on the trophy, Billy leaned in towards Savannah and asked her to let go and go check on her girls. And lock the door! He would handle the trophy. Flames shot from her eyes at the thought of him asking her to back down, but then realized her girls were her main responsibility so she nodded okay, and gave up her grip. Savannah disappeared into the dressing room and locked the door, but not before she heard the man yell, "Now asshole, you let go of our trophy!" and then he flexed his bicep and pulled.

Billy felt momentarily proud as he held tightly to the aluminum pillar that was still held in his hand until he realized the rest of the trophy had been separated from him by the beast of a man and was being passed back over the crowd. The only positive, Billy noticed, was that the majority of the crowd felt vindicated and thought they had gotten what they came for and were wandering out the gym holding the mangled hardware aloft as if it was the Holy Grail.

Unfortunately, the fireplug and about half a dozen of his cronies that all had the same weathered look one got from exposure out in the oilfield where the work was hard and the men were harder, stood in front of him, still not content.

"Now move so we can go up them stairs and shut those assholes up. Nobody disrespects us and gets away with it," Fireplug said as he pointed towards the Waymor fans that hadn't had the sense to leave or even tone down their celebration.

"I'm sorry I can't do that," Billy explained truly wanting to step aside and then follow them up the stairs and smack a few of the people himself.

"Well, you can step aside or be the first victim. Doesn't matter to me. We can go past you or over you. Your choice," Fireplug explained with cold eyes and a colder demeanor. Billy was sure the man would prefer to have any excuse so he could punch one more person along the way.

121

"Why don't y'all go on home? You got the trophy, and you can rewrite the scorebook to say whatever you want to say. There's nothing left to gain," Billy offered as an alternative.

"Like I said, by you or through you, Mr. Principal. Your choice," Fireplug spoke softer as his eyes narrowed and his features hardened even more. His pals moved to close ranks and prepared for the charge.

Billy spent the next few seconds praying for Gabriel the Archangel to swoop in and slay this beast. He figured the odds of that happening were about the same as his surviving the coming onslaught. He just couldn't in good conscience step aside and provide an opening to the girls, Savannah, or even his idiot fans that were still clueless to the peril that stood only a few feet away.

"I'm sorry. I just can't," Billy said.

The man grabbed the front of Billy's shirt while drawing back one of his arms that looked like a ramrod the police used for breaching doors. The surprising thing that crossed Billy's mind just before he suspected the man's hand would crush his face was that he was wearing his nicest shirt and hated the thought of getting blood on it. To his credit Billy didn't close his eyes, which was fortunate because he was able to see the hand of God reach over his shoulder just as Fireplug's fist was hurtling towards his face. The hand of God caught the fist in a massive hand of his own, and then used the man's momentum to pull him forward. Billy was bumped out of the way in the process, but saw that Boomer was actually the hand of God. Boomer had the Fireplug's arm twisted behind his back and was using his other arm, wrapped under the man's chin, to lift him off the ground about a foot.

Fireplug's buddies took a step forward until they saw Boomer flex his own arm and cut the air supply to Fireplug's brain. They stopped and reconsidered.

"This is what's going to happen. I'm going to give the rest of you 30 seconds. If all of you can make it out of the gym in that amount of time, I won't rip his arm out of socket and use it like the jawbone of an ass to beat this rest of you over the head. If you linger too long, this man won't being going back to work and

122

can't feed his family. There are not many jobs out in the oilfield for a one-armed man. If you or any of the other nutcases outside try to hurt our fans or girls, I'll rip your arms off as well. Any questions?" Boomer explained in a calm voice that left no doubt he could and would follow through. "Clock's ticking fellas!"

A mad scramble took place as the men raced across the floor and out the door. Boomer loosened his grip on Fireplug enough that the man could breath and touch the floor. "You seem to be the leader of the pack. You'll be the one I come looking for if any of our people are hurt. This is a stupid basketball game for gosh sake and not worth permanent injury. You need to work and both arms to do your job, I suspect. Keep that in mind and be smart for once in your life. Can I let you go now?" Boomer asked the man who nodded.

The man rubbed his arm and his neck as he walked for enough away to feel brave again and turned back towards Boomer. "You'd better bring an army if you decide to come after me!" Fireplug snarled still backing towards the door.

"I am the army," was all Boomer said. Not feeling the need to get into a war of words. He felt like his actions had said everything that needed saying.

"Thank you, Boomer," Billy said with as much gratitude as he could drum up. "You just saved my life, literally. You literally saved my life! If he had punched me it would have killed me. No doubt. Dead. I'd be dead!" the adrenaline in Billy's body had no place to go, and he was all motions and words.

Thank you, Billy," Boomer said.

"Me? For what? Getting killed?" Billy asked half laughing.

"For placing yourself between those jerks and our kids. That took courage," Boomer offered.

"I had no chance. He would have killed me. They would have trampled my body as they went past. You were the one that saved the day!" Billy said emphatically.

"All those things would have happened, and you knew it. Yet you didn't move. That's character man. That's courage," Boomer said. "I'm big. I just threw my weight around. It's not the same."

"Well, let's just be proud of each other then. You need to know that as long as I have you watching my back, I'll be full of character and courage," Billy laughed.

"I'll always have your back, Boss. You know that!" promised Boomer as they shook hands and patted each other on the back.

"You go check on Savannah and the girls. I have a few words to share with the fans upstairs. When the team is ready, bring them up to the bleachers, and we'll go out together." Billy said.

25

As Billy climbed the stairs, he noted how quiet it had gotten compared to how loud his fans had been only a few minutes earlier. He thought they might have all braved the crowd and left, which would have been just fine with him. Instead, when he walked up the stairs, he noticed all of the fans were at the top of the gym looking silently out of the windows. Billy slowly climbed up the stairs to see what was so captivating.

"They're trashing the bus, Mr. Masters!" one of the senior boys exclaimed.

"They busted out all the windows and now they're inside slashing the seats," explained one of the mothers that stood near him. She seemed more amazed than fearful.

"They cut all the valve stems on the tires. Every tire is flat. What the hell do we do now?" chimed in one of the more vocal dads that seemed to be accusing Billy for letting it happen.

That was it for Billy. He had no more patience for the mentality he had witnessed on both sides of the court during the game and the adrenaline was still pumping through him from his near death experience just moments before.

"What the hell we are going to do now is everyone is going to march down to the front row, sit your ass down, and shut your mouth. I will get us some law enforcement and when the girls are ready we are going to leave here together, with our mouths shut, and get the hell out of this place," Billy said emphatically leaving no room for doubt.

The sight of the mob destroying the bus and the tension in Billy's voice was motivation for each of the fans to back away

124

from the windows and start down the steps…except for one…there's always one.

"I don't think that kind of language is called for!" the man said as he squared around to challenge Billy. This was the same man that had been shouting right above Billy's head during the whole game at the referees and opposing fans, fanning the flames that had led to this particular moment.

"Let me be clear," Billy said in a low hiss that could be heard by the man, but not by anyone else. "I don't give a shit if they tar and feather you. I'll be happy to leave you as a hostage. What I do care about are the girls, and if you should in any way interfere with them getting home safely because of your words or actions, I will personally tie you to the bumper of that bus and leave you behind. Now go sit your ass down and shut the hell up!" Billy glared at the man who wanted to respond, but was pretty sure that Billy was unhinged at the moment. He walked down the stairs and sat beside his wife.

"Boomer will bring the girls up when they are dressed. We will need to send them with their parents, and any girl whose parents aren't here will be taken care of. If Boomer and the team show up before I get back, make that happen. " Billy instructed the group and then he walked down to the foyer to find help.

Leaning against wall by the concession stand was a police officer that evidently was assigned gym duty and crowd control. He was cramming popcorn in his mouth from the free bags that had been left over and placed on the counter for the taking. He ate as if the free bags would be gone before he could get his fill. Considering the size of his belly and that his gun belt hung below the vast expanse, Billy decided he would be eating a long time, and should he need to grab his weapon, he would have to lean side ways.

"Are you aware that a mob is outside destroying our school bus while you stand here eating popcorn?" Billy asked the officer.

"Better to let them vent on rubber and steel than your head," replied the officer.

"How about not letting them vent at all? Ever considered that?" asked Billy with contempt. "Any chance you can call for backup and clear those jokers out of here so we can get our girls home?" Billy asked hoping to help the officer formulate a plan.

Still cramming popcorn in his mouth and chewing as he talked the officer said, "You shouldn't have poked the bear. Folks here don't like losing."

"So all this is our fault because our girls played hard and won?" Billy asked incredulously.

"Wouldn't be happening if you lost," explained the officer confident in his analysis.

"Of all the things I've heard tonight that has to be the dumbest," Billy said, as he looked straight at the officer.

"You aren't going to win any friends here talking like that," the officer said with less cockiness and more meanness.

"With all due respect, officer, I'm not here to win friends. I wouldn't want to be friends with anyone that lives in this shithole. What I do want is to be able to leave…with my girls…safely. Any chance you can help me do that?" Billy asked with controlled anger.

"There you go with those insulting words. Nobody ever tell you about catching flies with honey?" the officer replied reaching for his third bag of popcorn and asking the girls cleaning the concession stand for a soda to wash down the hulls sticking in his throat. He didn't offer to pay her.

"One last question. Any chance there is someone on the local police force that's not a brother-in-law to those guys in the parking lot that might be willing to help us get out of town?" Billy asked knowing the answer.

"To be honest we're pretty much all related here in Rainwater. We have a couple of brothers, an uncle, and a father and son team that make up the police force and we do our best to protect the citizens of Rainwater, which is our sworn duty." The officer answered patriotically.

"Does "uphold the law" rank anywhere near the top?" Billy's patience exhausted at this point.

"You know mister. I've been patient and listened to your insults of my town and me. I'm starting to think you've verbally assaulted an officer. I might just have to arrest you and take you down to the station," the officer smiled at Billy with a look of malice in his eye. Billy wouldn't have been the least bit surprised had he pulled out his cuffs.

"Forget it, Junior. There's been enough nonsense tonight. We don't need to make it worse. " The words came from a Deputy Sheriff that had been standing off to the side listening to the exchange.

"Man's insulted all of us here and then expects a motorcade and parade out of town. I think he needs to learn some manners is all," the officer said to the Deputy and then turned to lift of his chin in Billy's direction that anyone would interpret as an insult and being dismissed all at once.

"I'd tell you to ignore him, but that's not the best idea. He's dangerous. When you're the Chief's son-in-law and married to his favorite daughter, you get away with plenty. Chief hates him, but loves his daughter, so he keeps him on. Sends him over to the gym as often as possible because he knows Junior will spend the whole night eating. When he's on the street, he has a tendency to let his power go to his head," explained the Deputy.

The man was old. Billy guessed close to 70 and wondered why he still was on duty. Reading his thoughts the Deputy explained, " I wasn't born here, but moved out here fifty years ago looking for work in the oilfield. Got hurt one day and needed to find another job less dangerous to support my family; so, I signed on with the Sheriffs department. Been there ever since. Could retire, but my wife died and my kids moved off. I keep doing this as a reason to get up in the morning. Sheriff uses me mostly to deliver paperwork and cover events not likely to escalate into mayhem. Think he misjudged tonight," the Deputy half smiled and shook his head.

"Any chance the Sheriff's department has men that could get us out of here?" Billy asked hopefully.

"Not really. We're as inbred as the police department, but I think I have some news that might make you happy," the Deputy smiled at Billy. "The two officials that fled to the dressing room and barricaded the door managed to break the glass in the coaches office to get to the phone. They called their chapter president in El Paso for help and he called the DPS. I just heard over the radio that two units from the highway patrol were five minutes out and closing fast. They'll be able to get you out of here. No doubt."

Billy smiled for the first time during this whole fiasco. He reached out and shook the Deputy's hand to thank him.

"I need to go get my people ready. Anytime you come over to Waymor, lunch is on me," Billy promised as he turned and took the stairs two at a time.

Boomer had escorted Savannah and her players up to the balcony where they had reunited with their families. All were talking in hushed tones until they saw Billy, and they all stopped. He evidently had made believers out of everyone. Billy stood in front of them and explained what would happen next.

"The Highway Patrol is coming to rescue us, and when they get here, everyone needs to be ready to go," he said.

Billy asked who had cars and who was riding with them. He saw that Boomer had adopted Savannah and three of her players whose parents hadn't come. Boomer drove a large Suburban to accommodate his size and had plenty of room for the extra passengers. Everyone else was accounted for and told to have their bags and equipment ready to move as soon as they were told to mount up. And to keep their mouths shut.

Billy walked to the top of the gym to watch and wait while Boomer loomed over the Waymor group. Billy had barely made it to the top when he saw the lights of the cruisers flashing as they sped into the parking lot with out so much as tapping their brakes. One car pulled to the rear of the bus and the other to the front. At the last minute brakes were applied, and the cars skidded to a halt on the asphalt. Expecting officers to tumble out with guns drawn, Billy was surprised to see nothing happen for what seemed like ages, but were mere seconds. Almost in a choreographed manner, the doors to each car opened simultaneously and an officer placed his left black boot on the ground and slowly eased himself out of the car. Each officer adjusted his grey Stetson on his head while they closed the car door and stood to their full height placing their right hand on the grip of their service revolver.

One riot, one Ranger was an expression that anyone that grew up in Texas or had lived there for any length of time had heard.

128

Texas Rangers were mythical creatures that secured the safety of the early settlers and protected them from the Comanche and outlaws. Most Rangers traveled alone or with a partner and many times found themselves outnumbered, but rarely outfought. The modern day Ranger was a division of the Department of Public Safety and to become a Ranger one had to be a highway trooper first. Most troopers aspired to qualify for the elite group and adopted the mentality that they could stand alone in the middle of a mob and control the situation. They were confident men and took their job seriously. One riot, one Ranger…. and the rioters in Rainwater noticed there were two standing in front of them. So when one of the troopers said in a voice neither raised nor threatening for everyone to just go on home, the Rainwater thugs knew they were outnumbered and began to comply. Being the idiots they were it was necessary for them to swear under their breath and posture towards the troopers who appeared not to notice or care. The troopers slowly moved forward herding the crowd out of the parking lot and into their cars.

When nothing but taillights was visible to Billy, he climbed back down the steps and told the waiting group to get ready. He walked to the railing in time to see one of the troopers come through the gym doors and speak to the Deputy Sheriff who pointed in Billy's direction. The trooper walked out on the gym floor in order to get a better view of the group waiting. He told Billy in a calm voice to get his people down to the front, and they would be taken out first.

When the group reassembled in the gym foyer, the trooper introduced himself to Billy as Officer Torres and explained that the trooper out front was Officer Grisham. Officer Torres asked for a show of hands how many cars were involved. With Boomer's Suburban, two carloads of boyfriends and football players, eight parent cars, and Billy's truck the caravan would be twelve long not counting their escorts.

Officer Torres was going over the instructions when Junior wandered over closer to the group interested in the details of the escape. Officer Torres sensed his presence and without so much as a word turned and glared at the policemen that stood behind him with popcorn hulls stuck in his teeth. The death stare took only seconds to convince the overweight officer to exit the building and walk to his patrol car.

Resuming the plan, Officer Torres explained he and Officer Grisham would take the group out north just to be on the safe side. He didn't expect any ambushes along the way, but stranger things had happened when idiots and alcohol collided. If an ambush were planned, it would most likely be east of town on the most direct route back to Waymor. Officer Torres explained he and Officer Grisham would escort them as far as the Interstate and then come back to get the officials. Once the Waymor folks hit the interstate, the troopers felt certain they'd be safe. It would be little bit longer trip, but in the best interest of their safety. No one argued. No one had any questions when asked.

Officer Torres keyed the mike on his shoulder to make sure the area was still clear. Officer Grisham who had stood guard outside confirmed all was clear and gave the okay to proceed. Officer Torres had explained that Officer Grisham would pull his car to the lead position, Boomer would put his Suburban directly behind the cruiser and everyone else was to file in behind to form a convoy. He asked Billy to make sure all his people were accounted for and then place his truck behind the last car. Officer Torres would bring up the rear. Each driver was instructed to stay as tight on the vehicle ahead of him or her as they could and still feel comfortable. Getting strung out over a long distance wouldn't be good for anyone. Everyone nodded.

With one last look, Officer Torres motioned for everyone to get to their vehicle and take their place. Billy walked out into the parking lot to monitor each vehicle as it filed into the parking lot behind the cruiser Officer Grisham had turned around and pointed east. Billy walked to the front in time to hear Officer Grisham giving Boomer last minute instructions.

"When we start out, stay tight. Don't slow down or stop at anytime. If there is trouble ahead, I'll stop and deal with it. You take the lead and get your people home. If we make it to the interstate without trouble, I'll pull over. Don't slow down. I guarantee you there's no one patrolling that strip of interstate all the way to your turn off. Got it?" Officer Grisham looked expectantly at Boomer.

"Yes sir! I'll make sure we all get there. Thanks for the help!" said Boomer extending a hand to the trooper.

Billy had no doubt Boomer would do what was necessary to protect the group. He just hoped it required nothing other than driving fast all the way home.

As the last car pulled in line, Billy walked past each car checking to make sure they were ready and had all their people. Each gave a thumbs up so he climbed into his truck and found his place. Officer Torres whipped his cruiser right in behind Billy and hit his roof lights. He must have radioed Officer Grisham in front since the cars began moving almost immediately. Every driver was ready and moved the instant they saw space in front of them. The gravity of what had taken place and their own perilous situation seemed ridiculous in light of the fact it was just a basketball game, but here they were in a convoy protected by troopers fleeing for their own safety leaving the empty scarred shell of a bus behind.

The lead vehicle eased out of the parking lot and slowly made its way east towards the edge of town. Officer Grisham gradually picked up speed to avoid the accordion effect, which would create gaps in their procession. Just as they got to the intersection where the Waymor folks would normally continue on east towards home, Officer Grisham turned left without braking and headed due north towards the interstate. Evidently on cue from Officer Torres in the rear that all cars had made the turn, Billy noticed a rapid increase in speed.

Before they had covered a mile, the rag tag group of citizens was traveling at 95 mph in a convoy that would make the Secret Service proud. Billy held on to his steering wheel and kept his eye directly on the bumper of the car ahead of him watching intently for the slightest variation. The speed was not unusual for people that lived in the desert. To get anywhere in a reasonable amount of time required high speed driving at all times on interstates or dirt roads. It didn't matter. It was the NASCAR like conditions without a margin for error that made

Billy uneasy, and he figured the rest might be feeling the same concerns.

In less time than normal, the interstate loomed ahead. Its overpass was silhouetted against the desert sky. The pace of the caravan slowed until Officer Grisham took the right turn and raced up the on ramp to the freeway. He immediately pulled onto the shoulder and came to a stop. Boomer took his cue swinging wide around the trooper's vehicle and hit the accelerator taking the group back up to racing speed. Focused on accelerating and the car in front of them, no one noticed the DPS cruisers wait on the shoulder of the highway until the convoy was out of sight. The troopers then backed down the on-ramp, made a J turn on the access road, hooked a left and speed south to rescue the referees that were still huddled in a dressing room.

Boomer led the cars as he had seen Officer Grisham do it. With the freeway clear of bumps and intersections, he set his cruise on 95 and drove east with everyone else in pursuit. After they had covered 75 miles in less than an hour Boomer hit the off-ramp having slowed only slightly. He rolled down the ramp and along the access road for half a mile bleeding off his speed before he turned right without stopping and only briefly checking for on coming traffic. He watched as the line of cars made the turn onto the farm to market road that would take them to Waymor. He picked up the pace again, but everyone notice they were traveling at a more reasonable speed. Boomer had decided their biggest threat at this point was wrecking as opposed to ambushes and chose to cruise back home.

Billy's knuckles were white from the last hundred miles of intense driving and fatigue was setting into his shoulders. The strain had taken its toll, so he was grateful for the respite. Half and hour later the cars rolled into Waymor from the north. As Billy watched, the number of cars in the caravan began to decrease as one by one they turned left or right heading for their homes and blessed safety and rest. When he found no one in front of him, he too turned into the parking lot of his apartment complex. He let out a deep sigh of relief and realized he had been gone less than a day and yet it seemed like a week. Holy hell, he thought as he drug his body inside.

Billy grabbed a beer out of the refrigerator and realized how very tired he was. He felt every muscle in his neck and back aching and knew that only adrenaline had kept him going the last several hours. As he leaned back in his recliner and replayed the events of the evening in his mind, none of it seemed real. When his first bottle was empty, he pulled himself up and started to the refrigerator for another. He passed his phone on the counter and decided he needed to let Cracker Jack know what happened. The next day was Sunday and everyone and their dogs would hear the story at church and Billy wanted the sup to hear it from him first and not be caught off guard. He realized it was late, but thought Cracker would forgive him.

After he had dialed the number, Billy doodled on the notepad he kept by the phone. After the fifth ring, Billy was preparing to hang-up when he heard Cracker's gravelly voice answer.

"Hello," Cracker said in a voice that everyone would recognize as someone wakened from a sound sleep.

"Cracker Jack, it's me Billy. I'm awfully sorry to wake you at this hour and on a holiday to boot, but I thought you might need to hear what happened over in Rainwater tonight," Billy explained quickly trying to smooth over any misgivings about the intrusion.

"Sure thing Billy. I wasn't in bed. I was just dozing in my recliner," Cracker explained either truthfully or trying not to make Billy feel bad. "If you've been in Rainwater on a Saturday night, I can only imagine."

"Well sir, with all due respect, I don't think you can imagine," Billy said and then proceeded to relay the entire events of the evening.

After hearing the story right up to the point his phone had rung, Cracker thanked Billy for the heads up and assured him he had done the right thing all the way around.

"You are making a principal after all. You got the people home in one piece and all our kids are safe...and you called me. Great job Billy," Cracker praised him.

Billy felt a little sheepish for the praise and tried to shrug it off by reminding Cracker Jack it was Boomer that had saved the day. Cracker wouldn't have it. He bragged on Billy's decision-making and decisiveness while agreeing he and Boomer made a good team. Cracker thanked him one last time and told him to get some rest. They agreed to meet Monday morning after Billy got the day started and decide what they needed to do about the whole situation. The last thing Cracker said to Billy was that he would call Leroy Perkins, their insurance agent, about having the bus towed and repaired.

"We pay thousands of dollars in premiums and now its time to collect on that coverage. It's just a bus, Billy. The important things are home in their beds. Don't ever forget that," Cracker said and he hung up.

Billy was drained. What a way to spend Thanksgiving. He was sure life had been better when there was football and turkey, but he had a feeling of satisfaction that surprised him as he brushed his teeth and threw his clothes into the basket he kept in the corner. He had faced the devil and lived to tell about it, and his boss seemed to think he did a good job. There was one last thing he needed to do. He picked up the phone and called Boomer.

"Hey Boomer, are y'all in bed?" Billy asked hoping he hadn't awakened them.

"No we were just finishing up. After we dropped the other girls off at their houses, Savannah has been calling all the rest of the players to make sure they were alright and to brag on them. She just finished. Hopefully you haven't tried to call before," Boomer reported.

"No. I called Cracker Jack to make sure he knew what happened so he wouldn't get blindsided at church. Before I crashed I thought I had better check on Savannah to see how she's doing," Billy explained.

"She's fine, but I'll let you talk to her yourself," offered Boomer.

"That would be great," said Billy. "Before you go Boomer, I want to thank you again. I believe you literally saved my life. I see no other outcome. Had you not been there this whole evening could have turned out a lot worse. I told Cracker that same thing. He's proud of you too. Thank you again."

"You didn't have to do that. My part was just a few minutes. You controlled the whole evening, but we've covered all that. Let's agree we make a good team and helped each other. That's what friends are for. Right?" Boomer said not waiting for a response before putting Savannah on the phone.

"Hello," Savannah's voice sounded like music to Billy's ear.

"Hey Savannah...uh, Coach Skinner. This is Bil. . . Mr. Masters. I just wanted to see how you were feeling after tonight. That was a little different than your average basketball game," Billy said.

"It was definitely an exciting evening. You sure know how to show a girl a goodtime," she joked.

"Well I try to make a good impression, but I think I might have disappointed you by not getting home with your trophy," Billy said a little embarrassed. "In the grand scheme of things it seemed like the best idea at the time."

"It really wasn't the trophy that had me upset so much as that Neanderthal thinking he could take it from me since I was just a pretty little lady. He has no idea how unladylike I can be," Savannah explained causing Billy to raise his eyebrows wondering what that could mean.

"I think everyone in the gym saw how well you can coach. No one can doubt your force of will and character. That was an incredible win for the girls in a very hostile environment."

"I was proud of them. They listened to me and never gave up. You can't ask for much more than that," Savannah said proudly.

"You can tell the girls they'll be getting a trophy. I'll make sure of that. I'll order it first thing Monday morning, and we'll have a school wide presentation when it comes in," Billy promised. "They earned it."

"The girls will be excited. I'd like that too. Thank you, Mr. Masters," Savannah replied.

"I'll let you go get some rest. I'll see you Monday morning. Sleep well," Billy said.

"Goodnight Billy," Savannah said as she hung up. Billy smiled for just a minute before replacing the receiver in the cradle.

He was out before he had even adjusted his pillow. The sun would be halfway across the sky before he had his next conscience thought, which was fine because it was Sunday, the last day of his holiday and the last chance he had for rest until Christmas. Surely to goodness no one played basketball during Christmas.

26

Billy had struggled to wake up and was moving very slowly when he walked into the office on Monday morning. He had seen a light on as he came through the door at the end of the hall. Ms. Dixie was already at her desk.

"Good morning Mr. Masters," Ms. Dixie called out in an unusually cheerful voice. "What an exciting weekend you must have had. "

"So you've heard," Billy guessed.

"Everyone has heard. It was all over town by the time church was out, and one pastor actually preached a sermon on standing up to evil!" Ms. Dixie informed him.

"You're kidding," was all Billy could think to say.

"No. It's true. By Sunday night the events in Rainwater had reached epic proportions that rivaled the rescue at Dunkirk and the fighting withdrawal by the Marines at the Chosin Reservoir. You, my friend, are a hero!" Ms. Dixie was almost jubilant as she related the gossip she had heard through her well-connected sources. "The best part that most folks like is when you told the city commissioner and the president of the bank to sit their ass down and shut up!"

"Yeah, about that. That probably wasn't the best way to handle that situation. I'm sure I'll hear about it again," said Billy feeling not so much a hero as someone with a bull's-eye on his back.

"Rumor has it both were heard in church saying they understood what you were dealing with and didn't blame you," Ms. Dixie assured him. "Their behavior during and after the game was also widely discussed. I think they are more than willing to put you in the spotlight and take the focus off

136

themselves. Everybody in town is envious. They've all wanted to say the same thing to those men so many times, and here you got them both at one time. Hero, Billy... Mr. Masters. I'm sorry, I guess I got carried away there," Ms. Dixie said.

She was both more excited and embarrassed than Billy had ever seen.

"Look, I understand office protocol, but I've seen you in your robe with no make-up, and you've seen me looking like Jack Nicholson riding behind your sister on her motorcycle. Maybe when no one is around we can say Billy and Dixie," Billy said hopefully.

"I think that might be alright. I'll give it a try and see how it goes," Dixie agreed almost relieved.

"Great...Dixie. I have to meet with Cracker once we get this day rolling to see what happens next with the fiasco of a weekend behind us," Billy informed her.

"Congratulations again...Billy. You did a good thing this weekend, and we're all proud of you," Dixie said with a smile.

"Thank you. "

The bell rang to start the day and as Billy stood in the hall, he found that he had become somewhat of a folk hero over night. He got more than a few high fives from the kids as they walked by on their way to class while several teachers walked up and simply shook his hand. Billy was embarrassed by the attention and wondered if this adulation was from the exaggerated accounts or the actual events. From what he remembered, the bravest thing he had done was not pee his pants in the face of certain death, and he was convinced that wasn't enough to qualify him for celebrity status. He finally decided to enjoy it while he could and realized the pendulum could easily swing the other way without a moment's notice. He smiled and waved and high fived until the last student was in class then excused the few that were tardy. He was in a noble mood, which meant forgiveness was the word for the day.

At 9:00 A.M. Billy walked over to the school administration offices to meet with Cracker Jack. Cracker's secretary greeted him more warmly than in the past and offered him a cup of coffee. He accepted and asked for a little cream. He was starting to get used to the celebratory feeling and walked into Cracker's office, when summoned, with a smile on his face.

"Morning, Boss," Billy said.

"It was a good morning, and then Leroy called," explained Cracker. "Leroy sent a wrecker over this morning to Rainwater to tow the bus back in for repairs, and when he got there someone had burned it to the ground. All that was left was the charred remains."

"You're kidding," Billy said in disbelief.

"I wish I were, but last night someone decided to come back and finish the job by covering the bus in gasoline and striking a match," Cracker said. "What's really got my goat is the superintendent from Rainwater just called accusing our people of burning the bus out of spite and ruining his parking lot. He's planning on sending us a bill for the repair!"

"He's sending us a bill? Did he offer to pay for the bus or for the damage his fans caused?" Billy asked

"I asked him the same thing, and he said he didn't have any proof people from Rainwater did the damage. He had the police look into it and they couldn't say for certain who was responsible, "Cracker reported incredulously. "I asked how he then could be so certain it was our people that had burned it. According to him the police were given a description of a vehicle fleeing the scene that headed towards Waymor."

Billy had nothing to say. He was stunned. Even after going through the events that happened Saturday night he wondered if this nightmare would ever end.

"I told the jackass to send us a bill...and hold his breath until we paid it. The bus or what's left of it is being held as evidence and circled with tape as part of a crime scene. Leroy said he had pictures and enough to file a total loss claim. We'll be getting a new bus and Rainwater can keep that pile of junk in the parking lot as far as I'm concerned. What we need to do today is determine what to present to the board at the next meeting in regards to further actions. That's why you're here. I'd like to have your input," explained Cracker Jack.

"Alright," said Billy. "My initial thoughts are that we never schedule another game with Rainwater so we never have to set foot in their town, and they never have a reason to come here. Should we ever have to play them in any kind of play-off, it would have to be at a neutral site. Should, God forbid, we ever wind up in their district, I'm for petitioning the UIL to move," Billy stated emphatically.

Cracker chuckled and said, "So how do you really feel?"

"Cracker, I really thought someone was going to die and that someone just might be me. Those people are insane," Billy said.

Over the course of the next hour, Cracker and Billy drafted a recommendation to the board, contacted TEA and filed a formal complaint as well as one with the UIL. Cracker called Waymor's police chief to find out whether not it would be worthwhile to file a police report and found that any evidence to support it would have to come from the Rainwater police and everyone agreed that would be a waste of time. When they finished, Billy and Cracker agreed that the girls had done a good job, everyone was safe, and they both would be happy to put the whole thing behind them. Billy's only regret was knowing he had more than likely eaten his last Roughneck burger.

27

Slipping quietly into the chair beside Dallas, Billy patted her on her thigh and smiled. Dallas smiled back and took his hand in hers patting it twice. He hadn't seen Dallas in days as a result of their conflicting work schedules, and the warmth of her touch reminded Billy what he had missed. She seemed truly happy to see him. Billy was running a little late and the pastor was already speaking about the role of the Christian in an unchristian world and referenced the events of the previous weekend with a slight nod in Billy's direction, and then had moved quickly on with the sermon.

Billy knew his fifteen minutes of fame was running out when an irate mother had verbally drawn and quartered him in his office just a few hours earlier. She was upset over his response to her daughter's skirt that would have needed to be twice as long to even come close to the dress code. Asking her to wear sweatpants that were kept in the office for just such an event

139

was demeaning and insulting according to the mom. Billy thought the girl bending over and letting pretty much anyone that wanted to look see all the way to glory land was more demeaning, but they agreed to disagree. Actually they hadn't since the mom wasn't agreeable to anything except the fact she considered Billy obnoxious and rude. Billy took the verbal beating until the mom ran out of steam, grabbed her daughter by the hand, and drug her out the door. He didn't expect to get the sweatpants back.

When he was sitting at his desk licking his wounds, he remembered it was Wednesday and prayer meeting seemed like a good idea. Seeing Dallas seemed like a good idea actually. Nothing took the sting out of a butt chewing quite like a large slice of cake and a beautiful woman. So here he sat, hand in hand, his thoughts swirling and his mind sinning faster than the faithful could pray. He did garner three mentions during the chain of prayer for his role in protecting the innocent, and blessings were asked to be bountiful in his direction. Each time he heard his name, he felt a little guiltier for the lust in his heart at the moment. He finally cleared his mind of Dallas and offered his own silent prayer of gratitude that he was still among the living, and the kids got home safe. He closed with asking forgiveness for his impure thoughts.

A lady that must have had dinner in the oven and harbored no doubts all topics had been covered fully closed the season of prayer. She simply stated that God knew what was needed and challenged him to get to work. Amen.

Dallas reached her arms around Billy's neck when they stood giving him a big hug.

"Long time no see, Billy Boy," Dallas said smiling.

"I know. It seems like years. I could not wait to get to church, which sounds kind of crazy, but...let's just say you look great," Billy said.

He realized she had taken his hand again, and a jolt of electricity went through him.

"It seems you've been busy," Dallas said with one eyebrow cocked.

"I wouldn't believe everything you hear. The stories have gotten a little out of control and reached mythical proportions, I'm afraid," Billy assured her. "Of course, my fifteen minutes of fame seemed to have passed.

"You're still my hero," Dallas said.

"Oh really?" Billy asked. "Why is that?"

"Not many men get in Dirty Mike's way and are able to tell about it," Dallas explained.

"Dirty Mike?" asked Billy.

"The guy you had a conversation with in he gym the other night. Short, stout, scar tissue, mean. Ring a bell?" she said.

"I know the guy. I just didn't know his name. We never introduced ourselves," Billy shrugged.

"Mike didn't get his name because of his hygiene; although, that's questionable as well. He works rigs during the week and picks up extra cash on weekends fighting bare-knuckle fights in the back rooms of bars across the southwest. No rules and completely illegal. He does whatever it takes to win. Dirty Mike," Dallas explained.

"He would have killed me if Boomer hadn't stopped him," Billy said.

"No doubt," Dallas responded without the slightest hesitation. "You're lucky to have a friend like Boomer. "

"No doubt? Just like that? If you're so sure I'd have died, how does that make me your hero?" Billy asked confused.

"You stood up to him, and you're standing in front of me tonight. Doesn't matter how. Dirty Mike doesn't care how he wins. You shouldn't either," Dallas said giving him a quick kiss on the cheek.

Billy thought about what she said and decided he'd take what he could get while it lasted.

"How about some cake? I made an Italian Crème tonight. It was a new recipe so I'm hoping it's good. Not too dry. " Dallas said as she led him toward the table where the cake and coffee were being served. Most of the gathering had served themselves while Billy and Dallas were catching up, so the line was short.

Billy scooped a piece of cake onto Dallas' plate as she held it out and then he dug out a large corner piece that he placed on his own plate. With coffee in hand, they made their way through the crowd to a table where they could eat and talk without interruption, or much interruption. Occasionally one of the loyal flock came by to praise Dallas' culinary skills, comment on how moist the cake was, and ask for her secret. She was obviously happy to hear this and shared what she thought they wanted to hear. Anyone can do it. It's in the mixing. I use real butter. Take it out of the oven a couple of minutes early. None of this would matter because the truth was that Dallas had the magic that the others didn't, but she wanted to give them hope.

Billy garnered a couple of pats on the back in the process. His status in the community, if not always at hero level, had risen to the point that people knew who he was. Billy wasn't convinced that was a good thing. He had liked the anonymity and the ability to move among the citizens without anyone paying attention. That had now changed forever. The price of fame Billy thought and shook his head.

"I'm on my days off. Do you want to come over for a night cap?" Dallas interrupted his thoughts.

"Absolutely!" Billy said just a little too quickly and a little too loud.

"How about I follow you to your apartment so you can park your car. We can go to my place in the jeep. You're a celebrity now and a popular topic for the gossip circles," Dallas said with the slightest bit of sarcasm. "We don't want to tarnish your new status as a white knight."

Billy just rolled his eyes as they gathered up the now empty cake pan and started for the door.

Later that night Billy buried his face in Dallas' back between her shoulder blades as she lay on her side facing the windows. They were covered with a quilt to keep them warm from the cold that had rolled down from the Rockies earlier in the day dropping the temperatures into the forties. In Minnesota no one would have noticed, but in the desert forties meant winter gear.

Billy had his right arm stretched across Dallas' hip and down her leg. She had her legs drawn up like a diver in tuck position so Billy slid his hand behind her knee and absent-mindedly ran his fingers back and forth across the silky smooth skin while he breathed in her intoxicating smell. Dallas wasn't big on perfumes, but she liked her bath soaps and body lotions. Billy found himself like Pavlov's dogs, panting ever time he caught the scent. It wouldn't be the best look in public, so he had to consciously refrain from giving into those feelings ever time she leaned into him near enough for him to catch a whiff of her.

"So do I have competition?" asked Dallas breaking the silence.

The question confused Billy who was mildly intoxicated from inhaling her for the last ten minutes or so. The question was also out of the blue, and he wasn't exactly sure what she meant.

"Competition for what?" Billy asked never moving his face away from her back.

"Your affection...and attention," Dallas said in a dangerously quiet voice.

"You have my undivided attention as we speak and have had it since the start of prayer meeting. The only time it might have wavered was when I tasted your cake. But then it was still your cake, so technically I was still focused on you," Billy said reassuringly. He pushed back slightly and ran his hand across her back massaging her shoulders before sliding it around to her stomach.

"I'm serious. Is there someone you are more attracted to?" she asked.

"There's no one else. I promise. I go to work, and I see you. That's about the sum total of my existence. My work is okay, seeing you is great," Billy assured her. "In fact, not having seen you in days made me sad. If I had to choose, I'd spend more time with you and less time at work. "

"Work is what I'm concerned about. Your new coach seems to occupy a lot of your attention. You stepped in front of a crowd of roughnecks to protect her. I'm just wondering if it's more than just work," Dallas explained.

"Savannah?" Billy asked surprised. "She's new and just a kid and any attention I've paid to her was trying to help her get settled so I don't have to worry about the girls teams or her classes. "

"And nearly getting yourself killed to protect her?" Dallas asked.

143

Billy realized he was in verbal combat at this point. He wondered how this evening that had been filled with cake and romance could have turned so quickly. When had he missed the signal?

"In fairness to me, I was also protecting the girls on the team that were running for the dressing room. Besides if I dated Savannah, I'd have to ask Boomer's permission. How funny would that be? And if I married Savannah, Boomer would be my uncle," Billy said thinking the whole thing was ridiculous.

"In fairness to me, I have a man in my bed that has his hands on my bare skin talking about marrying a younger woman and who his in laws would be," Dallas responded, her voice much stronger than before.

"In fairness to me, she's my teacher, and I'm her boss. I think it might be illegal to sleep with her and, if not illegal, then maybe immoral," Billy finally responded thinking maybe the professional route would be the best way to go. It wasn't.

"In fairness to me, you seemed to have given the idea of sleeping with her enough thought to determine the whether it was legal or not." Dallas was getting a little more intense with each statement. Billy felt the night slipping from his grasp and struggled to find something that might stop the bleeding.

"In fairness to me, I rarely see her except at games that I'm required to attend. The last time I talked to her was last Saturday night to make sure she was okay," Billy offered trying to slowly rub her stomach and leg in a sensual manner hoping to take her mind off the conversation.

"Was she?" Dallas asked.

"Was she what?" Billy replied once again confused.

"Was she okay?" Dallas said exasperated that he couldn't keep up.

"Oh. Yes. She was fine. She was just upset they had stolen the trophy," Billy answered.

"Good to know. So you won't be seeing her again until the next ballgame?" Dallas asked.

Billy started to assure her and then stopped. He just shook his head. He had been in arguments with women before and had even planned on being a lawyer, a trial lawyer. As good as he

144

considered himself to be with words, he had yet to win one argument with any woman. Not one time. How he was tripped up and tangled up he never knew. It had to be stuff women learned somewhere. They were all very adept at twisting words and finding insults in the smallest things. Damn! He thought.

"Actually, no. I ordered the girls a new trophy and promised to have an all school presentation when it came in. That will be in the morning," Billy confessed.

"So you are lying in my bed rubbing your hands all over me tonight thinking about seeing your other girlfriend in the morning?" Dallas said with fury as she took his roaming hand and flung it back at him.

"In fairness to me, she's not my girlfriend, and it's a school function where all the students and teachers will be present. I think your being a little dramatic," Billy said quietly.

"In fairness to me, why don't you get out of my bed, put on your clothes, and go home! How's that for dramatic?" asked Dallas as she yanked up the covers covering her head.

"In fairness to me, I don't have a ride," Billy said as he stood and started putting on his pants.

"Then walk!" came Dallas' muffled reply.

"In fai...." Billy started.

"If you say fairness one more time, jackass, I swear I'll throat-punch you!" Dallas yelled from under the covers.

Billy finished dressing and stood by the bed carefully considering the ramifications of his next words.

"It's freezing outside. May I at least borrow a coat?" Billy said quietly.

A hand came out from under the covers and reached across the nightstand. Billy didn't see the keys flying at his face until they had carved a nice gash across his eyebrow and fallen to the floor. He wiped at the trickle of blood that slid down his nose.

"Uh....," Billy started.

"Just leave it in the damn parking lot, and I'll get it tomorrow!" Dallas said anticipating his question.

"Good night," Billy said as he turned to walk out of the room. Dallas' response was muffled. It was not kind.

145

Chesty Puller and Gunny were waiting on the other side of the door and escorted him out. They evidently had been listening to the exchange in the bedroom and chose to take Dallas' side. Their disposition was no longer friendly and low, deep-throated growls followed as he made his exit.

Billy slid behind the wheel of the jeep and adjusted the seats and mirrors like he was taught in driver's ed. Billy realized too late that Dallas would probably be pissed about that as well when she came to drive her jeep home. How much worse could it be, thought Billy, and then he caught himself knowing full well that was a challenge to the gods of the universe, and he did not need any more insanity. He replayed the whole night in his head wondering exactly when the train went off the track.

Billy parked the jeep as far away from his door as possible to allay the suspicions of nosy passersby or gossips. He walked back to his door leaning over into the cold wind to protect himself as much as possible. He unlocked his door and even before he flipped on the living room light, he saw the red blinking light on his answering machine. He had a message. He closed his door behind him and walked over to the counter. Like a technician defusing a bomb, he gingerly pushed the play button.

"Hi Billy, this is Savannah. I got your message about the assembly tomorrow. The girls are excited, and I just wanted to thank you ahead of time for doing this. It means a great deal to the girls and well, its really special for me. Anyway thanks for looking after us the other night and caring like you do....uh...well...uh...I asked Uncle Corliss and Aunt Bev if they thought it would be okay if you came for dinner one night and I cooked. They thought it was a nice idea. I don't want to put you on the spot. It would just be my way of saying thank you, and, of course, Corliss and Bev would be here to chaperone.... ha...uh...not that we would need a chaperone.... oh...uh... I can make a great chicken spaghetti. Ha......Uh...well if you're interested, you can call me back, if it's not too late, or you can let me know tomorrow and we'll find a night you're free......Uh...I guess that's all.... uh, okay then...bye"

Billy played the message three more times before he reached into the refrigerator and pulled out a beer. It was closer to dawn than midnight, but he held no hope of sleeping the rest of this night. What had he done to get himself into the middle of this? How can two women that don't even know each other gang up on him and make his life miserable. Just days ago he was a hero. The whole town was singing songs about him. Preachers had preached sermons about his exploits. Pride cometh before a fall he thought. He had been too proud he decided. Now he was falling. And he never saw it coming.

Why is it that women made life special and painful at the same time? They smelled good. They felt good. They were fun to be with. Everything was better with a woman. Then everything crumbled like a sandcastle on a beach built too close to the ocean. Sometimes it went slowly, eroded over time, and sometimes it went all at once in the blink of an eye. A wave washes up, and the whole thing is gone. Tonight had been a rogue wave out of a calm sea. There had been no warning. It had come in the darkness like a silent killer. He just didn't understand. Then the phone call from Savannah. Was it a life preserver to save him or cinderblocks to be chained to his ankles making sure he drowned? He was a guy. He had no idea.

Billy walked into his office early the next morning clean, but disheveled, which matched his mood exactly. He was slightly hung over from the beers that had stretched from a late night snack to an early morning breakfast. He had given up trying to solve the mystery of women a little before dawn and caught a quick nap in his recliner before showering and throwing on some random clothes. When he looked at the trophy in the corner of his office he remembered he had an assembly first thing and decided he should have dressed up a little or at least worn a sports coat. Billy finally decided to take the coward's way out and let Boomer do the honors as athletic director since this was about basketball after all. It was also his niece. No one could gossip about that. Could they? He picked up the phone and dialed the field house.

When Boomer answered the phone Billy explained what he wanted and asked whether Boomer was up for some public face time and to practice administrating. Billy tried to sell it as an opportunity he was giving Boomer that would be a good thing for his future plans. Boomer acted like he was honored and if he smelled a rat he played the part of good friend and didn't let on. He said he would come by in time to get the trophy before everyone was dismissed to the gym. Billy hung up feeling slightly dirty after what Boomer had done for him the weekend before, but rationalized it as something actually good for Boomer.

"Oh my. What happened to you?" Ms. Dixie was standing at the door. "You look like you were in the middle of a cat fight. "

" I was. And it was a big cat," said Billy rubbing the cut than ran across his forehead. He hadn't looked close enough when he was dressing and now wondered if it was the shape of a key.

"Uh huh. Hmmm," Ms. Dixie said knowing she'd get the rest of the story sooner than later. "Prayer meeting must be rougher than I remember it."

"Prayer meeting was fine and Dallas' Italian Crème cake was delicious…. and then somewhere…somehow it went downhill from there," Billy said looking into the distance shaking his head still unsure as to what happened.

"If that's all the damage, then I would say you got off lucky," Ms. Dixie said with a reassuring smile. "I'd give it a day or two, and then it should be fine…unless it has to do with being unfaithful…then I'd leave town."

Watching Ms. Dixie turn on her heel and walk out, Billy couldn't help but wonder if he had been unfaithful. It seemed he had been judged and sentenced without any evidence that he could recall. Everything that had happened up to this point had been job related and his responsibility as a principal. There had been no touching, no intimacy; certainly no one had been naked. He shouldn't have to apologize to anyone. He certainly didn't deserve to be maimed and almost blinded.

The more he thought about the whole thing, the madder he got. He had swiveled around in his chair and was looking out the windows cursing under his breath when he heard a knock on his doorframe.

"Hey. Billy...uh...Mr. Masters. I hope you got my message. I really do appreciate what you're doing for us this morning and that trophy looks amazing," Savannah said as she pointed towards the corner. "It's ten times better than the one Rainwater tore apart. "

"Good morning.... Ms. Skinner," Billy said swiveling around to face her. Her smile melted away all the fury that had been building up in him. "I'm glad you like it. I asked for the best they had. The score's engraved right there on the plate along with tournament champs. I thought we might like to remember this for a while!"

"That's awesome," Savannah replied as she walked over and looked at it closer. The trophy stood over four feet tall and had all the bells and whistles that Billy could think of. He told himself when he was ordering it that the girls deserved it for having to go through such an ordeal just to win a game. Now he felt a little embarrassed by its ostentatious appearance. It didn't help that Savannah stood beside it and declared it was almost as tall as she was.

"Well...you guys deserve it," was all Billy could think of to say.

After a few moments of embarrassed silence on both their parts, Billy told her how the assembly would work and that Boomer would present the trophy since it was about athletics, and he was the athletic director. He found himself rambling and finally stopped.

"The girls will love it. Thanks again," Savannah said as she smiled and offered a little wave as she left the office. Remembering at the last moment, she stopped right in front of Ms. Dixie's desk, leaned toward his door, and said loud enough for him to hear as well as everyone else in the office, "Oh, about dinner. You let me know when you can come and I'll make sure its special. " She added another wave, a bigger smile, and tossed her ponytail as she bounced out of the office.

Billy sat at his desk with his hands folded in his lap and his eyes cast down. He didn't know how she did it, but he knew she was standing in front of him. Ms. Dixie placed a folder on his desk with papers that needed signing.

"I'll be leaving town," Billy confessed.

"Ummmmhuh"

Billy had observed the presentation from the back of the gym. Boomer handled the crowd with surprising ease. He got different groups cheering together and then in competition with each other. When they had reached a fever pitch, Boomer introduced the girl's team one player at a time. He finished with Savannah who was all smiles. The trophy was presented and the girl's captain said thank you on behalf of the team mentioning Mr. Masters at the end for his help and support. Savannah followed with her own thank-yous and she too managed to point out Billy in the back of the gym while offering her praise for his handling of the situation and also for the fine trophy he was responsible for getting. Everyone cheered. Billy's plan to go unnoticed was working about as well as everything else in his life.

After fifteen minutes of missing class, the students were directed back to their first period classroom to resume the education of their young minds. They walked slowly hoping to kill as much of the period as possible. Billy didn't rush them or challenge them, but simply slipped back in his office where he hoped to hide the rest of the day.

Boomer knocked on his doorframe.

"Hey Boss, you got a minute?" he asked

"Sure what's up?" Billy said.

"First of all, thank you for the opportunity. That was fun. About the only speaking I do is at the annual sports banquet. Other than that, it's just talking to the team in practice or on game night. I need to get better if I ever plan to be more administrator than coach," Boomer offered.

"You did a great job and believe me, I'll be happy to find more opportunities for you to practice. You may even want to take my job. I've been thinking about leaving town," Billy said with half a laugh.

"Yeah right. You're doing a great job. You're a hero. Kids love you and the faculty does too. What more could you want?" Boomer asked.

Billy knew his fame had fled, and he didn't feel loved at the moment. He actually felt miserable and had no idea why other

150

than his argument with Dallas the night before was weighing heavy on him.

"You may just be coming down with the flu or something," Boomer offered. "You don't look very good this morning. Maybe it's just a cold. Anyway, thanks again. Look, if you've got time I wanted to talk to you about going over to Sul Ross and starting our hours for certification," Boomer said.

Billy perked up when he mentioned the hours since he had pushed that thought into the back of his mind. He knew he and Cracker had talked about needing to get some hours for a temporary certification, but that was the last time it was even mentioned. He really never considered his current position as anything more than temporary, but he was interested. The idea of going back to college was attractive for several reasons and most of them juvenile. He remembered some of the best times of his life had happened at college. Maybe it was time for another round.

"I've got all day. I sort of cleared my schedule...since I might be coming down with something. Let's hear it," Billy said.

"Great. Like I told you I've done some research, and if I want to be an athletic director in a bigger school or even a principal like you, I need to get an administrator's certificate. You need one too, so you can keep doing this job," Boomer explained.

Billy thought keeping this job wasn't high on his list at the moment, but he would need to work somewhere, so having a certificate wouldn't hurt.

"I called over to Alpine and talked to an advisor. He walked me through the details, and it's pretty straightforward. We need to get our Masters and then a few hours more for the admin certificate," Boomer said lightly. Billy thought he might be joking.

"Is that all? Get our Master and few hours more?" asked Billy sarcastically.

"It's really not as bad as it sounds. The program is set up for people that are already working and supporting families. You attend class on Saturdays and Sunday mornings. You can still keep your job and get certified too," Boomer said with confidence. "It'll be a breeze."

151

"So every weekend for how many years?" Billy said still unconvinced.

"It's really up to each person. You go one weekend a month for three hours, two weekends for six and three weekends a month for nine semester hours. We can also pick up some hours in the summer. If we worked at it steady, like every other weekend, we'd still have some time for ourselves, and the advisor thought if we used some of our summers it would take a year and half or two years max," Boomer said encouragingly.

"Really? We spend two weekends a month in Alpine for a year or two and we can get our Masters and an administrator's certification?" Billy asked unconvinced.

"That's the way I understand it. It doesn't interfere with our job and we might even enjoy the weekends away. For a change you know," Boomer said and smiled. "If you're interested, we need to get an appointment with this guy. He can set us up a degree plan, and we will know exactly what we need to take and how long to do it. I can schedule that for next week if you're ready," Boomer offered.

"My calendar seems to be perfectly clear for the near future except for games, of course. See what you can do. It won't hurt to at least go and talk to the guy. I could use a road trip anyway," Billy said starting to warm up to the idea.

"I'm on it! Soon as a I get it worked out, I'll let you know," Boomer clapped his hands and stood.

Boomer extended his massive hand across the desk towards Billy. The same hand that rendered a very mean man helpless. Billy took it and thanked Boomer again, for everything. Halfway across Billy's office towards the door, Boomer turned back around.

"Oh I forgot. Sunday. Come to our house for lunch, Savannah's cooking. From what little I know about what's right and wrong when it comes to being a boss and all, the invitation is from Bev and me. You'll be coming to eat with us at our house. Alright?" Boomer turned not waiting for an answer and assumed it was settled.

"Uh...alright...what time and what can I bring?" Billy asked reluctantly.

"Let's say one. That gives everyone time to get home from church and change. We can watch the Cowboys afterwards, if you want or you can leave at anytime. A good meal might make you feel better, and Savannah wants to cook. Don't bring a thing," Boomer said, and then he was gone.

"Oh crap," Billy said under his breath. He realized he was running his hand through his hair. At this rate he'd be bald by May.

Billy walked to the door and look out into the office. No one was waiting or milling around.

"Dixie, I'm going over to Boomer's house for lunch on Sunday. He and his wife invited me, if anyone asks. Its Boomer's house and his invitation," Billy said.

Ms. Dixie made it a point to write a note on her calendar repeating Billy's word a little more dramatically than he would have liked.

"Lunch Sunday. Boomer's house. His invitation," Ms. Dixie dotted the i's rather firmly, looked up, and smiled a most insincere grin. "Got it. If anyone asks."

"We're going to talk about going back to school. To get our Masters…. and administrator's certification," Billy offered weakly.

Dixie looked back down at her calendar and added, "talk about college." Once again the insincere smile. "Anything else? The menu? Will you bring anything?" she asked.

Billy just looked at her. He knew this would only continue to go downhill.

"So you decided against leaving town?" she asked.

28

Church was really not an option for Billy. He was pretty sure Dallas' days off had passed and she was back at work, but he couldn't take the chance of running into her and the awkward moment about whether to sit with her or not and the questions from the faithful that had seen them all lovey dovey at prayer meeting. It wouldn't' take long for them to get the gossip mill going about an apparent riff between them.

Billy had thought about calling Dallas everyday, but just couldn't bring himself to do so. He didn't know if he was apologetic or not or whether he should feel guilty or not. He did feel bad which made him feel mad since he felt unjustly accused. Each day had passed as he wrestled with his emotions, and now he was dressing to go to lunch. Boomer and his wife Bev had invited him he kept telling himself. But it always ended with...and Savannah's cooking.

Billy wondered what he actually felt for Savannah since he had spent more than hour showering, shaving, using extra deodorant, a splash of cologne, and even creasing his jeans with an iron. Billy finally admitted to himself in the mirror that he wanted to make a good impression, and if Savannah wanted to thank him, he should be happy to let her. Dallas had chosen to start the fight, and she could choose to stop it. Until then he had a lunch date...with Boomer...and Bev. And Savannah was cooking.

At 12:59 Billy rang the bell as he stood on Boomer's porch. He had chosen his favorite blue shirt to go with his boots and jeans. He wore a fleece vest to ward off the lingering cold that had settled in and hoped he looked respectfully casual and relaxed. In his left hand Billy held a bottle of a dry red wine he had saved for a special occasion and thought this qualified. Boomer opened the door wearing sweat pants and a Cowboy jersey with the number 54 and the name White on the back. Boomer loved Randy White. The Manster. Half-man, half-monster. Billy thought that seemed fitting for Boomer.

"You're still dressed up," Boomer said as he held the door open for Billy to come in. "Church run long and no time to change?"

"No, I just thought...uh...being company and all..." Billy waffled around and finally held out the bottle of wine.

"I should have told you we're really casual here on weekends. You can run change if you want," Boomer offered.

"I'm good. Boots and jeans are my favorite clothes," Billy lied. He knew if he'd been at home, he'd had on a raggedy pair of sweats himself left over from his coaching days.

154

"Alright then, come on in. The girls are in the kitchen, and lunch is almost ready," Boomer said.

Billy followed Boomer as he walked towards the back of the house. They passed through the dining room where the table was set for four and glasses were already filled with iced tea.

"Guest of honor is here, and he brought wine!" Boomer announced to the ladies in the kitchen.

"Hi, girls. This smells delicious," Billy greeted them.

"Well, Savannah's the cook. She just let me fix the garlic bread. The rest is all her," Beverly explained as she leaned in as Billy gave her a one-armed hug.

Savannah dried her hands and came over and gave Billy a straight on full frontal two-arm hug as she thanked him for coming, and she was so glad he had. Billy instinctively wrapped his arms around her as well and squeezed slightly, but quickly let go. Quicker than Savannah did, creating an awkward moment where he had his hands out to his side and she was still attached. It didn't seem to bother her. Uncle Corliss and Aunt Bev didn't seem to notice.

"Why don't you open the wine Uncle Corliss and we'll have a toast before lunch," Savannah suggested.

"You got it," Boomer said as he fumbled through a drawer looking for a corkscrew.

"Is there anything I can do to help?" Billy asked.

"Oh she's not going to let anybody help. She's already told me a dozen times," answered Beverly. "I'm not sure if she's trying to prove she's special or talented, but we already know she's both. I'm sure you've figured that out as well by now, haven't you Billy?"

"Yes ma'am. She's quite the young lady," Billy replied as diplomatically as he could.

"My Savannah here is going to make some lucky man a fine wife. She..." Beverly was interrupted as she was prepared to list the many virtues of her niece.

"Aunt Bev, you're going to embarrass me and probably Billy as well. He may think you're trying to be a matchmaker," Savannah admonished her aunt halfheartedly. She actually appeared to be smiling at the thought.

155

"Billy could do a lot worse, and I'm not sure he could do better," Bev looked Billy straight in the eye as she made her final pitch.

"Uh… no ma'am. I'm sure you're right. Savannah here is definitely special," Billy agreed.

"I know I'm right," she finished quite convinced and turned back to slicing the Italian loaf.

Boomer had managed to get the wine bottle open and poured four glasses. He passed them around and offered a toast.

"Here's to friends and family and friends who become family. Skol!"

Billy had the glass to his lips as he digested Boomer's words and almost choked. He managed to recover before spewing wine across the kitchen. He sipped slowly looking over the rim of his glasses to see the faces of everyone in the room. It appeared to be a normal day in the Skinner household, and he seemed to be the only one uncomfortable. Maybe he was reading too much into what very well could be a lighthearted conversation. Fortunately the food was ready, and they all took their places at the table.

True to her word, Savannah's chicken spaghetti was delicious as were the grilled vegetables. Billy loved the flavor and the noodles were cooked to perfection. He and Boomer each had a second helping, and then the dishes were cleared to make room for dessert. Lemon meringue pie was set on the table and Savannah cut large slices for him and Boomer. Bev's piece was slightly smaller as was hers. Coffee was poured and they all dug in. Billy had eaten his fill a while back, but could not resist the pie. He had finally relaxed and the conversation during the meal never once brought up marriage, love, husbands, lovers, or anything else that might have convinced him he had been set up.

Most of the topics had to do with Savannah's family and her growing up. Some of the stories were funny and some embarrassing for Savannah, which made them funnier for everyone else. Billy found he was enjoying the family moment and laughed right along with everyone else. Savannah was a good sport and took the ribbing in stride.

Billy offered to help with the dishes and after some convincing and support from Savannah, Boomer and Bev agreed. Bev went back to her room, and Boomer placed his large body in his recliner to watch the football game. Billy chose to wash while Savannah dried and put away. The kitchen looked like a disaster area. Billy never realized how many dishes and pans it took to cook just a few things. He mainly used the same pan to cook everything, and most of the time, he simply piled all his ingredients together and cooked them at the same time. He guessed that to do it right required a different approach and resulted in a much different outcome.

Billy briefly regretted offering to wash dishes until he realized this would be a nice innocent way to have a conversation with Savannah and spend some one on one time. Over the course of the next hour, as he scrubbed pots and pans, grease and baked on grime, he and Savannah relived some of the stories that had been told over spaghetti about her and her family, and she gave him some background on why a lot of them happened. She told him about growing up and the things she liked and what she wanted to do with her life. She thanked him again for giving her a chance to teach and coach and questioned him non-stop about his life.

Billy initially glossed over many of the details of his past and gave her only the high points, but she seemed to see through him and continued to delve deeper until he had pretty well given her his life story in explicit detail. Her squeezing his arm when he held out and bumping him with her hip to encourage spilling his guts broke down his defenses. Her massaging his back when he cramped up from leaning over the sink too long pretty much assured her that he would tell her anything.

When the last dish had been cleaned and put away, they walked into the living room to find Boomer fast asleep, snoring like a hibernating grizzly. Bev was nowhere to be seen and Savannah whispered she usually napped on her bed after church as well. She took his hand, held a finger to her lips and led him down the hall to her room. Boomer's snoring drowned out any sound they might have made and could have easily covered the sound of a jet taking off.

After his uneasiness earlier, he found himself quite enchanted with Savannah's laughter and self-confidence. She had touched him several times during the afternoon, but each time it seemed to be the friendly gesture of someone that is at ease with herself and trusts the person she's with. He was enjoying listening to her talk almost non-stop, and each time she laughed, it made him laugh because it was unforced and unrestrained.

Billy had not overlooked her brown eyes that sparkled like those of a mischievous child who had secrets running through their heads. Nor had he failed to notice she was attractive. Her brown hair was pulled back again in a pony tail that bounced as she threw her head around during the telling of her stories. Occasionally, without thinking she would reach up and pull on her hair with one hand as if she was trying to straighten it. Billy decided it was probably more of a nervous habit, although she gave no evidence of being the slightest bit nervous.

Savannah offered to show him her high school yearbooks, which convinced Billy that she was definitely a confident person. Few people offered to show pictures from their past especially going back to high school. Savannah laughed right along with Billy as they covered her teenage years and all her glory from choir, to Ag, and, of course, sports. She had been the Valedictorian of her class and voted Most Beautiful. The combination of beauty and brains made her the natural choice for Most Likely to Succeed.

When they had gone through the yearbooks and laughed one last time, they sat in silence on her bed. Billy looked at her and found himself quite attracted. He smiled, and she smiled back without looking away. She reached with her left hand and slid it inside his left hand while clasping her right hand over the top encasing his hand in a firm double grip.

"Look, Billy. This may sound silly, but you coming over today has been fun, and something I really needed. I know you have more important things to do than babysit me, but as you know there aren't a lot of people in Waymor my age to be friends with. As much as I like my kids and the people I work with, I miss having someone my on age to just talk to and laugh with. It's been a little tough to have a social life here in Waymor. Most of the girls my age are married, and those that aren't married are looking for husbands and the guys...well you know what they're looking for, I imagine," Savannah explained. "Anyway thank you for today. Hopefully we can do it again."

"It's been my pleasure," Billy assured her. " I haven't enjoyed myself so much in a long time. I think I'd almost forgotten what it was like to laugh, and I didn't see it as babysitting at all. For starters, you're far from a baby," he finished with a laugh. "I'd love to do this again...soon."

"Maybe next time I can fix you my famous mushroom steak and rhubarb pie," Savannah offered.

"Why don't I just marry you right now and get it over with?" Billy suggested without even thinking. Even though they both laughed, an uncomfortable silence filled the room as they sat on her bed with their hands clasped together. Finally, to break the awkward silence, she pulled herself closer and kissed him on the cheek.

"You're sweet," was all she said.

This seemed like the right time to thank her for a lovely afternoon and make his exit. She held his hand as they tipped toed up the hall, past the still sleeping Boomer, to the front door. Billy thanked her again for the tenth time, and it was her turn to say it was her pleasure. They stood looking at each other for a minute longer than was called for until Billy backed away and walked down the steps to his truck. Savannah was still leaning on the screen door as he slid the truck into reverse. He waved as he backed down the drive. She waved back.

As he drove slowly home, Billy dissected the entire afternoon word by word, touch by touch. He finally concluded he had no idea if he had a new best friend or was engaged. He decided he would be fine with either.

29

Billy slept better that night than he had in years. He felt completely happy and dreamed...good dreams.... not the nightmares that usually plagued his sleep. He realized that the whole setting with family around the table and an afternoon of talk and laughter was something he hadn't experienced in years. He felt drawn back to his days as a kid and decided that was why he was so happy. Then he thought of Savannah and her brown eyes and laughter that shook her whole body and decided that didn't hurt either.

He slept so hard, he was late getting up and by the time he walked into the office, Ms. Dixie and Boomer were both waiting on him.

"Hey, boss. We were thinking about calling for a welfare check," Boomer said.

"It appears that sleeping late looks good on you. Maybe you should try it more often," Ms. Dixie added.

"I'm not sure what happened," Billy said. "I went to bed early and slept all night long. I even slept through my alarm."

"It must have been that home cooked meal you got yesterday. I know it knocked me out. I didn't even know when you left. I'm sorry for being a bad host, but Savannah said she took good care of you," Boomer shared.

Billy glanced at Ms. Dixie who was shuffling papers, but listening to every word.

"Don't worry about it. You were sawing logs. We did the dishes and then she showed me her yearbooks," Billy replied making the whole afternoon look innocent.

"So Savannah can cook?" Ms. Dixie asked not wanting to be left out of the details.

"Can she!" Boomer replied. "I've gained ten pounds since she's been living with us. Billy probably gained five pounds yesterday. I'm pretty sure he had a second helping of spaghetti and pie!"

"So there was pie, too?" Ms. Dixie asked.

"Lemon meringue," Boomer once again answered for Billy.

"No wonder you look so happy. Home cooking, pie, and a good night's rest. That seems to be just what the doctor ordered," Ms. Dixie said. Her smile looked a little less than sincere.

"Probably why all those statistics say married men live longer," Boomer added.

"It could be single guys doing stupid things has more to do with it than pie," Ms. Dixie suggested. Her eyebrow cocked daring Billy to challenge her.

"Let's just say the meal was nice, the pie delicious, the company enjoyable, and its time to go to work how about?" Billy said trying to bring an end to the inquisition. "What do you have on this beautiful Monday morning Boomer?" Billy asked as he walked into his office turning on the lights and taking off his coat.

"School! I was going to tell you yesterday, but it seemed you were enjoying talking to Savannah and well, I slept all afternoon," Boomer chuckled.

"What about the school?" Billy asked, now concerned.

"Oh, not this school. Our school. Sul Ross. Where we get to be students. I called the advisor, and we have an appointment Wednesday afternoon. We have to be there before four, but I thought we could probably slip out of here a little early. I know you have prayer meeting, but that was the best day to meet with him between your schedule, my schedule, and his. Will that work for you?" Boomer asked.

"Wednesday's not a problem," Billy said. "I haven't been going to prayer meeting lately. I probably should, but..."

"Great," Boomer said. "Also listen to this. The guy said there's an intersession that starts the weekend before Christmas and meets four times. We would go that weekend, the weekend between Christmas and New Years and then the first two weekends in January and could get our first three hours." Boomer said.

"That does sound good. Four weekends and three hours. I might be able to do this after all," Billy said starting to understand Boomer's excitement.

"The only difference is that because it is compacted in a short period of time, we would have a Friday evening session each weekend. Normally that isn't the case, but to meet the number of classroom hours required we would go from 6-9 P.M. on Fridays."

"The only thing I can see wrong with that is basketball games in January that one of us has to be at," Billy said trying to work out the details.

"I've got that covered as well," Boomer said. "Paddy! He's going to be the admin in charge for those games and also for the Christmas tournament. "

"What Christmas tournament?" Billy asked puzzled.

"The basketball tournament. Boys and girls. Just like at Thanksgiving," Boomer explained.

"We play basketball over the Christmas holidays?" asked Billy. "What kind of communist organization is that?"

"Everyone has a holiday tournament. They're afraid of the layoff and having players celebrate too much," Boomer said.

"So this has always happened? Not just this year? What an ignorant sport," Billy said disgustedly.

"Like I said, don't worry about it. Paddy's got it covered. Also if you're worried about a repeat of Rainwater at Thanksgiving, don't be. The tournament is in Seminole. I checked the brackets and every team except us is from the Panhandle. Those teams come to play and will be well coached while the fans have more sense and class than the gyp water heathens in Rainwater. The Seminole boys are good and will win the whole thing as expected. Seminole's a volleyball school, and they see basketball as off-season conditioning. As long as the volleyball trophies keep stacking up, no one will be concerned about scores. It'll be fine and you don't have to be there," Boomer assured him.

"So how is Paddy doing and why would he do this?" asked Billy.

"Paddy's great. His new teeth are a great party trick and have helped to raise his ability to entertain to a new level especially when people are around him for the first time," Boomer laughed. "I've even heard that on a couple occasions he has slipped his dental bridge into an unsuspecting lady's drink at a bar and has scared the life out of them. His wit and charm along with sharing how he's a bull rider manage to soothe them, and from what I'm told, everyone ends up happy and satisfied before the night's over."

"So I have a person who picks up women using his false teeth, makes a joke out of everything, and his best quality is that he can outrun danger monitoring the safety and well being of our kids. That about right?" Billy asked skeptical.

"As crazy as Paddy is you know he is responsible when it comes to his job. He would look after our kids as well as you and I would. Besides, he's been talking to me about become an athletic director sometime in the future and actually asked to help out for the experience," Boomer explained.

"Paddy. An AD?" Billy said with a half laugh.

"Yeah. I've actually considered recommending him to replace me when the time comes for me to move on. You know people have a tendency to step up when you give them responsibility. Look at you. You weren't exactly the poster boy for leadership when Cracker gave you a shot. He saw something in you and you proved him right." Boomer said seriously.

"Thank you....I think," Billy said.

"Look man, it's all good. Let's give it a shot, and if it doesn't work out what have we lost?" Boomer said. "And if it does...look what we've gained!"

Billy sat thoughtfully for a few minutes, digesting everything Boomer had told him and began to like the idea. He would get to leave town most weekends, no basketball games over Christmas, and he could still make it home to see his family. Billy decided not everything had been lining up in his favor lately and he needed to be thankful for the things that did. He owed Boomer once again.

"It sounds like you've thought of everything. Anything I'm missing? It sounds too good. " Billy finally said.

"It is all good. No hidden surprises. We go back to school, get our Masters, get certified. Onward and upward," Boomer assured him.

"OK. I'll drive Wednesday. That's the least I can do. Lets leave about 1:30. I'll make sure things here are covered," Billy said.

"Sounds like a plan. I for one am excited," Boomer said as he rose and offered his giant hand to Billy. They shook, and Billy walked him to the door.

As Boomer walked off down the hall, Billy asked Ms. Dixie to clear Wednesday afternoon's schedule and briefly explained the plan he and Boomer had concocted. He passed it off as simply meeting the expectation of the superintendent. Billy didn't let on he couldn't wait to leave town and breathe.

Billy was back at his desk signing papers and humming under his breath. During the second verse of **Cocaine Blues** he became aware that Ms. Dixie was sitting in a chair across from him, and his door was closed. He had no idea how she did it. She had to be a ninja.

"How long have you been there?" He asked with a laugh.

"How long do you think?" she responded with a straight face.

"Remind me never to play hide and seek with you," Billy said.

"I can promise you that won't ever happen," Ms. Dixie assured him.

"Billy," Ms. Dixie started, and he realized fun and games were over. "You know from the first day you walked into this office I've been on your side. I know sometimes I may have come off as harsh and demanding when it comes to this school that's important to me, but I also want you to do a good job."

Billy felt like she had rehearsed her speech and needed to get it said, so he listened without interruption.

"I think you're a good man, and if you do a good job the school benefits, I benefit, and we all are better off…so if I seem bossy, it's only because I want you to succeed…. okay?" she asked.

"Sure. I know that, and I appreciate all the help you've given me," Billy said thinking she was through. "You've been a Godsend, I swear. "

"Okay, then listen," she started again with more firmness to her tone. "My sister is a good person. She has a rough side to her, and she is tough as nails, but she also has a gentle spirit and a kind heart. She's been hurt and betrayed by men more than once, so she has a chip on her shoulder when it comes to relationships. She can be stubborn when she gets her mind set on something and apologizing is very difficult for her. She's my sister, and I love her, and she deserves a good man to treat her right."

164

Billy was at a loss for words. He had expected a lot of things, but this was not one of them.

"She threw me out in the middle of a freezing night and cut me across the forehead. Granted I'll have a great looking scar, but she could have blinded me just as easily," Billy responded feebly. He wasn't sure why he felt the need to defend himself.

"She did. And she could have. And she could break you in half if she got really angry. I know none of that makes her more enduring, but given the right person treating her the right way, she could really be happy," Dixie said.

"I also know Savannah is as sweet a young lady as I've ever met. She's as cute as button and has the personality to match. From the carrying on I've heard from you and Boomer, she's also a great cook and single which makes her very appealing, I would imagine, to a young man like yourself," Dixie said.

"She is all those things, and she can cook. She's also lonely. She told me she's having a hard time finding someone her own age to be friends with and it was nice to have someone to talk to," Billy said thinking he was helping himself. He was not.

"I can see why she would be attracted to you, and you definitely seem attracted to her," Dixie observed.

"I'm really not sure…." Billy started.

"Look, lets be honest. There are two eligible women that are vying for your affection. Each has her strengths and weaknesses. I assume Savannah does have a flaw of some kind if we looked close enough," Dixie said with a little edge to her voice. "And remember I said from the beginning, I'm on your side. You have a problem, a nice problem, but a problem nonetheless. You can't win if you don't choose. You'll lose them both and make enemies in the process. You may not think this is my business, but it is. Let's review. I want you to be successful. I want you to stay. I want to be able to work with you for many years. None of that can happen if you don't fix this…okay?" Dixie said. Her voice rising as she spoke.

"Okay," said Billy meekly. "Any thoughts on how?"

"I certainly can't make that call for you, but I can tell you this. If you don't want to see Dallas anymore, you need to make that clear to her and do it by phone…from another town. I can

165

probably protect you during the day, but after dark you're on your own. She's a wild thing, but like I said, the right man that is willing to grab on and hold on will be glad they did. There might be a few bumps and bruises along the way, but not all of them bad. I don't know Savannah that well, but she seems sweet, kind, and precious. I can see you two making a nice couple, raising a family and eating peach ice cream on Sunday afternoons while the kids play in the back yard. You're a lucky man. You have two great choices that will lead in two different directions. Be man enough to pick one and be nice to the other one," Dixie finished quietly. "You owe them that, and you owe yourself that. And you owe me that."

Billy could tell Dixie had invested herself in this problem and figured she had spent the weekend thinking about it. Hearing the replay of lunch from Boomer first thing on a Monday morning hadn't helped. He also knew she was right. He just didn't know what the answer was.

"Thank you," Billy said. "Too bad you're already taken, being the sensible responsible one."

"I'm attracted to men that can make decisions," Dixie said and winked as she walked out the door. "Impress me."

30

The program advisor at Sul Ross had been very helpful and encouraging. He assured Billy and Boomer they were the perfect candidates for the Masters of School Administration program, and that they would find most of their classmates in similar situations as themselves. He also promised they wouldn't regret starting and they sure wouldn't regret the benefits of finishing. He had helped them enroll in Equity in Excellence for all students, the intercession class, and gave them forms to send into their respective colleges to have transcripts sent. He promised to have a complete degree plan in place by the end of the intercession in time for them to enroll in the spring semester and estimated two years for completion of all course work if they maintained a steady pace. He shook their hands and wished them well.

Billy and Boomer had driven back to Waymor in high spirits after seeing the possibilities and knowing they would take their first steps in graduate school in a little over a week.

The days leading up to a major holiday always went far slower than an average class day. The anticipation by everyone reached its peak the last week. Billy found that just like at Thanksgiving, parties were held in an attempt to keep from having to introduce a new chapter or unit prior to the break and as usual a couple of kids got to start their holidays early because of a sugar fueled escapade that even pushed Billy to his limit of patience. He threatened to suspend the teacher as well, but Ms. Dixie talked him out of taking on that battle. She also explained that if kids and teachers alike thought they might get sent home early he would be facing chaos of epic proportions. The punishment needed to be extending their time at school as opposed to shortening it. He grasped what she was saying in time to avert complete disaster.

The last day before the holidays fell on Friday, and everyone was dismissed at noon. This gave Billy and Boomer plenty of time to make sure all the students left campus and the custodians had locked up. He didn't worry about the teachers leaving other than fearing they might run over the students in the parking lot. By 2 P.M., with a burger basket special in their laps and a large Dr. Pepper, they set off for Alpine with high hopes and a sense of adventure. Billy really didn't know what to expect, but unlike his first time through college he actually felt like he had a reason for going that was important. He figured he would find out soon enough.

They made good time, and it was early when they drove into Alpine so they decided to drive through town and take a look. Both of them had been through Alpine at one time or another, but neither had really paid attention. They had traveled across a hundred miles of flat land only to be surprised to see mountains rising right out of the desert floor. Billy and Boomer found they could drive up a mountain road to an overlook and see the campus, the town, and probably to Mexico. It was still desert and lacked any kind of vegetation other than scrub, but the unique scenery gave Billy and Boomer a sense of vacation. It provided decompression from the past several weeks for sure. They found themselves laughing and acting like....college boys.

Billy had rented a room over the phone for two nights at the local motel. They would learn that it would be important to do this well in advance once the regular semester started since most of the graduate students drove in just for the weekend. They intended to share a room since availability was limited and this caused Billy a little concern after having heard Boomer snoring in his recliner on a Sunday afternoon. They checked in and placed their small overnight bags in the room and took care of a little business before class.

Dressed and refreshed, they parked near the building that was on their registration form and located the classroom, which turned out to be an auditorium. Billy and Boomer looked at each other and wondered how many people would actually be taking the class. Several other students evidently had forgone the city tour and come straight to class. They had scattered themselves around the whole auditorium making sure to leave plenty of personal space for themselves and anyone else that might sit near by. Billy and Boomer picked what they thought would be a fairly safe spot about five rows up and on the teacher's left side. According to research Billy had read, this was the overlooked zone should there be a lot of questions or expectations for audience participation. Billy wanted to get his credit and his hours, but didn't intend to be the valedictorian. He was fine just passing and moving on. They left a space between them for elbow room and to be able to breathe. This was really for Billy's sake since Boomer needed a chair and a half minimum.

As the clock moved closer to 6 P.M., more and more students showed up. Some had the deer in the headlight looks that Billy figured he and Boomer had, but most showed the relaxed confidence of someone that had done this before. They were the veterans Billy assumed. The professor walked in at straight up 6 P.M. wearing black leather boots, a black leather skirt of modest length, and a black leather dress jacket over a white silk blouse. Her hair, which she had piled on her head, was salt and pepper and complimented her outfit. She wore black glasses and carried a black leather briefcase.

After she had unloaded her briefcase on the table at the front of the room, she addressed the crowd that had filled about a fourth of the room.

"You folks are all adults, and I won't treat you like children. This is as loud as I intend to talk, and if you can't hear me I would suggest you move closer." No one did. Either they didn't hear her or didn't won't to move.

"My name is Dr. Lucia Cruz. I am an adjunct professor, and you will see me more than once if you complete the School Administrator's program. I'm a retired superintendent from the El Paso area with forty years in teaching, campus administration, and district leadership. Since I'm Hispanic, the school thinks I'm the logical choice to teach Equity in Excellence for all students. So my first question is why this class?"

Hands flew up from the first two rows that were filled with the teacher pleasers. Dr. Cruz called on a young lady she must have had in a prior class.

"Margaret, good to see you again. How's the new baby?" Dr. Cruz asked.

"Good to see you, Dr. Cruz. The baby's growing like a weed. She's almost four months old now. " The class was all caught up on the personal life of the chosen student before Dr. Cruz asked again what she thought the purpose was for the class. Margaret, having obviously gotten the book and read ahead, quoted the textbook answer verbatim, "It is our responsibility as educators and administrators to ensure that each student has an equitable opportunity to received an education and be successful. All kids can learn and should have the chance to do so."

"Outstanding as always Margaret," Dr. Cruz said, pleased to have a go to person should the rest of the class languish behind.

Dr. Cruz paused for affect and to let the answer soak in. As she looked in Billy's general direction he heard her say, "So my second question is what do you think about that?"

Completely defying all research about the overlooked zone and the overwhelming statics published about how teachers always focus on the front and the right of a classroom, Dr, Cruz looked back and left, pointing directly at Billy.

"Young man, the one with the blue pearl snap shirt. Tell me your name since you appear to be new. We'd all like to get to know you," Dr. Cruz instructed as Billy tried his best to slide down in his seat out of sight. "I can still see you. Name?" Dr. Cruz scolded.

"My name is Billy...uh...William Robert Masters on your roll, ma'am, but my friends call me Billy," Billy stumbled and fumbled as the others looked on in amusement.

"We are all friends here so we shall all call you Billy," she stated without waiting for consent. "Now what are your thoughts about equity in excellence?"

"Ma'am, I uh...I...guess I'm just surprised that this is something that has to be taught." Billy finally managed to say fearing he was going to alienate the teacher within the first five minutes of the first class.

"And why are you surprised, Billy?" Dr. Cruz asked.

"I guess to me it's something everyone should being doing anyway. I've just always thought of my students as all the same, well except the ones that cause trouble. They have a tendency to make me less pleased to see them," Billy offered sheepishly.

Dr. Cruz had folded her hands and placed her thumbs under her chin as if balancing her head while she stared directly at Billy for what seemed to be an eternity. He squirmed uncomfortably in his chair. No one else was moving. Margaret looked at him with disdain.

"Mr. Masters, Billy, you are either the most naïve man on this planet or possibly the most enlightened. I think over the course of the next few weeks we all shall see which," Dr. Cruz said.

"Ma'am, I apologize. I'm pretty sure I'm just naïve. I'm just learning how to do this principal thing, and I'm not very good at it, yet," Billy said.

"Sir, do not apologize and do not concede. I am truly hoping for enlightened," she said with a wave of her hand. "That would be a refreshing change."

Billy simply nodded and found he could scrunch down just a little bit further into his chair. The lesson continued on for the next hour and half without him being singled out again. He was just starting to breath normally when Dr. Cruz announced a break. They had fifteen minutes to stretch, relieve themselves, and grab a snack.

Billy and Boomer exited out the door closest to them, but not before Dr. Cruz had walked in their direction. Oh Lord, thought Billy, she's going to ask me not to come back. He saw his graduate school career coming to a sudden halt.

Extending her hand, Dr. Cruz said, "Billy, I like to get to know my students. I don't recognize you two from previous classes."

Yes, ma'am, Billy Masters and this is my friend Boomer.... Skinner. We're from Waymor and this is our first class. Hopefully, not our last," Billy said.

"Nice to meet you. Boomer. I assume my roll will say something different?" she asked.

"Corliss. Ma'am. It'll say Corliss Prescott Skinner," Boomer said.

"Alright then Billy and Boomer, you can call me Lucy when we're out of class and just talking. Glad you guys are here. Please feel free to speak up. A different viewpoint always makes for a more lively discussion," Dr. Cruz said and walked back to her table and drank coffee from a thermos.

The rest of the weekend was uneventful other than the snoring at night. Billy used the extra pillow on his bed to muffle the sound to some degree and finally exhaustion allowed him to sleep. He wasn't sure the sleeping arrangement was going to work and wondered about calling Bev to see how she handled it. During the Sunday morning session prior to winding up the first week, Dr. Cruz assigned the students to eight different groups with five or six people to a group. She explained that sometimes the best way to understand another culture is to experience their customs and traditions. Each of the eight groups was assigned a culture that was represented in Texas and the group had to research the traditions of the culture as they related to Christmas. In addition to an oral report, the group was to provide three food dishes to represent the culture assigned.

Class would meet at her home in the mountains above Fort Davis on Friday night the following week and everyone would celebrate Christmas as a class and as a learning experience. She passed out maps and gave the groups the remainder of the

171

morning to organize and prepare while she sat in the front of the room swinging her crossed leg and reading the paper. When groups had their plan in place and responsibilities assigned, they were dismissed.

No one felt the need to have Billy do any of the heavy lifting on the project and since he was the only rookie in the group, he was assigned to bring two dozen tamales. He was fine with that and wasn't at all offended being assigned to "right field." He didn't trust himself either to not screw something up. How he was selected to be in the group that celebrated the Mexican culture, he wasn't sure, but felt like it was pretty much a slam-dunk since his partners were all Mexicans from Pecos, Van Horn, and a couple that rode together from Canutillo. They were finished and heading home before 11 A.M.

Billy waited for Boomer in the hall. On the way home, it was apparent to Billy that Boomer was found guilty by association and given little responsibility as well. Since the group was assigned African Americans and Kwanza, Boomer would be having Beverly make sweet potatoes with marshmallow topping. Overall they decided the weekend was almost fun. They had made a couple of new friends, and the homework wasn't taxing so far. Billy and Boomer decided they liked Dr. Cruz, Lucy, and agreed unanimously that for a woman of her age she had held together fairly well. They even considered her attractive in a mom's friend sort of way.

31

Christmas fell on a Tuesday. On Sunday Billy loaded his car and drove north to his parents house. Before he left he had called Marbella, the snack bar lady that sold tamales on the side, to see if she would do his homework for him. She agreed to have a dozen each of chicken and beef tamales ready Friday morning. He had not seen or spoken to Dallas or Savannah since his heart to heart talk with Ms. Dixie and convinced himself it had a been a crazy busy week as opposed to pure cowardice on his part.

Billy had missed the family Thanksgiving and missing the family Christmas wasn't an option. Even though it was a six-

172

hour trip, July was the last time he had been home and he was a little embarrassed he had been so caught up in his own life that he had failed to do more than call home every couple of weeks. Hopefully all would be forgiven when he pulled into their drive.

Billy's mom and dad were standing on the porch when he arrived. He had no idea how long they had been there. It wasn't going to be a white Christmas, but it wasn't warm either. He hoped they had been peaking though the blinds waiting for him to turn down their street as opposed to simply camping out so they wouldn't miss his arrival. His sisters remained inside wrapping presents and making pies.

After the initial hugs and glad to see yous, they settled into the usual routine of catching up while drinking hot chocolate. Billy could have used Scotch or tequila, but this was an alcohol free zone imposed by the religious beliefs practiced fervently by his parents. He knew later on when he would make a grocery store run, his sisters would pile in the car with him and nip from the bottle he kept under the seat. The party always got livelier after the trips to the store. His mother enjoyed the upbeat in celebration and probably didn't care if its origins were in a bottle of alcohol. She just liked having her kids home.

Billy was the oldest and his two sisters were several years younger as if his parents were reconsidering the idea of children after Billy came along. One of his sisters had just graduated from college and the other had two years to go. None of them were currently married which eliminated any in-laws or even the promise of grandchildren, much to their mother's lament. It provided a direct line of questioning that took place as Christmas Eve drew nigh.

His mother made a few inquiries about his sisters' status as far as promising boyfriends or possibilities, but spent very little time on the topic. She realized they were serious students with great futures ahead of them and actually doing the right thing- not getting involved with a boy or the distractions that came with a relationship. The idea of the girls and grandchildren never even crossed his mother's mind. There would be a wedding before any of that would take place. Her world allowed for no other scenario.

Billy was a different story. He was an easy target, and his mom never missed.

"Have you heard from Crystal lately?' his mom asked.

"No mom. I haven't," Billy said playing his part in this recurring dialogue.

"Well, that's a shame," his mother said.

Billy waited.

"Have you tried getting in touch with her?" she asked.

"No, mom. She made it clear when she left that she really didn't want to hear from me," Billy explained.

"Well, that's a shame," his mother smiled a sad smile.

Billy waited.

"I always liked her. I thought y'all made a great couple. I keep hoping you can apologize and get back together," his mom said wistfully.

"There's really not a chance that's ever going to happen mom so you probably need to accept it," Billy said with a little less compassion than he should have.

"Well, that's a shame," his mother said shaking her head.

Billy waited.

"Are you seeing anyone else?" she asked with renewed hope in her voice.

"Not at the moment I'm afraid," Billy confessed.

"Well, that's a shame," his mother said.

"I am going back to school," Billy offered hoping to lift her spirits.

"That's nice. Maybe you can meet a nice college girl," she said filled with hope once again.

"Maybe, but the women in these classes are probably married and have families. I'm taking courses for professional educators," Billy explained.

"Well, that's a shame," his mother said.

Christmas Eve passed into night and his folks went to bed. He went to his car and brought the bottle into the house. He and his sisters told stories and jokes until well past midnight. His dad came out of the bedroom on the way to the bathroom in the hall close to 1 A.M. Seeing the light still on in the living room and hearing muted laughter, he hollered down the hall that they

174

needed to go to bed so Santa Claus could come. They giggled behind their hands, and Billy assured him they were headed that way.

Christmas Day was spent exchanging gifts and emptying stockings. His mom reminded each of the kids after every present that they could exchange it if they didn't like what they got. She kept all the receipts. They all assured her they loved their gift. Food was served all day long and everyone dozed off in front of the fire in the afternoon amidst wrapping paper and scattered gift boxes.

Billy enjoyed the time he had with his family, but was ready to get back to his apartment. He had no idea why, but he felt a connection to Waymor he hadn't felt before. He knew it wasn't the town; so it had to be the people, a select group of people. When he told his mom and dad he had to leave the next morning, his mom said it was a shame, but she fixed him a care package of leftovers to take with him. The gallon baggie filled with chocolate chip cookies rode in the front seat, and he ate the last one as he drove into Waymor six hours later.

32

Billy picked up his tamales from Marbella on Friday morning, and then waited for Boomer to come by to pick him up for class. He questioned coming back a day and half early once he got home and found no one around he wanted to see. He had puttered around his apartment and finally put a jigsaw puzzle together to help pass the time. People were the attraction he felt for Waymor. He now had no doubt. Those people were nowhere to be seen. Thankfully Boomer arrived a few minutes early and they raced across the desert towards Alpine and a weekend of college. Billy's spirit rose dramatically.

Dr. Cruz's house was actually in the Davis Mountains above Fort Davis, which was on their way and about thirty minutes closer than Alpine. As Billy and Boomer turned and twisted up the mountains, their eagerness to leave town had them arriving almost an hour early. They decided they could help set up. Rounding the last curve, both were surprised at the mountain home in front of them. Billy and Boomer had assumed Dr. Cruz lived in a small weekend cabin based on how she mentioned it, but what they saw looked like an alpine ski lodge complete with an A-frame wall of windows to greet visitors. They looked at each other and simultaneously mouthed, "Wow!"

Surprisingly enough, they weren't the first ones to arrive. Several cars were parked out front, and people could be seen through the wall of windows walking through the main area of her home. Dr. Cruz met them at the door wearing red leather boots that came to her knee, a red leather skirt that was slightly less modest than her black one, and a red leather vest over a white silk blouse. Her blouse was unbuttoned two buttons, but she had a modesty scarf tied around her neck. It was red.

She brushed off their apologies for arriving early. She also dismissed their offer to help setup. She explained that she volunteered for the intercession course each year for several reasons, but the Christmas party was the highlight. She dearly loved having her students over and started decorating in November just to be ready. Those that had been in her classes before knew they could show up at anytime or come visit for no reason. She considered her students her family, kids she never had. Margaret, for instance, had been here since mid morning. Big surprise, thought Billy.

She had shown them where to put their food dishes and the alcohol they had each brought. An email had been sent out the previous day that assured the students that alcohol was acceptable and each student could bring their own. Billy had opted for Tequila in keeping with his cultural experience and Boomer had brought a cooler with a case of Lone Star packed in ice in keeping with his drink of choice. They set their food down and offered Dr. Cruz a drink. She declined, but showed Billy where a glass was and offered any mixer he might want. He assured her straight up was fine. Boomer popped the top on a can and refused the offer of a coozie. He explained he never held one long enough for it to get warm.

Billy had complimented her on how nice her home was and when they had a drink and were settled, she took his arm and offered a guided tour. Boomer opted to go out on the patio and

176

take in the view that stretched for miles. Over the course of the next hour, Dr. Cruz held tightly to Billy's arm and shared her home and her personal life in great detail seemingly unencumbered by modesty or privacy. She treated Billy as a long lost friend and confidant. He didn't mind a bit.

Billy learned that the house was once the family's vacation retreat. The family's meant her and her husband's. She was married and had been for almost thirty years, but lived alone since he was serving time in a federal penitentiary. She had grown up in Pecos in a family of immigrants that found steady work on the farms and ranches. She had always loved the area around Fort Davis and Balmorhea. Her family "vacations" usually involved a trip to the swimming hole where the water was clear and inviting in the summer or camping up in the mountains nearby. She had no idea what Colorado or even New Mexico looked like and for her this part of Texas was heaven. It was all she needed.

Her career in public education culminated with her being named the youngest superintendent in Texas. She was a woman, a minority, and a rising star. She served first in Van Horn, then Socorro, before being summoned to El Paso ISD, where she met her husband who was a banker and investor. As their combined incomes grew, she asked for a house in the mountains for a get away from the stress and strain of daily life. He was eager to accommodate her. She was the love of his life, but also provided him respectability that was a nice front for his business ventures. To make her happy, he built her the alpine lodge they were currently touring as her private retreat.

When the FBI knocked on their door four years ago and took her husband away in cuffs, Lucy was as surprised and stunned as anyone. She had no idea that his investments had expanded to what the government called racketeering. In a quest for more money and a lavish life style, his deals and partners became shadier and eventually involved fraud, swindling, drugs, gambling, and a multitude of other sins. Lucy had thought all the money came from his keen business sense and real estate development.

As part of a plea bargain her husband's lawyer had worked out, she was allowed to keep one home and her own personal possessions including her paychecks and retirement. She had chosen to resign her superintendent's job, humiliated by the scandal that played out on the front page of the newspaper for weeks. She retired from public education and walked out of their upscale El Paso home with three suitcases, which she loaded in her Audi after the FBI had gone through and fingered each item she had packed. Everything left behind was impounded to pay back those swindled. She moved to Fort Davis.

Her retirement check was enough to provide for her needs, not in the way she was used to living, but in a way that was light years better than her childhood. What she didn't share with Billy was that the "emergency kit" her husband had put together and hidden for her to use, "should anything happen", would make a huge difference in her lifestyle. She had thought the "anything happens" meant like a heart attack or kidnapping. He had shown her the hidden vault in the floor of the mountain home knowing it would be the last place she would give up. He had added to its contents dramatically she discovered when she had unloaded her few belongings and made herself at home. She had no concerns about her future. Cash in small denominations and diamonds would take care of her now.

When the dust settled, Lucy explained to Billy, she had applied to teach at Sul Ross. They were excited to hire her as an adjunct professor, and here she was. She explained with a laugh.

Billy asked a little hesitantly about how long her husband would be gone. She never blinked when she had said she didn't expect to see him again in this lifetime.

"You people are my family now," she said as she pointed at him and to the group at the foot of the stairs that had grown considerably larger during the tour.

Billy had seen four guest bedrooms, a master bedroom larger than his apartment with a king sized bed covered in a white duvet and dozens of white pillows stacked in rows. Each bedroom had it own bathroom and hers resembled a very plush spa. It was open with a walk-in shower where spray nozzles

178

could massage you from the ceiling or on three different sides. There was a wall length mirror and dressing table filled with bottles, tubes of creams, and makeup. Her closet was filled with clothes, many of them leather, and could have been a converted bedroom with two levels of clothes hanging racks and shelves for her shoes and boots that covered one wall.

The downstairs was made up of almost an entire open area that served as a den, kitchen, and dining area. While the kitchen was tiled, the rest of the area was hardwood flooring that had been polished and waxed to a fine shine and covered in part with thick rugs of western design. The furniture was heavy leather chairs and sectionals complimented by rough wooden tables stained dark. Strategically placed couches and chairs divided the living space into small sections while the kitchen would have made any chef happy with the array of hanging copper pans, a commercial grade gas stove, and double oven. A marbled top counter ran in a semi-circle separating the kitchen from the dining area while providing seating for at least ten people with poolroom style barstools set underneath.

As the tour wound down, Billy and Lucy stood at the base of the stairs as she pointed at the wall length windows that exposed the scenery on the east and south sides of the house.

"As nice as this house is," she said unnecessarily, "the windows are my pride and joy."

"Oh really?" Billy said surprised considering all he had just seen. "Why is that?"

"I love the view and being able to sit just about anywhere in my house and look off down the mountain. That was what I wanted more than anything, but we live right below the McDonald observatory. Any light at night creates light pollution and interferes with the use of the telescope. This whole area has extreme restrictions on the amount of light that can be visible any night of the year. As much as I have cursed my husband over the years for the lies he told, I have to give him credit for finding the special glass that diffuses the light coming from inside which allows us to meet the restrictions by the government. I got my view," Lucy finished triumphantly.

"He would never say where the glass came from. I'm more convinced now that he probably came by it illegally. Maybe so, maybe I'm not going to tell," she finished with a wink and led him towards the large group of students now gathered.

"Thank you Lucy for the tour and sharing your life like you did. That's all...well, that's amazing. Your house and your story," Billy said as they walked and he patted the top of her hand that still gripped his bicep. It had never loosened its grip the past hour.

"Any time. You're always welcome here. Do plan on coming by," she said as she smiled.

Margaret came rushing up to let her know that most everyone had arrived and all the food dishes had been set out. She cut Billy a look that could have killed for so selfishly dominating the hostess the way he had. Billy thought the tour had been Dr. Cruz's idea, and he had just been along for the ride. Either way, Margaret wasn't buying it and reached for Dr. Cruz's hand to lead her away.

Boomer must have been tracking the time as well since he came alongside of Billy where he had been left standing at the edge of the room and raised his eyebrows and said, "That must have been some tour. I was beginning to wonder if you'd gotten lost in a bedroom." His eye's laughed like a frat boy wanting details about a friend's exploits.

"Boomer you wouldn't believe this house and when I tell you the story I just heard...you won't believe that either," Billy said shaking his head.

"I can't wait," Boomer said.

Billy had refilled his glass and Boomer started on his second six-pack while the rest of the class made themselves comfortable in chairs or in the floor on cushions as they scattered around the den. Dr. Cruz welcomed everyone to her home and reminded her guests that they were family. She extended an invitation to each of them to come back and visit whenever they wanted. She appeared to be looking at Billy when she covered this part. When Billy saw Margaret's gaze of death, he decided he hadn't imagined it.

180

Dr. Cruz then explained the ground rules of the lesson. The oral reports could be no more than five minutes long or she would cut them off. If they could say it in less, good for them. Be precise, informative, and quick she encouraged. The food and fellowship was the focus of the evening it appeared. Equity could wait until the following day. No one seemed bothered by this format, and within thirty minutes, all eight groups had briefly covered their topics and lines were formed to begin dishing food onto their plates and refilling their drinks.

The remainder of the night the students ate, drank, and mingled. Billy met as many of his classmates as he could while he stood by the kitchen bar and visited with those that came back to refill their plates. He also had easy access to the queso dip and tequila. He managed to speak to just about everyone before the night was over and even Margaret grudgingly responded when he asked about her child, whether it was a boy or girl, and where she lived. He considered the night a win all the way around.

People began saying their goodbyes around 10 P. M., but neither Billy nor Boomer was in a hurry to leave. All they had to look forward to was the four walls of a motel room thirty miles down the road. When the last six people began picking up their dishes and coats, Dr. Cruz came by. Billy extended his hand which she grasped firmly while he thanked her again for the invitation. He offered to stay and help clean up, but was immediately interrupted by Margret who assured him and Dr. Cruz, that she and her girlfriends would be staying and cleaning Dr. Cruz's house.

Dr. Cruz gave him a wink and squeezed his hand and promised to see him in class the next morning. Billy decided that was their cue to leave.

Boomer was still working on the case of beer, but Billy had no qualms about him driving. Boomer's capacity was mythical and he was nowhere near his limit. Billy, on the other hand, was on the fine line between being buzzed for a good time and a drink or two away from too much. He decided to save the rest of his bottle for the next night. To make the trip down the mountain and over to Alpine pass faster, Billy told Boomer the story Dr.

Cruz had shared with him. He didn't feel he was violating anyone's trust since she didn't appear to think any of it was a secret. She had shared freely with Billy unsolicited and Billy shared with Boomer.

"Holy crap," was all Boomer said when he finished. "That sounds like some kind of Godfather movie!" Billy couldn't agree more.

When they had checked into their room and taken care of their nightly rituals, Billy produced a set of earplugs he had purchased on Beverly's recommendation. She assured him they had saved her marriage. He hoped so.

Billy had a better night and only heard what he would describe as a low roar coming from Boomer's side of the room. He managed to sleep almost all night and was rested the next morning. Class had gone smoothly and mostly consisted of reliving moments from the night before between comments about the importance of making sure every child regardless of race, creed, color, or national origin had a chance for a quality education. Once again Billy seemed surprised that people had to be taught this. He hoped he was treating his kids fairly.

There were two things everyone must do in Alpine Billy had learned the night before at Dr. Cruz's house as he talked with his classmates at the counter by the food. One was to eat at Patricia's, and the other was to see the Marfa lights. The consensus of the group was that only a loser would pass either of those up. He and Boomer weren't losers. For lunch on Saturday, Billy and Boomer had followed the directions across the railroad tracks to the east side of town and a small house that had seen its better days. Cars were parked two deep around it and down the block.

When they finally managed to get a table with enough room so Boomer wasn't a fire hazard, they were starving. The smell alone was intoxicating. Without looking at a menu, Billy ordered two meat and potato burritos with green sauce and Boomer ordered four of the same. The choice of burrito with beef and potatoes had been made for them the night before as well by group agreement. Hands down. No argument. Iced tea with lemon was brought out to drink while they snacked on chips and salsa, both of which were advertised as homemade in the kitchen they could see from their seats. A little old woman was stirring a pot over a flame and they wondered if that might be the famous Patricia. Before they could ask, their ordered was placed in front of them and all thoughts of conversation disappeared. With each mouthful, their respect for their classmates' judgment grew immensely. They had high hopes for the Marfa lights.

Saturday night Billy and Boomer took the remains of Boomers cooler and what was left of Billy's bottle and drove over to see the Marfa lights. These were unexplained lights that popped up in the desert that people swore were caused by UFO's or alien life form. The stories had been around since the 1950's and had grown in legend each year. Scientists had assured everyone they simply were reflections of campfires or car lights on the highway caused by desert heating and cooling. People assured each other that the more scientists discounted the sighting, the more the government was covering up. Who could forget Area 51 or the UFO at Roswell, New Mexico? Regardless of whether a person fell on the side of science or truth, everyone that got within fifty miles of Marfa had to drive out east of Marfa and take a look for themselves. Boomer had asked a couple of guys in class how to find the right spot during the afternoon break. He was told there was a pull off about ten miles east of town, and he could park out of the way of traffic and get the best view.

After a second helping of Patricia's burritos for dinner, Billy found himself in Boomer's front seat in the pull off east of Marfa facing south. Darkness had fallen before they had even left Alpine since the days were so short. Billy and Boomer spent an hour visiting and drinking with an occasional hard look to make sure they weren't missing anything. They actually didn't know what to expect so anything bright caught their attention. They noticed several cars had joined them and that a couple had already given up or seen things Billy and Boomer had missed and left. One car a few feet away had the windows fogged up and was rocking rhythmically and with enthusiasm, which made Billy wonder how serious that couple was about the lights.

After two hours of vigilance, the last beer can squashed in Boomer's massive fist and Billy's bottle bone dry, they convinced themselves they had seen lights dancing across the horizon in the area that was all desert and far away from the highway. When the rocking commenced after a lengthy break, they started the engine and drove back to their motel with another check on their bucket list.

Sunday's class time focused on data mining to determine how successful students were. The results would eliminate any doubt on how effective a school was doing educating minority students. Homework was assigned to pull up data from the last five years and bring it back the following week to discuss in groups. On the way home, Billy volunteered to pull the information since it was probably in his office. They agreed he'd do this assignment, and Boomer could do the next. Boomer asked if he wanted to come over for New Year's Eve and celebrate with him and Beverly, but Billy saw all kinds of problems coming from that scenario, so he made up an excuse to decline.

"I talked to Beverly during the break this morning, and she said Savannah came in last night holding the second place trophy from the Seminole tournament and was thrilled," Boomer said. "They played Levelland in the finals and actually held their own right up to the final minute. Everyone knows Levelland is a powerhouse when it comes to girls' basketball and to just stay on the court with them...well that's impressive."

"Good for her," Billy said sincerely. "She's definitely done wonders for those girls."

"She's a special kid that Savannah. Always has been," Boomer said.

"No doubt," Billy said in full agreement.

33

Billy ate his second bowl of Frosted Flakes as he watched the flower covered floats make the turn onto Colorado Boulevard in Pasadena. The overly excited host dressed in stocking caps and mufflers to ward off the extremely rare cold snap for a Rose Bowl Parade, described the process of placing millions of flowers by hand over dozens of floats for the viewer's pleasure. Billy had

184

been up since 6:30 A.M. and was glad to have something to watch other than daytime TV and news.

Billy knew his mom had been up much longer making cinnamon rolls and chocolate fried pies for his sisters and dad. The New Year's Day tradition had been around as long as he could remember. By now his sisters were snuggled under blankets on the couch watching the parade with his mom as they licked the sticky icing off their fingers and reached for another roll. Nothing would happen for the rest of the morning until the parade was over. The one day of the year his mom put herself first, at his dad's insistence, was from 10-Noon on New Year's Day.

The paternal decree had been issued the first year the family had gotten their first television. The colorful floats that shimmered in the California sunlight mesmerized his mom, but she had a hard time grasping that every bit of the decorations were from flowers and plants. Each year after that his dad announced first thing to start the new year that their mother would have the TV until noon. Of course as kids, the parade was great entertainment while eating cinnamon rolls and fried pies. It wasn't until the NCAA expanded their bowl schedule and backed up their start times that Billy began to chafe. If his dad ever regretted missing the first half of the Gator Bowl or Peach Bowl, he never let on. He had decreed, and he held firm. The parade was Billy's mom's yearly treat.

The Frosted Flakes were a poor substitute for homemade cinnamon rolls and turnovers. Billy left the parade halfway through to catch the lead-in to the first game of the day. He felt a pang of guilt, but since he had spent New Year's Eve at school working on his college homework and the evening celebrating alone before going to bed at 10 P. M. the whole new year new beginnings thing was somewhat of a disaster already. What a loser he thought. To make matters worse, Billy realized while reaching for the milk earlier he had no black-eyed peas to eat for lunch, and the stores were all closed. He was no doubt out of luck.

At halftime of the Gator Bowl, with Georgia leading Michigan State 17-7, Billy closed his eyes and dozed off while the analyst replayed the first half. His blood sugar was trying to counter balance the overdose of Frosted Flakes, and he was enjoying a very pleasant dream while his body fought to right the ship. The knock on his door startled him awake. Billy sat up quickly trying to get his bearings and clear his head as the knock repeated itself. He made his way to the door having no idea who would possibly stop by on New Year's Day, or any day for that matter.

Opening the door, he saw Dallas standing in front of him holding a wrapped Christmas present. She wore jeans and a white sweater that clung tightly to her body. Her knee high suede boots made her almost as tall as Billy. She smiled when she saw the surprised look on his face.

"Don't be afraid. I come in peace," she assured him. "No weapons. "

"Hey, good morning. Come in," Billy said coming to grips with her presence.

"I don't mean to be rude, but you kind of look like crap," Dallas offered with a smile as she stepped inside the doorway.

"Yeah, I guess I do," Billy said, as he looked himself over standing in his ratty sweats and a holey t-shirt. He knew he hadn't combed his hair or brushed his teeth. "I guess I wasn't expecting company. "

"Evidently not. Rough night last night?" Dallas asked as she walked past him and placed the package on the counter.

"Actually I did homework and was in bed by 10 P.M. I guess my body's not used to being treated to a decent night's sleep," Billy said as he tried to mash down his hair that was sticking in several different directions.

"I'd heard you were dating Boomer now. Leaving town every weekend together and doing homework on New Year's Eve," she said laughing at the thought.

"I guess that's right, other than New Year's Eve. I spent that alone. Just so you know he doesn't smell near as good as you and snores to high heavens," Billy said and noticed they were just standing in the middle of the room. "Sorry, would you like to sit down? Do you want something to drink?"

"No, I've got to get going. I just wanted to bring by a peace offering," Dallas said as she pointed to the package on the

186

counter. "My sister told me I was a jackass, and needed to get over myself. "

"Dixie called you a jackass?" Billy asked a little surprised.

"She said mule headed, but she meant jackass," Dallas replied.

"Thank you. I'm sorry, but I don't have a gift for you," Billy looked around as if a present would suddenly appear.

"This isn't a gift exchange at a Christmas party. This is me saying maybe sometimes I get a little carried away, and maybe this is one of those times. I'm sorry. Especially about that scar above your eye," Dallas explained looking everywhere but at Billy. "Don't shake the package. It's a pie. Keep it right side up when you open it."

"Thank you. Good to know," he smiled. "Look, I've been meaning to call and see if we could talk this through, I just...."

"Dixie called you mule headed, too. She said we were both acting childish and one of us had to be the bigger person," Dallas offered. "So there's a peace pie. I'm the bigger person. Maybe sometime you can take me to dinner. "

"Sure. I'd like that," Billy said. "Are you sure you don't want to sit down and stay?"

"I'm actually driving to Arlington today. I have some friends that have invited me to visit during my days off. They're starting a security firm and wanted to talk to me about joining them," Dallas said. "I know you have class and all, and I'll be gone until Saturday night, then back to work. Just call me sometime down the road and...uh... I'll pick up."

"So you have a job interview? Does that mean you might be moving?" Billy asked surprised. "I never thought about you leaving Waymor. "

"I'm just going to see old friends and listen. I'm not gathering up cardboard boxes just yet. Maybe I need a change. I'll let you know," Dallas said as she walked towards the door. Billy followed her completely caught off guard. She leaned over and kissed him on the cheek and said, "Don't dump the pie, okay? It's coconut crème." And she was gone.

187

34

People in the desert of West Texas didn't need a calendar or an understanding of the equinox to know when it was spring. Spring started the day they all woke up and looked to the west-northwest and saw a brown wall of dirt blowing in their direction. Spring lasted until the winds calmed down and the skies cleared which usually occurred about the third week in May. And then it was summer.

Spring in the desert usually meant track meets were canceled because no one at the finish line could see the starter or hear his pistol. Discuses had been known to disappear into the brown and never come out, confounding those that went in search. Softball and baseball games were canceled for lack of visibility in the infield, and the outfielders had to use voice cues to find their way back to the dugout.

Everyone in town was irritable and cranky for weeks. Dirt seeped into cracks around windows settling on furniture and even getting into beds. The grit and grime that could not be wiped away became an irritant as much psychologically as it was in underwear and socks. Spring in the desert was hell week, week after week. But not this year.

On the third Saturday in February, the brown wall rose to the west and began boiling down off the foothills of the Rockies. The vast majority of Waymor weren't even aware of it, and if they were they didn't care. They were in Big Spring, Texas in the gym at Howard College. They filled the visitor's side almost to capacity. In a couple of hours they hoped to celebrate a regional championship with their Lady Sand Crabs. A lunar landing was less rare than what the good folks of Waymor were experiencing at the moment.

Three weeks before, to the amazement of everyone, The Lady Crabs, under the leadership and inspiration of Coach Savannah Skinner had breezed through district play with a record of 9-1 and qualified for the playoffs for only the second time in school history. Now all they had to do was win one playoff game to make Savannah and the girls basketball team the most successful program in school history. They had accomplished that goal during the bi district round as they traveled east followed by half the town.

The next week they rode the bus west to meet their opponent from the El Paso area in Van Horn. The string of car lights following the bus to and from the game stretched as far as the girls could see as they peered out the bus's back window. Stores had shut down in Waymor, and the streets were empty. History was being made, and no one wanted to miss out. A new level of excitement never before experienced by anyone in Waymor, even in the throes of passion, engulfed the town when the girls advanced to the regional finals. The Lady Crabs were one win away from the state tournament!

Billy had brought in Boomer and Paddy to help with crowd control for the afternoon game. He had never seen the Waymor bleachers filled to capacity, but he didn't expect any trouble other than a couple of mouthy parents that felt entitled to correct the referees and coaches, since they themselves had once dribbled a ball. He was afraid that his people had no idea how to act in this situation. He really couldn't blame them since it was new to everyone. He had to admit he was overwhelmed as much as anyone. His only hope was that in their rudimentary ways and unbridled enthusiasm that they didn't break too many social norms and offend those that actually had been here before.

Unfortunately, when the girls made two free throws with no time on the clock to win by one, several of the opponents and their fans along with two of the tournament host were knocked over in the mad dash of the Sand Crab faithful to storm the courts. Cutting the nets down became secondary to trying to rip the backboards apart to salvage a piece of plexi glass. Only when the local police were called in to provide back up to the campus cops was order restored, and the fans ushered out of the gym. Billy had a cut under his left eye and Paddy had blood on his lip and a gap where his dental plate had been. Fortunately he had taken his magical teeth out prior to the melee and secured them in his pants pocket. Boomer was unscathed.

Cracker Jack would get a bill from Howard College the following week for damages in the amount of a $2,876. He called the school board president as a courtesy and with his support, Cracker gladly wrote them a check.

Savannah and the Lady Sand Crabs were going to Austin in less than two weeks.

35

When Billy and Boomer had learned that Dr. Cruz was teaching school law in the spring, they registered for her class that met the first weekend of each month. They also signed up for an additional three hours in a political science class that fit into the degree plan their advisor had created. It met on the second weekend of each month. They would go two weekends on and two weekends off to see how that worked.

On the first Saturday of February, Billy and Boomer had strolled into the auditorium looking like the veterans they now were. They had earned three hours toward their degree during the intercession and both made an A. Currently they each had a 4.0 in graduate school and felt accomplished. How they had done it neither was sure, but their "A" had been printed on the report card they received in the mail right next to the "4.0".

They'd had little sleep the night before following the dramatic basketball win that clinched district for the girls, but their spirits were high, and they each waved at friends they'd made during the intercession. Billy even stopped to speak to Margaret in an attempt to start off the semester on the right foot. She was seated front row center and regarded Billy coldly until he asked if she had any new baby pictures to show. She brightened considerably. After he offered the appropriate oohs and aahs, Billy and Boomer found their usual seats in the now disproven overlooked zone and waited.

Dr. Cruz's arrival had not been disappointing as strode across the front of the room as the clock struck 10 A.M. with her hair flying behind her. She did not disappoint in her leather boots, skirt and jacket over a white silk blouse. All pink. A dark pink. For Valentine's month she explained. The month for lovers.

"Good Morning!" she said to get everyone's attention and received a few feeble responses in return. She pointed and waved at familiar faces around the room, which of course included Margaret who beamed with the attention. Having covered most of the room, her gazed moved left and she spotted Billy and Boomer in their familiar seats.

"Hey guys," she said as she pointed and waved. "Good to see you! Welcome back."

Boomer tilted his chin to acknowledge her, and Billy gave a half wave with his right hand, but both smiled at the attention as well. Margaret made a note of the extended greeting, and it appeared to Billy all his goodwill and baby cooing had been for naught.

"Good Morning," Dr. Cruz said again. This time with a loud voice that commanded the room and demanded a response in return. The entire class replied.

"Welcome to school law. This is the single most important class you will take during your course of study, and the most important information that you will use during your careers. If I teach it, you write it down. If you write it down, you learn it. When you learn it, don't forget it. When you make a legal mistake, you are screwed."

The room was silent, and she paused for effect. She had everyone's attention including Billy and Boomer who had straightened up and opened their notebook to a blank page.

After an appropriate amount of time to allow her words to sink in, she continued.

"You must know the law. Any person that becomes unhappy with you these days will show up with an attorney. If it's determined you have violated the law, you lose, they win. Know the law. If you know the law, you can bend the law. You bend the law to get done what you need to get done. Most of the laws aren't written to help you. They are written to protect the students, which is how it should be. Know the law and bend the law to get your business done. Bending the law is not breaking the law. Learn to bend without breaking. If you beak the law, learn how to say "do you want fries with that?"

Another silence fell over the room. This woman knew how to engage students. Billy and Boomer had been excited about the law course. Billy really liked Dr. Cruz for all the right reasons

191

mostly, and he and Boomer both had Social Studies backgrounds. They felt their knowledge of government and history would make this course a breeze for them. Billy wasn't so sure now. He started to doubt his commitment to being an administrator.

"Now before all of you go running to your advisor and getting your schedule changed, know this. Each district should have a school lawyer on retainer. Find out who they are and how to get in touch with them. Then use them. It cost money every time they pick up the phone, so you can image your superintendent doesn't want you calling on a daily basis. I am here to help with that. We will learn the law and where to look to find the answers to the usual questions. The big stuff? Call your attorney."

The rest of the day's lesson alleviated most of their fears. Evidently a lot of common sense was involved. In addition to relaxing a little in class, Billy and Boomer filled up on Patricia's burritos. It had been weeks since they had last tasted the homemade goodness, and they were in full-fledged withdrawal. They asked to place an order to go so they might take several with them to eat later. The little waitress, who had answered the question a thousand times, repeated what obviously she'd been taught straight from Patricia herself.

"Food to eat. Food not to take with you. Food only good hot and right off the stove. Order what you can eat and eat it. If you can't eat it all, order less next time. No orders to go. No carry out. You not finish your plate, you leave it and do better next time" and she looked at them to see if they understood. They did, so they ordered one more to eat there just to be safe.

36

The week leading up to the state tournament was chaotic for Billy. His biggest problem was keeping kids in class and teachers out of the hall. The only group discussions going on centered around the basketball tournament. Had there been a test over anything tournament related from the amount of tickets set aside for each school to where in East Texas Hardin-Jefferson was located, all his students would have aced it along with the faculty. Once again Billy had to be forgiving since this might be a once in a lifetime experience. It was definitely a moment in time to savor. He had no intentions of being a party pooper.

The first game of the tournament was scheduled for Thursday night. Waymor would be playing Hardin-Jefferson at Frank Erwin Center more commonly referred to as the Drum he was told. Billy had to look on the map to locate their opponent. Once he found out the school was actually located in the town of Sour Lake and named after the two counties it served his search was made a little easier. From what he read, he decided the people he would see across the gym on Thursday night would be similar in many ways to the citizens of Waymor. The two schools had oil as a common denominator and Billy figured the language of the oil field was universal. That could be either good or bad.

Tickets to the game were being sold out of the superintendent's office and by the looks of the line on Monday morning when Billy drove to work, a stranger might have thought Willie Nelson was coming to town for a concert. Billy felt sure the seating for the fans from Waymor would be adequate for everyone to sit together in the assigned section of the gym, but then again he had been surprised each week at the number of people showing up.

Billy's ticket was in his billfold. He would be on the front row in the southwest corner section of the upper deck in front of all the Scand Crab faithful. Hardin-Jefferson fans would be located directly opposite in the northeast corner of the gym. His placement was intentional. Cracker had seated him so that he could hear any grumblings or malcontent from the locals behind him and address it before an official had to. Cracker had sorted out seats for him, Boomer, and Paddy scattering them throughout the town's section to help with crowd control. Boomer was in the back poised to move forward and address anyone that appeared to be standing or moving in the wrong direction. Paddy was smack in the middle. He would spend most of the night entertaining those around him with jokes and stories, but would be alert for disruptions and expected to help.

Cracker felt the check he had written to Howard College was worth every penny, but was more concerned with Waymor getting a reputation like Rainwater as a town of derelicts and thugs. Cracker desperately wanted a better showing from the townsfolk in Austin. Howard College had filed a formal complaint against the fans of Waymor and their administration. The UIL had sent Cracker an overnight letter condemning the behavior witnessed at the regional tournament and outlining the expectations of the UIL, the University of Texas, and Austin police department concerning the fans attending the state tournament.

Cracker had the letter printed in the paper that came out on Wednesday of tournament week. Along with the letter, Cracker implored the Sand Crab faithful to be positive in their support of the team, but restrained in their exuberance. He ended by assuring the readers that the world needed to see actions that reflected the qualities that made Waymor the beacon in the desert, a light for others to use as a guide. The letter was well intentioned, but many readers had to ask what exuberance meant and, of course, by then the whole train of thought was disrupted. Most agreed the beacon of light in the desert was poetic and did sound like them. They were leaders for sure since they had the only team in the whole desert going to Austin.

Billy found out later that each school also received eight administrators' passes for courtside seats during their game. These tickets were mailed separately to the athletic director, which was Boomer, who had turned them over to Cracker Jack as soon as they arrived. Boomer felt that distributing them was above his pay grade, and he was right. As it turned out, Cracker and his wife Betty occupied the first two seats. Next to them was the Board president and his wife. The remaining six seats went to the lesser board members whose spouses sat among the unclean in the upper deck with Billy.

Billy had no illusions of scoring a courtside seat. After all, he was only the principal of the school represented on the court. He knew Cracker had to keep the board happy to keep his job and as long as Cracker had a job, Billy would have one as well. He would be more at home among the fans in the upper deck and enjoy the game more he kept telling himself.

School was canceled for Thursday and Friday of tournament week by order of the superintendent using whatever ruse

194

necessary to make it happen. Cracker Jack's stock rose even higher among the parents wanting to travel to the game as well as the school personnel that enjoyed days off anytime they were offered. No one had wanted to stay behind and for the few that chose not to make the six-hour trip down Interstate 10, they would have the run of the town.

On Wednesday morning the entire town turned out to send the girls' bus off in style. Savannah had gotten permission to travel a day early so she could hold a practice in Austin to help the girls get their legs back under them after the bus ride. She could have asked for anything and gotten it at that point. Fortunately for Cracker and the school budget, an extra day was all she wanted. Each school lined up along the single block that housed all three campuses to let their students stand on the curb to wave and shout as the decorated bus passed by with the girls hanging out of the windows waving and shouting back.

From kindergarteners to seniors, the students and their teachers made an unbroken chain of waving arms supported by shouts and whistles. A fire truck led the procession with it's lights flashing and horn blasting a piercing sound that caused a couple of the younger kids to cry. Two police cars followed the bus with their lights flashing and random 'whoop, whoop, whoops' of the sirens being switched off and on.

The sound of sirens in such near proximity surprised the three sophomore boys that had snuck behind the Ag building during the mobile pep rally hoping for a quick smoke. They prematurely snuffed out their cigarettes and darted back around the building to blend into the crowd before any officers arrived. Only too late did they discover their mistake. Premature responses have always been the bane of teenaged boys.

The bus and their escorts were followed by all the parents and fans that had opted for the full experience package and were planning to follow the bus down, attend practice, and enjoy every minute of the adventure. The rest of the town would follow Thursday. Most expected the town to be deserted by noon.

37

After the parade had passed and students were herded back to class, it dawned on Billy that he and Boomer had class the coming weekend. They were scheduled for their second session in school law. If the girls won their first game on Thursday, the finals took place on Saturday afternoon and there was no way they could miss the finals. School law was the most important class they'd take. Dr. Cruz had emphasized that point over and over. Missing wasn't an option for class either. After worrying about it the rest of the morning, he mentioned it to Boomer at lunch. They couldn't come up with a solution. They knew they wouldn't miss a championship game if there was one and they also knew they needed to be in class. Billy finally decided he would call Dr. Cruz that night and let her help them figure out what to do.

When he got home from school after the three days of nonstop preparations, Billy was as tired as he could remember being his whole life. The mental strain seemed to take more of a toll on his energy than a good hard physical workout. After dropping his briefcase on the counter, he sat down in his recliner with a cold Lone Star allowing himself a few minutes of convalescence before doing anything else.

Halfway through his second beer it dawned on him it was prayer meeting night and wondered if Dallas was there. He knew without a doubt the basketball team and tournament in Austin would take up most of the airways to God during the prayer session. God would be beseeched for traveling mercies and victory in Jesus, should he see fit, and if it was part of his overall plan, for the salvation of the nation and the rest of the heathens in the world. Billy also wondered what kind of cake he was missing since he had skipped lunch talking to Boomer. Instead of getting up and starting dinner, Billy opened a third beer and thought back to the last time he had seen Dallas.

Billy had finished his intersession course in January and for the first time in weeks had a weekend free. He remembered Dallas' invitation as she was leaving town on New Year's Day and decided it would be nice to see her and find out if she was taking the new job. He had worked through the possibilities of life with her and without her the remainder of the Christmas break, but then had shoved it to the back of his mind when his life went back to high gear after the break. Realizing he had a free weekend, an evening with Dallas seemed like a good choice.

He had called at noon and she accepted his offer to provide dinner that night and they agreed to meet at her house at 6:30 P.M. Holding a bag of two-dozen of Marbella's homemade tamales with two cups of special green sauce and another with an avocado, a head of lettuce, and two tomatoes, Billy rang the doorbell. The bottle of red wine was secured under his arm. Gunny and Chesty Puller were on either side of Dallas as she held the door open to let him in. They chose to growl deep in their chest to let Billy know they still harbored a grudge against him even though the lady might be willing to take him back. Billy hoped they stuck to verbal abuse and not turn to violence.

Dallas stood beside him at the cabinet with an amused look on her face as Billy unloaded dinner from the plastic bags and prepared to start "cooking". He opened the wine first and after Dallas produced two glasses, poured and offered a toast.

"To two mule headed jackasses, peace pies, and tamales. "

"I'll drink to that," Dallas said. They tapped their glasses lightly together and took a drink.

The meal had been enjoyable. They had eaten casually at the counter each consuming their share of the tamales. The conversation had been light. He talked about his course work, and she covered the events of the oilfield. As they were cleaning up the few dishes that had been used, Billy finally worked up the nerve to ask her about her job interview.

Refilling their glasses while emptying the bottle, Dallas pointed to the sofa currently occupied by her guard dogs that still refused to forgive and forget. Billy suggested that ladies should go first being a gentleman and for his own safety. When Dallas began to sit, the dogs took her cue and dropped to the floor moving to a rug where they could still be within striking distance should the need arise. Billy sat a respectful distance away from Dallas, which seemed to please the dogs. They relaxed enough to lay their heads on their paws, but never shifted their gaze.

Dallas explained that her friends in the Arlington were from her Marine Corps days and had been kicking around the idea of starting a security firm. They hoped to focus on security for businesses and also supply personal bodyguards to anyone who was a celebrity or had a need to be protected. The skills they had learned in the military seemed to make them highly qualified for such an endeavor. Dallas, being highly skilled and a woman, only added to their sales pitch since many time females guarded by males were vulnerable when they had to visit a restroom or during times they were alone dressing. Those were gaps in the coverage that put people at risk, Dallas explained. Dallas and one her of girlfriends would be an advertising gold mine.

Arlington was right in the middle of the Ft. Worth-Dallas area, which had a number of high profile athletes and celebrities from the movie and music industry. The metroplex also had a concentration of oilmen and businessmen who were not public figures, but were extremely wealthy which made them targets to anyone that was greedy. She had been assured she would be extremely busy, but extremely well paid. Her estimated income if she came in as a partner was more than triple what she was making in the oilfield.

Billy listened quietly as she went through the proposal and the opportunities it provided. She never mentioned any downside and Billy assumed other than leaving her friends and family behind, there wasn't any. When she finished, Billy asked if she had made up her mind. Hearing her go through the sales pitch as she had probably heard it left little doubt it was appealing and something he couldn't see her turning down.

"I told them I'd think about it. They hope to launch in June, so I have until April to let them know if I want to invest and be a partner," Dallas explained. "If I don't want to put up any money and bypass the headaches of management, I can go to work for them anytime I want at a moment's notice. The salary would be the same; I just wouldn't get the dividends from an owner's share."

"Are you leaning one way or the other?" Billy asked.

"I have until April so I'm just letting it sit there for a while. I figure I'll know when I know," Dallas said.

They had sat in silence as Billy thought about what she had told him, and he noticed Dallas was lost in thought as well. He had no idea if she was thinking of moving to the bright lights of the big city or something completely different. He stood and took both their empty glasses to the sink and washed them. He helped her up off the couch, kissed her on the cheek, and thanked her for the evening. As he started towards the door, Chesty and Gunny escorted him out happy to see him leave. Dallas thanked him for dinner, but didn't offer a nightcap or ask him to stay. Billy hadn't expected one so he climbed in his truck and made the slow drive home.

The half empty can of Lone Star slid sideways and poured its cold contents onto Billy's crotch. His nerve endings overreacted to the assault on his reproductive organs and sent dire warnings of panic to his brain that kicked an enormous amount of adrenaline into his blood stream to fight or flee. Billy fled as far as standing up before his rational sense was able to rein him in and explain that he had fallen asleep. His hand had relaxed in slumber from around the can of cold liquid, which was now dripping on his boots. His heart was still pumping rapidly; Billy grabbed a dishtowel and sopped up the seat of his chair and the front of his clothes. He opted to rip off his pants and underwear and toss them in the hamper replacing them with his old pair of sweats.

Billy noticed it was past ten, and he hadn't eaten, but, more importantly, he hadn't called Dr. Cruz. Food could wait, he decided, and searched for the business card she had given him the night of the party. He hoped he wasn't about to flush all the goodwill he had built up with her down the toilet. He dialed and waited still trying to get his heart rate back down to normal.

"Hello," Dr. Cruz answered on the fourth ring.

"Dr. Cruz, I hope I didn't wake you. I'm really sorry to be calling at this late hour. This is Billy, William Robert Masters. I'm in your law class," Billy managed to get all that said in one breath.

"Oh, hi, Billy, silly boy. I know who you are," she laughed.

"Oh good," he said. "Did I wake you, Dr. Cruz?"

"It's Lucy. Remember. In social settings, it's Lucy. I'm in my bed and that's about as social as it can get, don't you think?" she asked.

"Oh, you're already in bed. Look I can call back tomorrow if it would be better," Billy volunteered.

"Billy, take a deep breath and relax. I'm in bed, but I'm not asleep nor will I be asleep for sometime. I love my bed, and at night this is where I read or work. Tonight I'm reading. Okay?" Lucy said. "Now, what can I do for you?"

Billy took the next five minutes explaining about the girls' basketball team, their trip to state, and his dilemma about missing her class or missing the championship game. He finished by asking if she had any ideas how to solve the problem.

He heard her laugh under her breath as he rambled to a close. "You poor man. I hope you haven't wasted much time worrying about this. It's really not a problem. First of all, congratulations! Go and enjoy the game. If your girls lose, I'll see you Saturday morning. If they win, then give me a call and sometime next week, say maybe Wednesday evening, you can drive over to my house, and we can have a make up session while we have a nice dinner together. How does that sound?" she asked.

"That sounds great. Thank you. That helps tremendously," Billy said. "This would have to be for Boomer as well, you know."

There was brief pause before Lucy replied, "You can bring the big fella, or you can come get the lesson and take it back to him," she said speaking a little lower than before.

"Did I mention I like spending my evenings in bed?" she asked. "Do you know why?"

"Uh...no ma'am, I'm not sure I do," Billy said unsure of how to respond.

"Egyptian cotton. I have sheets with close to a thousand little threads woven together every square inch. Do you have any idea how soft that is?" Lucy asked, her voice becoming fainter.

"I really don't. I'm afraid I buy my sheets at Sears and get what's on sale," Billy confessed.

"There are very few things I have found in life that feel better than Egyptian cotton on my skin. Sliding between the sheets each night is almost like a romantic experience in itself. Let's pray your girls win; then, you can feel the softness for yourself," she said.

"Uh... I'd like that," Billy finally responded. "Thank you again, and I'll let you know how things go. "

"The pleasure's all mine," Lucy said as she hung up.

"What the hell was that?" Billy said to himself as he placed the phone back in the cradle.

38

Billy sat in the front seat of Boomer's Suburban as they joined the caravan of cars headed east on I-10. Beverly was in the back reading a magazine where she insisted she'd rather be "while you guys talk. " Most of the conversation, which had been minimal at best, was about Billy's conversation with Dr. Cruz the previous night and class the upcoming weekend. Billy hadn't shared the details, but assured Boomer that regardless of the outcome of the game, there was an option for them to still get credit for class. He did say that Lucy was very willing to accommodate.

Once they hit the interstate, Boomer had focused on finding the right speed to stay within the convoy and maintain enough space between him and the car in front. He knew passing would be an exercise in futility considering the mile long parade that stretched ahead of him unless he wanted to floor it until he took over lead of the convoy, which didn't appeal to him at all. He set a comfortable speed on his cruise and sat back with his left hand hanging over the top of the steering wheel and his right arm stretched across the back of Billy's seat.

Billy occasionally commented on the black and gold streamers tied to the reflectors along the highway at regular intervals and the signs that declared "Crabs!" "Lady Crabs!" and "Sand Crabs rule!" He wondered who had the patience to stop every mile or so to place the spirit lifters and if he would see them all the way to Austin. Billy was really more interested in the thoughts of people traveling from California to Houston, not being aware of the significance, and how they might interpret the signs. He laughed to himself imagining the conversations in the cars when the kids in the back asked dad what a crab was or a lady crab.

"Bev, do you know about Egyptian cotton and thread count?" Billy asked out of the blue. He had been replaying his conversation from the night before and asked the question before he realized he was talking out loud.

"Sure. Why?" she answered. Which caused Billy to have to get creative quickly.

"Well...uh...I think I need some new sheets," he responded. "Looking at some of the information, I keep seeing things like thread counts and cotton from Egypt. What does that mean?"

"Egyptian cotton is supposed to be softer than regular cotton. Do you know what kind of sheets you have now?" Bev said trying to be helpful.

"Cheapest thing Sears had on sale the last time I bought any," Billy confessed.

"You sound like a guy. I bet you have those little pills or rolly balls all over your bed," Bev said pretending to be disgusted.

"Well, since you mentioned it there might be a few," Billy said.

"You guys would sleep on sawdust if women weren't around to take care of you," Bev said. "You need at least a 200 thread count minimum to make the sheets soft. Four hundred is obviously better and, if you go higher, well you can figure that out. The more thread woven together the softer the sheets and less likely to pill up or scratch. If you want me to go with you to Bed Bath and Beyond while we're in Austin to help you find some, I will," she stated.

"No, I can do it, but thanks. I was just trying to get my information straight. We have a basketball tournament to win first," Billy turned and said across the back of the seat.

After ten miles of silence Billy said absently, "So 1000 thread count would be..."

"Overkill for a single guy, but any lady would appreciate the luxury. It would be like sleeping in melted butter," Bev finished his sentence for him.

"Melted butter," Billy repeated under his breath. "Hmmm."

A few miles past Junction, the line of cars from Waymor turned left onto Highway 290 that took them through Fredericksburg and Johnson City, home of LBJ, and on into the southwest corner of Austin. Several of the cars stopped to eat traditional German food in restaurants lining the highway through Fredericksburg while the majority pushed on to Austin. Billy and Boomer had agreed to wait and eat a little later so they could try out a place that had come highly recommended. It was called Chuy's and was located across the river and west from downtown on Barton Springs Road. The jalapeño dressing was supposed to be delicious and could be used to top any food a person ordered or eaten on chips by the bowl full.

The line of cars began to disperse once they drove into Austin city limits. The team was assigned rooms in a downtown hotel, but Billy and Boomer were staying out near Round Rock in an Embassy Suites that had happy hour every afternoon. It was also away from their fans and wasn't where the superintendent or board members were staying. The amount of money they would save on drinks and an evening meal would almost pay for their room.

Each car had a destination in mind for restaurants or to check into their selected hotel and found their exit as the dwindling convoy drove up Loop 1. Once everyone was settled, they met back at the Drum in time to be seen and be heard. Chuy's didn't disappoint and the Embassy Suites had two rooms ready when Boomer drove them into the drive. The happy hour would have to wait for the next night. Time allowed for drinking or basketball, but not both. The girls took top billing this weekend.

The buzzer sounded, ending the first game in their bracket as Billy found his seat on the front row overlooking the floor of Frank Erwin Center. Waymor's opponent on Saturday would be Devine who sank five free throws in the last minute to clinch the victory and a spot in the championship game. From what Billy had seen walking up the steps, he felt confident the Waymor girls could play with Devine. No doubt. Now they just had to get past the Hawks of Hardin-Jefferson.

The Waymor crowd had been on their feet since the girls ran out of the tunnel for their warm-up. Billy noticed a couple of extra police officers placed below them on the floor who were giving his fans extra attention while trying to decide who would be the troublemakers in the group. Located as they were in the upper deck, Billy felt confident no one would go over the railing. If the impulse struck a fan to attack, by the time anyone made their way up the stairs to the exit then down the stairs to the court, they would be met by force if they still had enough oxygen left to try to breach security.

The Lady Hawks supporters were equal in number, but this wasn't their first rodeo. They were no less excited, but had a controlled enthusiasm and were pacing themselves for the duration. Billy hoped that someday he and his crowd knew to do the same. It turned out to be a blessing that the Lady Crab fan base had shouted, whooped, and hollered during warm up. There were few opportunities for excitement and joy once the game began.

Savannah had her girls fundamentally prepared, but there was nothing she could do to prepare them mentally to handle a state play-off game. Their eyes were big as saucers, and they moved about the court as if they were in a daze. The Lady Hawks controlled the tip and scored a fast break layup taking a lead they would never relinquish. The Waymor girls turned the ball over the first three times up the court, once dribbling it off their foot and the other two times the defense took it away for easy layups. Savannah called her first time out less than two minutes into the game already trailing 8-0. The Lady Hawks bounced over to their coach while the Lady Crabs walked completely shell-shocked back to their bench.

Billy watched Savannah spend the entire time-out in the face of her players. She smiled, she screamed, she hugged them and patted their backs. She managed to get a half smile out of a couple of her girls, but still hadn't calmed all their nerves when the whistle blew to resume play. The Waymor fans did their best to help, loudly encouraging the girls as they walked back onto the floor. Pulling out all stops, the fans reached deep trying to

204

instill confidence and ward off the panic that had begun to creep in.

Waymor stabilized enough to stop the bleeding, but trailed by twelve at half. In what was a small victory, the Lady Crabs had been down fifteen, but hit a basket with a foul making a three-point play just before half. Using the momentum, Savannah clapped and praised them as they ran off the floor. Championships are won and lost during the first three minutes of the third quarter she told her girls after they had taken care of their business and sat in the chairs arranged in a semi circle inside the dressing room. Teams that came out and took control right after halftime won games and won championships. She promised her team if they won the championship minutes, they'd be playing on Saturday. They believed her and ran back on the floor determined.

The Waymor fans that had spent the last twenty minutes in the restrooms or at the concession stand were back in their seats ready to support their girls and were thrilled to see a different look in the eyes of the players. Energized with new hope the chants started immediately and lasted until the Lady Hawks ran off six straight points and Savannah called time out. She had been right about champions. She had just been wrong about who it would be.

The remainder of the game passed quietly. The Lady Hawks were methodical as they dissected the Lady Crabs defense. The Hawk defense occasionally allowed points but only sporadically. Subs were eventually sent into the game to gain experience for the Lady Crabs and make sure their names showed up in the box scores for historical reasons. The Lady Hawks had a game on Saturday and rested their starters most of the fourth quarter. Neither crowd wasted much more energy, but watched confident of the outcome. Then it was over.

Coaches argued all the time whether it was better to get beat by one or by twenty. Does a good old fashion tail whuppin' take away the doubts and the questions about what might have been? In the end it didn't matter which was better. The Waymor Lady Crabs and their fans had been beaten fair and square with no doubt left as to who was the better team. It didn't stop the tears and the sadness for parents who had watched their child play their last game. It didn't stop the hugs and emotional support they shared with each other. While the girls ran to the dressing room after the handshakes, wiping tears from their eyes, the fans spent several minutes assuring each other that the season had been amazing, and their girls were still number one in their hearts.

Once an adequate amount of mourning had been done, the majority of the Waymor faithful left to explore the haunts of Austin looking for cold beer and live music. They would have to go home the next day, back to the life they knew and weren't necessarily happy with. One last fling was necessary. The parents and a few of the loyal fans closest to the girls walked out of the Drum and waited patiently by the dressing room door for Savannah and the players to emerge. The men jingled the change in their pockets and the ladies talked about the food they'd had for lunch and discussed how it might have been made. Billy stood off to the side by Boomer and Bev.

The girls eventually emerged dressed, carrying their game bags, but with red swollen eyes. As they found their parents, the tears and hugs began all over again. Savannah was the last one out, and her eyes showed signs of tears as well. She accepted a few congratulations for a great season from the fans closest to the door, and then she skirted the crowd to make her way over to Bev and Boomer. Billy watched as she allowed Bev to embrace her and pat her back for several seconds while whispering softly in her ear. Boomer lifted her off the ground in a giant bear hug as he told her how proud he was. When he finally set her down, Billy leaned over and wrapped one arm around her shoulder and offered his congratulations as well. She looked at him through tears and thanked him for coming.

The next few minutes were spent reliving the game and since the highlight reel was fairly short that conversation died quickly. Several of the girls came over to ask where the team was planning to eat so their parents could follow and one asked if she knew yet when they'd be going back home. Savannah promised a group wide report shortly.

"Uncle Corliss, do you think it would be alright if I let the girls stay for the rest of the tournament? It would be good for them to see the other teams play and honestly I really think they earned it," Savannah asked. She could have asked for a new car and he wouldn't have refused her.

"I think that would be a great idea," Boomer said. "Do you have a problem with it Billy?"

"I think it's a great idea as well," Billy agreed.

"Let me run it past Cracker Jack. We budget funds for play off travel each year and have never had a chance to spend them. I think it's high time we did," Boomer said as he took Bev's hand and started walking around the crowd where Cracker Jack was talking to a couple of the board members.

Savannah scooted next to Billy and leaned against his side. "I just feel so bad for the girls. They were so upset with themselves and felt like they had let me down. It took a long time before they were convinced I wasn't mad at them and was actually proud," Savannah told him as he wrapped his arm around her shoulder again.

"You should be proud. What a run you had. You'll never have to buy another meal in Waymor that's for sure. The fans love you, the girls love you, you can write your own ticket," Billy said as he hugged her closer with his right arm emphasizing his words.

"What about you, Billy?" she asked.

"Me? My fifteen minutes of fame were up a long time ago. I'll be paying my own way from here on out," he laughed.

Silence was not what he had expected. Maybe a punch in the arm or sarcastic comeback, but silence was all he got.

Savannah turned to face him running her arms around his waist. He looked down and saw that she wasn't in a joking mood. He put both arms around her to steady himself and hold her close as well.

"What about you Billy? You said everyone loved me, does that mean you love me as well?' she asked quietly looking straight into his eyes.

"You know I do," Billy said after a moment.

"Do I?" she asked. "Sometimes I don't even know if you are my friend or just my boss. I haven't seen you in weeks, and I really thought we had a good time the Sunday you came for lunch. You said we could do it again."

Billy decided to put a little thought into his next response. He realized this conversation had moved away from basketball and the ramifications of a misspoken word could be huge.

"You need to remember that you've have been awfully busy becoming a legend in this town. With your schedule, and Boomer and I taking classes, there just hasn't been a lot of free time. I haven't forgotten the offer of rhubarb pie," Billy said hoping to justify his obvious avoidance of her the past two months.

"So do you love me?" Savannah asked again direct and unblinking.

Billy never got the chance to answer. Boomer walked up with Bev in tow to find them locked in an embrace.

"Are you okay, Sugar?' he asked thinking Billy was having to console her.

"I guess I'm taking this as hard as the girls," Savannah said as she wiped a tear from her eye and disentangled herself from Billy.

"It's hard, but you'll see. The sun will come up tomorrow and everyone will remember how much fun it was to get here," Boomer said offering his best pep talk. "Anyway, Cracker Jack gave the okay, with the blessing of the school board president. Use the credit card you have to cover your meals. Just remember to keep it reasonable, get receipts, and no alcohol on the tickets."

"Uncle Corliss!" Savannah said as she rolled her eyes. "Thank you for letting us stay. I know the girls will be excited."

Savannah waded into the crush of players and parents to let them all know where the team would be eating dinner and surprised them with the news about staying through Saturday. Spirits brightened considerably. The players piled on the bus and a smaller convoy of parents and fans followed it south across the river towards the restaurant.

Early the next morning Boomer loaded his and Beverly's suitcase into the back of the Suburban and held the door while

208

Billy placed his suitcase along side. Beverly was already in the back seat thumbing though her choices of reading material. They had chosen to eat at the breakfast buffet before checking out and wistfully looked over where happy hour would be in full swing in a few hours. Maybe next time Billy thought.

Billy had intentionally chosen not to call Dr. Cruz until later in the morning to insure she wasn't in the process of having a romantic experience with her sheets.

They stopped in Junction a couple of hours down the road for a stretch break and to get gas. Billy used the pay phone and dialed Lucy's number from the card he carried in his billfold.

"Lucy, this is Billy," he said when she answered.

"Hi, Billy. How's Austin?" she asked.

"Austin is great, but our girls are not I'm afraid. We lost last night so Boomer and I will be in class tomorrow," Billy explained.

"Well that's a shame," she said.

"It is. They're heartbroken," he replied.

"Maybe you can come by and see me some other time," Lucy said.

Billy realized they were having two different conversations.

"Hopefully so," he said. "I'll see you in the morning. "

They said their goodbyes and Billy walked back to the Suburban thinking about thread count and Egyptian cotton again.

39

The weekend in Alpine had passed uneventfully. He spent a lot of the class time thinking about his conversation with Savannah. It had unnerved him, and he realized he had been too casual with her and her feelings were stronger than he realized. When he reached a point that he found himself going in circles, he switched topics and thought about Dallas and whether she would be leaving town.

During the first break of the morning on Saturday, he had tried to talk to Dr. Cruz, but Margaret had an extended question that dominated the entire break. Billy had stood quietly by for a few minutes until it became obvious she wouldn't be finished anytime soon, so he went on to the restroom and grabbed a bottle of water.

When the class was dismissed for lunch, Billy hung back until he could have a minute of Dr. Cruz's time.

"Hi Billy. Good to see you," she said.

"Look, I want to thank you again for being willing to work with us about missing. I was going to tell you earlier, but Margaret seemed to need extra attention," Billy said with a touch of spitefulness.

"Now Billy, you be nice to Margaret. Somebody needs to be the teacher's pet and try as I might, you don't seem to be interested in the job," Dr. Cruz said with a smile as she snapped her briefcase closed and started walking towards the door.

Billy followed her out.

"Anyway, thanks. It's nice to know you were willing. That might be helpful down the road," Billy said.

"Being willing could be very helpful down the road," Dr. Cruz said as she climbed into her car and shut the door.

40

There were five days left before spring break. Billy was secretly glad the whole basketball extravaganza was behind them and as he stood in the hallway on Monday morning, Billy hoped the week would pass quietly. It would not. Every student and teacher wanted to relive each moment of their trip to Austin and some even went back to the playoff games leading up to the state tournament. The girls were hailed as heroes and, since the agony of defeat had long since passed, celebration filled the hallways.

Billy listened and responded to each comment that was made in his direction, but was glad when the tardy bell rang to start first period. He walked back to his office to drink coffee and stare out the window. Savannah was sitting in the chair across from Ms. Dixie who was asking her questions about the trip. Both ladies smiled when he came in.

"I guess having celebrities in the house makes for a rowdy morning," Billy said.

"This little celebrity would like a minute of your time," Ms. Dixie said nodding in Savannah's direction.

"Sure. Come on in," Billy said leading the way.

Savannah followed Billy into his office closing the door behind her and took a seat facing him across his desk. She looked at him and smiled as she picked at the nail polish on one of her fingers. She appeared to be extremely uneasy and not knowing what was coming, Billy decided his best bet was to wait. Savannah was working up the courage to say what needed to be said.

"I needed to talk to you first thing this morning...uh.... hmm... Johnny B Good is watching my class. Just so you know," she said still hesitating.

"Okay. This seems serious," Billy said.

"I think it is," she agreed and then waited.

Billy waited patiently and then said, "You remember we're friends, right?"

She nodded.

"You can talk to me. I've seen your high school yearbook, and I know about your senior prank," Billy said as he tried to relax her.

She smiled halfheartedly.

"I've been offered another job," Savannah finally blurted out.

Billy had been expecting a confession about being arrested in Austin, maybe getting drunk in her hotel room. Her buying the girls drinks on the school credit card. He was not expecting that. He was relieved at first, but then realized why it was difficult for her to share. She was leaving.

"Congratulations," he said and stopped, not sure what else to say.

"Yesterday the athletic director at Frenship called and offered me a job. Frenship is a school district right outside of Lubbock. Its small now, but has a high growth rate, with the population of Lubbock moving in their direction. He's projecting they'll move up in classification every two years with the realignment until they are in the large school division," Savannah repeated the sales pitch like she had heard it the day before. Once she had started talking, it seemed she couldn't stop. "I would be the head girls' basketball coach and the girls' athletic coordinator. One

211

sport and an administrator's job. He assured me this would be a career move that would set me up for years to come. He had heard how successful our year was. Also, if they build more high schools, I would be first choice for the district girls' athletic director's job. That's something he suspects might happen in the next six to eight years. " Savannah kept ticking off the boxes of all the plusses. "I would be minutes away from Lubbock where many of the teachers actually live. I could shop in Lubbock and have access to all the entertainment available not to mention Texas Tech is there. A college town."

At this point Billy felt like she could have been the Chamber of Commerce Director for the town. She had the presentation down pat.

When she finally stopped to catch her breath Billy said, "That is an amazing opportunity. Congratulations again. You earned it."

Savannah had been talking to her hands that were in her lap and occasionally still picked at the irritating piece of nail polish that had come loose. She had never once looked up to see Billy's response. She just nodded at his praise.

"Do Boomer and Bev know?" Billy finally asked.

"We talked about it last night," Savannah said.

"What did they think?" he asked.

"They're excited for me. They'll miss me. It's an opportunity of a lifetime. I'm like their kid leaving home. They'd be sad, but glad," she said basically replaying the back and forth they'd had.

"I can see how they'd miss you. Having you stay this year had to be good for them, but you know this is how it works, right? You do well; you get promoted. Getting promoted means better jobs and better pay. You did super so people are noticing," Billy said. "And yet, you don't seem that excited."

Savannah shrugged her shoulders still staring at her hands.

"No one is going to be mad at you," Billy tried to assure her.

"I'll stay if you ask me to," Savannah said quietly never raising her head.

Billy finally understood.

After silence dominated the room too long, Billy stood up and walked around the desk. He reached down for her hand, which

212

she placed in his. He lifted her to her feet and pulled her into an embrace. Only then did she look at him. She had tears welled in each eye being held by the slightest resistance, poised to roll down her cheeks.

As he held her firmly, Billy said, "I love you too much kiddo to ask you to stay. " He heard a sniff and knew the tears had won. "You've out grown us here in Waymor. You're a star that is too bright for the desert. It would be selfish on my part to even think about asking you to give up the chance to shine. We can't come close to offering you anything better."

After a couple of more sniffs Savannah said, "If I could have you, it would be worth it."

Billy waited for a long moment trying to find the right way to say what he needed to say. "It may seem like a good idea now, but down the road you would hate me. You would. I'd hate myself. You need to go. You'll meet friends and people you can talk to your own age. You'll have a social life in addition to a great job. You have to go," he said plainly.

Her tears continued for a couple of minutes. Billy felt the wetness seep through his shirt. He didn't mind. He suspected this would be the last time he held her. He felt like crying himself. She finally patted his chest with both hands and backed away, rubbing her eyes with her fingers. Billy reached for the Kleenex box he kept handy for students that found themselves overwhelmed by the unfairness of his office. She took a couple and blotted her tears dry and then wiped her nose. She was a mess of swollen eyes and a runny nose, but didn't seem to care.

"Okay," she said.

Billy asked about the details and found Frenship wanted her to start the Monday following spring break if possible or as soon after that as Waymor would allow. They needed her to be part of the hiring process for other girl coaches and spring practices coming up. Billy nodded. He had gotten her to the point where she needed to be. He couldn't afford to get emotional about her imminent departure.

"Look. You go write up a letter of resignation explaining your opportunity and address it to the superintendent. I'll work with

Boomer and Cracker Jack to see how soon we can let you go. I'll come find you when I have an answer, okay?" Billy asked.

She nodded and wiped her eyes once again. He took her hand one last time and assured her this was best. She was doing the right thing. She smiled weakly as she let go, opened the door, and left.

Ms. Dixie waited until Billy had followed Savannah out into the hall and watched as she walked away. When he turned back to face her she said, "Can I assume the world has found out about our secret?"

"I'm afraid so. It's hard to hide talent," Billy said. "I need to call Cracker."

Cracker took the news almost as hard as Billy. He not only had been proud of the job Savannah had done, but knew a young lady of her caliber was hard to find. She would not be easy to replace.

He agreed that if Billy and Boomer could cover the rest of the year, they'd release Savannah to take the job. The consensus was she had earned it, and one didn't hold back a rising star for selfish reasons.

Boomer was as moody as an old woman, and Billy felt sure Bev was distraught. Doing the right thing didn't make letting her go any easier. Billy sympathized as they went through the motions. The long-term sub that had covered for Billy at the first of the year was brought back to finish the year. Johnny B Good agreed to move back over for the spring to cover the girls.

Billy didn't see Savannah after letting her know the district would release her with gratitude. She would work with Ms. Dixie to check out.

Billy had planned on taking a trip during the break. He hoped to go back to Austin for a couple of nights of happy hour and live music followed by some beach time at South Padre Island. Thinking of the coeds that migrated south during the annual bacchanal had excited Billy. Instead, he found himself wandering around his apartment lethargically for several days. He sat in a lawn chair dressed in gym shorts and a tank top in the parking lot to catch some of the spring sunshine in between sand

214

storms and finished more than one bottle of tequila. His meals were sporadic and sparse.

He told himself that not having to drive the hundreds of miles and avoiding the stress and worry of work was like a vacation. Plus it was cheaper. And required less effort. He was very convincing.

On the Wednesday of spring break, a card arrived in the mail. It was a thank you note from Savannah. The words were meaningful and signed with a heart. She was gone.

41

Just as quickly as it started, spring came to an abrupt end during the first week of May. This was earlier than normal, but nobody seemed to mind. Each day large clouds gathered in the southwest and promised refreshing rain to the sand covered town that needed a cleansing bath. Billy stood on the steps of the high school gym at 7:30 P. M. sharp on the second Saturday of May dressed in his only suit. He stood next to Dallas who looked the part of a June bride. She was golden brown and glowing. She wore an evening gown that fit her like a picture in a magazine. Billy had less than expertly pinned a corsage of white roses to the thin strap that served more as decoration than actual support. Dixie was kind enough to fix it correctly once they had arrived.

Billy and Dallas stood at the top of the red carpet that was unfurled from the curb of the bus lane to the gym door. Students arrived as couples in the best ride they could beg or borrow, were announced like royalty, and had their walk recorded for posterity by a paparazzi of parents and neighbors needing a night of excitement. A waiting valet drove the car away to make room for the next set of celebrities.

Prom was the highlight of each school year. Graduation was a close second, but then that was caps and gowns with boring stuff like diplomas. This was prom dresses and red carpets, a chance to feel special for the whole night of eating and dancing before finding an after party where the punch was spiked.

The week and half after spring break Billy had gone through the motions of his job and responsibilities without much enthusiasm. When people had asked, he waved it off as flu like symptoms even though flu season in the desert had long since passed. On a Wednesday afternoon at straight up four o'clock, Ms. Dixie dropped her folder filled with papers needing a signature on his desk and said, "You need to get your head out of your ass," and walked out. She didn't see him nod in agreement.

Billy sat in the back row of chairs set up in the fellowship hall for prayer meeting. He was early, one of the first to arrive. He had showered, put on pressed jeans and his favorite blue shirt. With the weather still cool, but warming, Billy chose not to wear a jacket. With the circulation problems the majority of the faithful had, the thermostat was regularly turned well past comfort level for the young and healthy.

Billy had not been to prayer meeting since Dallas had carved up his face with her keys except for a couple of rare occasions. Even though they had seen each other several times since January and peace pies and tamales had been exchanged, an uneasy truce seemed to linger. Her job offer hung in the air like the other shoe waiting to drop. He had no idea if she had made up her mind, but remembered her deadline was fast approaching.

The older members stopped to shake his hand reintroducing themselves and welcoming him, unaware they had met before. He didn't fault them. He was the one that had been negligent and erased himself from their memories. The pastor was kind enough to tell him what a great year the school was having and how about those basketball girls. He finished with what a shame about losing "our" coach. Billy agreed with his observations.

Dallas walked in carrying a large cake dish five minutes before the scheduled start time. After placing the cake on the serving table next to the coffeepot, she made her way to where Billy was sitting. He wasn't sure she had seen him, didn't know whether to wave, and was anxious as to how she might respond. Dallas never missed step and slid right into the chair next to him.

Over the course of the next forty-five minutes the pastor spoke of the opportunity that spring brought, a chance for new growth, and a renewal of spirit. Many of the congregation still had sand behind their ears, in the corners of the eyes, and in crevices of an undisclosed nature from the most recent wave of dirt that had swirled across the desert. Those present chose not to scoff, but to understand he was speaking metaphorically about a place they had all read about where trees and flowers bloomed from the refreshing rains. Eden they assumed.

Prayers for rain dominated the prayer chain; refreshing, cleansing rain. A few mentioned the sick, the elderly, and one parent prayed for a new basketball coach to help the girls go back to Austin. She received more Amens than the rain did. The prayers were offered and received, Billy assumed, so they were dismissed for coffee and cake.

"Haven't seen you around here in a while," Dallas said as they stood apart waiting their turn. "Word on the street is you've had the flu."

"I'm okay. It's has been a while, and I've missed it ... and seeing you." Billy said.

They stood quietly for a few minutes both searching for the right words and tone.

"I came to ask you a favor," Billy finally said.

"Okay," Dallas replied turning to face him giving him her full attention.

"Would you go with me to prom?" he asked.

Dallas almost burst out laughing. If she'd had coffee, she probably would have spilt it. The she saw he was serious.

"You really mean it. Me go with you to prom," She said.

"Yeah. I'm going and would like to take you as my date. I'll buy you a corsage and everything," Billy added with a smile.

"Seriously?" she asked waiting for the punch line.

"Would you like for me to get down on one knee?" he asked.

"Absolutely not. I think that's just for marriage proposals any way. There might be a few older people here that might not live through the shock," she said adamantly.

"So will you?" he asked again.

"Look, I don't even have a fancy dress to wear. I don't know if I even have a dress period. Can't you ask Dixie or one of the teachers?" Dallas asked.

"Well, for starters, Dixie is married. And so are the other teachers at school. I'm not sure that it would be appropriate for me to ask out a married woman. Secondly, you're the one I want to take," Billy explained.

"Oh brother. Where's that little coach when you need her," Dallas said more to herself than anyone.

"I would like for you to go with me, and I would like to buy you a dress as well. And a corsage," Billy stated.

Dallas stood and looked at Billy for a while, the debate raging in her head. Billy waited patiently not planning on being denied.

"Okay," she finally said.

After they had eaten their cake and cleaned up the empty dish, Billy walked Dallas to her car and thanked her for accepting his invitation. They made plans to drive to Midland to find the perfect dress the following weekend. It had taken the whole day. Dallas would have bought the first dress she tried on, but Billy wasn't prepared to settle for any thing less than the perfect dress. He insisted that she continue to try on and model each possibility. She finally embraced the insanity and each new dress became a whirl and twirl event spiced up with runway poses of the rich and famous.

Billy finally found what he had been looking for in a bridal shop even though Dallas had almost refused to enter. The dress that caught Billy's attention looked white at first glance, but was the lightest shade of pink that the sales lady called rose gold and was accented with small designs of lace. The sales lady described the material and design in detail to Billy while Dallas whirled and twirled in front of the mirror. She could have been talking a foreign language as far as he was concerned. Billy imagined it was the kind of dress someone getting married barefoot in a meadow or on the beach might wear. It was simple, ankle length, and flowed over Dallas' body like water. The sales lady assured them it was a wedding dress, but could be worn as an evening gown if they chose to use it that way.

All Billy knew was that it fit Dallas perfectly. It was simple, elegant, and the prettiest dress he had ever seen. Maybe it was Dallas that made the dress beautiful, he thought. Either way it was the look he had been waiting for. The sales lady happily

218

rang up the sale. After finding the right shoes to match the dress in case Dallas chose not to go barefoot, they celebrated with steak and cold beer before driving home in the dark across the desert. Billy was exhausted, but pleased. Dallas spun the knob on the radio hoping to find one clear station. Her expression alternated between happy and bemused.

As they stood next to the gym door, more than one person mentioned that they looked like the topper on a wedding cake. "What a nice couple they made" was the comment of the rest. Billy was proud of his date and for himself for making sure she had the right dress. And corsage.

The afternoon cloudbank that normally slid around to the north or south held steady as the red carpet procession continued. A cool breeze swept though the crowd off the front of the storm as a warning. Dresses that had cost parents a semester's worth of college tuition along with their hairdos that had taken hours were in jeopardy.

Billy left Dallas standing under the awning and started with the emcee that happened to be the pastor with the most officious voice. He then moved to the parents overseeing the drive up and unloading. Word was spread rapidly down the line that the process was about to speed up for their own sake and not to tarry getting out of their cars. No longer was one couple at a time allowed on the red carpet. As soon as one car unloaded, another pulled up.

Double-timing the unloading, the last couple entered the gym as the first raindrops fell. Billy, who had moved Dallas and her dress inside earlier, stepped up and closed the doors behind the last students like Noah in the Ark before the flood. He watched the great mass of citizens being pelted with raindrops as they grabbed their aluminum folding chairs and scrambled for their cars. Inside, the music was loud, the food was delicious, and everyone was dry. His job was done. With a beautiful woman on his arm, he could now stroll through the crowd, snack on a wide variety of food, and simply be present. Teachers and sponsors were assigned to make sure the evening went well, and he would allow them to do their job.

After circling the dance floor a couple of times acknowledging the adults posted randomly around the gym, Billy steered Dallas to a dark corner and found them a chair where they could sit and eat their shrimp, stuffed crab, stuffed baked potato, and chocolate covered fruit chunks. They sipped on lemon flavored sparkling punch.

"Do kids still spike the punch bowl?" Dallas asked.

"As in when you were growing up?" Billy half yelled over the music.

"Maybe," she answered with a smile.

"I have Boomer and Paddy both assigned to the punch bowl table. Only one can leave at a time. If someone can get past them, I guess they can spike it if they want to," Billy announced proudly.

"You're such a spoiled sport. Where's the fun in that?" she asked.

"It's hell being the responsible one," Billy assured her.

"So what if I wanted to spike my own drink?" Dallas asked teasingly.

"Then you would have to go to my office and open the third drawer on the left side of my desk. You would find a bottle of vodka confiscated earlier this evening from a student trying to subvert tonight's pleasantries," Billy explained. "At least that's the official story should anyone ask why there's a bottle in my desk."

"You do plan ahead cowboy, now don't you?" Dallas said admiringly.

"It could be a late evening with the storm and all. Shall we?" Billy asked as he stood and held out his hand. He led her through a gym door located behind the bleachers and into a back hallway. Having a master key allowed them to circumvent the crowd and arrive across from his office unseen.

With the lights off, enjoying the ambient light from the street and the occasional flash of lightening, Billy and Dallas sat side-by-side and sipped from their plastic glass of spiked punch. The music that was filtered through several walls and down a hundred feet of hallway was now playing at a comfortable level.

"I'm not leaving," Dallas said out of the quiet that had engulfed them. "I called my friends last week and took a pass on the security job."

"I've been wanting to ask, but I decided you'd tell me when you got ready. Are you okay with that?" Billy asked.

"I am. I gave it a lot of thought, and realized I've seen the world, and the people I like the best are here. I would have made more money, but I make enough and I'd rather be happy." Dallas explained.

Silence settled in once again. Lightening continued to flash followed by rolls of thunder. The streets were almost covered with water. Wet refreshing cleansing rain.

"Can I ask you a favor?' Billy broke the silence after several minutes.

"The last time I said yes to one of your favors I wound up in a wedding dress sipping vodka out a plastic cup," Dallas said shaking her head.

"Winner, winner," Billy said. "Double or nothing?"

With feigned disgust Dallas said, "Sure. Why not?"

"Just hear me out," Billy said as his opening statement. He wasn't sure how organized his thoughts would be on the spur of the moment, but he had ever intention of saying them. "First of all, you look beautiful. I said it earlier, but I need you to know, I can't take my eyes off of you."

"Is that you or the vodka talking?" Dallas asked.

"It's me, with the vodka giving me permission and a nudge," Billy said. "I've screwed up the last six months terribly, and I'm sorry. I had a great time with you last fall and to be honest didn't see our...uh... breakup coming. I know now that I probably gave you good reason to smash me in the face with your keys, carving me up like a turkey."

"Oh, brother," Dallas said as she rolled her eyes.

"Anyway, since you told me you might be leaving on New Years Day, I've been struggling. I wanted to ask you to stay. I wanted to ask for another chance, but I never could decide what was the right thing to do. I needed you to make up your own mind. Now that you have and you're staying...can I have another chance? I'll do it right this time. I promise," Billy said.

After several minutes of silence, Dallas asked, "What about your little coach friend?"

"Fair question," Billy said. "I've asked myself the same thing. She's a sweet girl, attractive, and has a great personality. I enjoyed talking to her...."

You're not helping yourself. I don't have keys, but I do have that stapler on your desk," Dallas said.

"Please, hear me out," Billy said and hurried on. "She's perfect in everyway except...she's not you. You see every time I was with her or thought about her, I found I was always using you as a measuring stick. Comparing. I've known all along that you're the one. You're the one."

"So why the moody blues when she left?" Dallas asked. "Maybe I'm the one because I'm the only one left."

"I assumed you were leaving from the start, and then when Savannah left, I guess I was feeling sorry for myself," Billy said. "I was losing a good friend, and also the woman I loved. I had my own little pity party. Dixie kind of kicked me in the rear, and I decided I should at least go down fighting. Look, tonight, the dress... was about several things. I wanted to show you what I do. I think I'm good at this job. I wanted you to see me among the kids and adults I work with everyday. I like it...and I think they like me. This is what I want to do. I also wanted them to see you. With me. Dressed up. The most beautiful woman in the room. I wanted you to see us as a couple and how well we fit together. Honestly...I was hoping it would make you want to stay."

Billy looked out the windows at the receding storm. The rain had stopped and he noticed some of the students were already leaving for an after party.

"I don't expect you to take my word for it. I'm only asking for a chance to prove it," Billy said.

Dallas sat quietly as he refilled their glasses and took a sip from his. She finally stood up and faced Billy, hiking her dress up to her knees and straddled his legs. She took his face in her hand and kissed him hard on the lips as he wrapped his arms around her and pulled her tight.

After several minutes she sat back on his knees with her palms on his chest and said, "I may have been a little irrational at times.... and might be again. If you can handle that, then...."

He pulled her close and kissed her again.

42

Betty Daniels walked the senior class through graduation practice on the football field Friday morning. The maintenance crew had erected a stage, chairs, and a podium at the fifty-yard line facing the east bleachers. The idea was to start graduation on Saturday morning by 9 A.M. so the crowd and graduates were shaded by the bleachers long enough to finish the ceremony before the sun rose high enough to do much damage. Adjustments had been made over the years to cut down on the number of heat related casualties. The graveside burial tents from the local funeral home had ironically proven to be a lifesaver for many of the elderly who were seated in the shade on the track. If they perceived foreshadowing, they didn't show it. Blessed shade was their main focus.

Betty was the student council sponsor in addition to her duties as department head and teacher. She had steered over thirty graduations successfully. Her advice to Billy was to pay attention and stay out of the way. He promised to do both.

Friday was a workday for teachers while the students had been released for the summer. Teachers that weren't part of Betty's elite graduation squad could leave when their grades had been turned in along with keys and others items on the end of year checklist. Many left the parking lot soon after 9 A.M. Some had tried to turn in their grades before finals were even over. Billy kept his mouth shut and stayed out of the way. Dixie handled the faculty.

After Betty was sure the students understood what they were supposed to do and when, she dismissed them with a reminder about arrival time and dress code for the following day. She then called Billy over and asked if he knew where to sit, when to stand, and what to say. He felt fairly sure he did, but when he didn't readily assure her with his words or body language, she reminded him she would be behind the students directing the program to its finish. She could cue him if he got lost. Billy thanked her for her dedication and diligence as he started the walk back towards his office. He really needed to think about what he was going to say. Tonight he really should get on that.

It was almost 11 A.M. and the line out of the office door had dwindled to a relative few waiting for Ms. Dixie to sign off on their form and set them free. The English teachers were still hours away from even thinking about checking out and a couple would have to come back on Monday to finish up. That would forever remain a mystery to Billy.

As he slipped past the line and through his office door, he saw a large box on his desk. It was wrapped with a red bow, and the card read Happy Boss's Day. He wondered what the gift was all about as he opened the card and saw signatures of a number of the teachers, some adding comments. He skimmed the messages and when he got to the bottom he noticed Dixie's and surprisingly, Dallas' signatures and comments.

As he finished the card he looked up and saw Ms. Dixie standing beside him. Ninja. How she did that he did not know.

"So what's with the present?" Billy asked as he calmed the adrenaline rush she had caused by sneaking up on him once again.

"Boss's Day," she said.

"I always thought we use to pitch in a dollar for the boss in the fall sometime," Billy said.

"Normally we do. And some pitch in more than a dollar. This year no one expected you to last, so we didn't bother getting you a gift. By the time everyone figured out you might make it, well, it just never seemed to be the right time until now," Ms. Dixie explained.

"I appreciate the overwhelming vote of confidence," Billy said sarcastically. "With so many pulling for me, how could I have failed?"

"If you're honest, you didn't believe in yourself," Ms. Dixie said.

"No ma'am. I didn't think this day would ever come. I have you to thank for that. This present should be yours," Billy said. He reached over and gave her a hug.

Dixie smiled and patted his back. "Congratulations. One year as a high school principal. Open it."

Billy untied the large bow and slipped a fingernail through the tape. He lifted a pair of leather pants out first and then a leather top. He realized it was motorcycle leathers. In the bottom was a pair of gloves.

"We got your sizes from Boomer from when he ordered your coaching gear. We added in a little extra for all the pie you've been eating this year. The boots are on you. We didn't even consider trying to pick those," Dixie explained.

"I'm tired of people staring when we ride down the highway. No more riding in back dressed like a clown. Who knows, maybe you'll want to get your own bike," Dallas said from where she stood just inside the door. He hadn't heard her walk in either. Damn these Grant women.

"Wow. I don't know what to say. This is...well...it's very generous," Billy finally said.

"Donations covered some of it. Dallas and Cracker Jack made up the difference. We all are happy for you. You've come a long way," Dixie said.

43

Graduation was a day everyone looked forward to, mainly because it meant the end to another school year and the beginning of summer or at least work with no students around. Billy had always been ready for the end of a school year as a coach and graduation was something the coaches attended to show their face, but as soon as the hats went in the air, they were gone to the golf course to celebrate. This year...Billy had to be on stage...and speak. He had dreaded the day simply because he wasn't sure how he would respond to standing in front of the crowd seated in the east bleachers of the football stadium with the students on the track in front of him...and the superintendent and school board behind him!

Betty Daniels and her crack squad of graduation specialist were ready and every movement had been scripted. Student Council members did most of the setup and different teachers had the responsibility of lining students up and checking for unneeded items or possible shenanigans. Billy's main role in the overall scheme of things was to welcome everyone and present the class.

When Betty handed him the program for the graduation ceremony a couple of weeks ago, he was surprised. It never occurred to him he might have to speak. When Betty went over the program with him, he decided, "Welcome. Thanks for coming" and "here is this year's class" would suffice. He could handle that. Ms. Dixie came in about a week ahead of time to make sure he understood the "depth" of his role after he had may more than one casual remark about "welcome" and "here you go." She had not been amused.

Ms. Dixie's dedication and love for Waymor High was well known. Billy had understood that more and more with each passing day she had spent mentoring him throughout the past year. She expected him to represent the school and himself in the best possible light. Ms. Dixie had sat across from him and asked him to respect the ceremony and to plan to offer heartfelt thoughts about the parents and townsfolk present as well as extended family that had traveled to attend. Most of all she felt he needed to speak of encouragement and hope to the graduates, giving them words to take with them as they leave. She was impassioned and he was convinced, but at a loss as to what he might possibly say.

Dixie really put him on the spot by talking about how The Rock had marred the whole ceremony with his apathetic and pathetic presence. Coming from Ms. Dixie these were as harsh of words as he had heard her speak. He could tell she felt betrayed by Donnie C and had placed her hopes in Billy.

Billy had promised to do the very best he could and allowed her to offer any suggestions she might have.

"Mr. Masters, I have watched you and listened to you for the last nine months. I can say this with no hesitation. You have a good heart, you were raised right, and you have a compassionate spirit. I would suggest you look at the parents in the stands as they sit proudly, and you look at the faces of the seniors on the track, and speak from the heart…and you'll be just fine," Ms. Dixie had assured him.

Billy hadn't slept since.

He made some notes and wrote several variations of what he thought sounded good, but each time they turned out lame or stilted. He used references and quotes that sounded wise and inspiring. He tried serious, and he tried funny. He did not find what he wanted. Billy finally decided that this whole year he had trusted Ms. Dixie, and she had never been wrong.

When the time came he found himself nervous, but very much in control and motivated to honor those present…and Ms. Dixie. He spoke a warm welcome to all those that had joined them on a bright sunny morning and prior to presenting the class, he talked to them as if they were his own children. He finished several minutes later by wishing them well and asking for God's blessings on them. Betty Daniels, standing behind the students on the track with her binder opened and marked like a director of a Broadway play, gave him a thumbs up. The diploma covers were presented, the band played, the students prayed, hats were thrown, and that was that.

After shaking hands with Cracker Jack and the board members who congratulated him on his year and a fine ceremony, he walked back to the office, loosening his tie and carrying his jacket over his arm. The sun now imposed itself on the day. Sitting at her desk, Ms. Dixie was clearing away the last remnants of the school year. She smiled when he came in and simply said, "Thank you, that was a refreshing change." She couldn't have said anything that would have meant more. He thought he might like graduation more than he had imagined.

Cracker Jack poked his head in the door just as Billy filed away his notes and locked his desk.

"Great job, Billy Boy! I believe you are a natural!" he boomed. "Another year in the books!"

"Thank you," Billy said with more than a little satisfaction. "Betty's a life saver. She's a real pro."

"She definitely can organize your life, if you let her. Believe me, I know. Now what the hell are doing here? We tee off in one hour, and you still have to pick up your lunch at the clubhouse. If you're going to be my partner, I need you ready to go. I'm undefeated and sure as hell ain't going to start losing by dragging your sorry ass around the course," Cracker exclaimed.

"I guess I'm not sure what you're talking about," said Billy a little confused.

"Hell, it's the annual graduation day golf scramble out at the country club. You coaches ain't the only ones who sneak off and play. All administrators, board members, and a few town folks are lined up because today we graduate. Then we celebrate, and you're with me so get moving!" boomed Cracker.

Billy didn't wait to be asked twice. He rushed out the door stopping only long enough to ask Ms. Dixie if there was anything else he was supposed to be doing. She smiled, told him to have fun and help Cracker win, and not show up on Monday until 8 o'clock. After thanking her once again, Billy dashed down the hall smiling as went to change clothes and grab his clubs.

Cracker Jack Daniels slid into the chair opposite Ms. Dixie's desk and said, "So Dixie girl, what do you think of our boy? Do we want to try and keep him around for another year?"

"Absolutely. I believe he's a keeper," Dixie said with a smile.

"Do you see any problems we need to fix," asked Cracker.

"I only see two problems," Ms. Dixie said. "He's dating my sister, which is always dangerous and soon another district will try to entice him away with more money, a bigger school, and brighter lights. Just like they came for sweet little Savannah."

"Now darlin'. If that's all you're worried about, I can take care of both of those really easy," replied Cracker. "I suspect his name's already on the trophy for today. He'll be a winner. I've also heard there's a sizeable raise for our Billy on the agenda at the next board meeting. He's through working for a teacher's salary. As far as Dallas, you know I have a way of talking to that girl where she understands. I'll make it a point to do just that. We want our Billy Boy to stay healthy and happy, right, Sugar?" Cracker answered with a sly smile on his face. "You know I love you girls and want you happy as well."

"Thank you, Uncle Jack, we love you too. We also appreciate how you look out for us," Dixie smiled and said.

"I'm proud of you girls, and I know your daddy would have been proud as well," replied Cracker. "Now I have a tournament to win and a principal to keep." Cracker wedged his frame from the chair, kissed his niece on the cheek, and walked off down the hall whistling and jingling the keys in his pocket.

Ms. Dixie finished clearing her desk, smiled to herself knowing her job just got a lot easier. She had someone that would represent Waymor High the right way and take good care of the folks there by instinct. She decided they had at least one more year together. Billy still had to finish his college work, and he did buy Dallas a wedding dress. She still hadn't figured that one out, but Dallas seemed happy about it. Dixie decided if life was fair, she might get to retire without ever having to train another principal.

Dixie had her own celebration to get to. Each year on graduation Saturday, her husband Ken took the day off. With the kids at her mom's house for swimming and a sleepover, their afternoon and evening were filled with grilled steaks, tequila, and a celebration that lasted well into the night. Smiling happily, Dixie took her purse from the filing cabinet and turned out the lights.

As Dixie walked down the hall she remembered her daddy telling her as a child, "The rocky road provides the best scenery."

About the author

Gene Suttle is retired after 35 years in the Texas Public School System. He was a Teacher, Coach, and Principal during his career while serving in ten schools in seven different school districts across north Texas. During his last 14 years he was principal at four different high schools. As many have, he vowed to write a book about the crazy life of an educator. And now he has....three times.

Gene is married. He and his wife Lisa have two children who are also married and have children of their own. He currently is a full time Papi and part time writer.

Acknowledgements

The My/High Trilogy began in 2011. I am grateful to family and friends who have stayed faithful and offered support and encouragement throughout. To my critical readers and editors, thank you for your feedback and efforts. Any errors that still exist are mine and mine alone.